Kayla was laughing so [...] attempts to impress her that it took a few moments to notice the pair of businessmen loitering just outside the school's wire fence. Loitering and watching them. A moment later she noticed their ears.

Their long, curved, pointed ears.

"Uh, excuse me, guys," Kayla said. She walked quickly into the closest building and stood there for a moment, leaning against the row of metal lockers. *It's the elves. They know I'm here. What am I supposed to do now?*

As if for an answer, Kayla saw one of the business-suited elves walk into the building, scanning the hallway. He saw her, and for a brief moment, they stared at each other. Then Kayla turned and ran.

She didn't hear footsteps running behind her, but a split second later there was the startling crackle of displaced air and then the elf was standing ten feet ahead of her, right in the middle of the only doorway out of the building. He smiled at her. Kayla didn't lose a step, but slammed into him at full speed like a football player. The elf had time for one startled expression on his finely-chiseled features before he was knocked flying. Kayla heard him crash into a locker as she fell, then she rolled to her feet and kept going.

I can't believe it. Elves invading my new high school, and it's only my first day here!

Baen Books By Ellen Guon

Knight of Ghosts and Shadows
(*with Mercedes Lackey*)

Summoned to Tourney
(*with Mercedes Lackey*)

Wing Commander: Freedom Flight
(*with Mercedes Lackey*)

ELLEN GUON

BEDLAM BOYZ

This is a work of fiction. All the characters and events portrayed in this book are fictional, and any resemblance to real people or incidents is purely coincidental.

Copyright © 1993 by Ellen Guon

All rights reserved, including the right to reproduce this book or portions thereof in any form.

A Baen Books Original

Baen Publishing Enterprises
P.O. Box 1403
Riverdale, N.Y. 10471

ISBN: 0-671-72177-1

Cover art by C.W. Kelly & Larry Dixon

First printing, July 1993

Distributed by
SIMON & SCHUSTER
1230 Avenue of the Americas
New York, N.Y. 10020

Typeset by Windhaven Press, Auburn, N.H.
Printed in the United States of America

Dedication

This book is for my family, with love: Mom, Dad, Micki, Laura, Reuven, Eial, and Danna.

With special thanks for moral support and technical support: Steve Beeman, Stephanie Bergeron, Charles Cafrelli, Rey Castro, C.J. Cherryh, Kim Davis, Larry Dixon, Jane Fancher, Bill Fawcett, Nancy Feldman, Beverly Hale, Robert Herrick, Natalya Johnson, M.J. Kramer, Mercedes Lackey, Katherine A. Lawrence, the Los Angeles Police Department, Christy Marx, Mike Moe, Jody Lynn Nye, Nonie and Bob Quinlan, and, of course, Lisa Smith.

Chapter One

Sunset Boulevard was a blur of lights and noise, too many radios and car stereos, too many people talking and shouting and laughing. Kayla jammed her hands in the pockets of her denim jacket and wished all of it would just go away.

At midnight, it seemed like everyone was on the street, all the weird and lonely and "professional" residents of Los Angeles: the punks and the pretty boys in tight black leather, the women in brightly colored miniskirts, the dealers with too many gold chains beneath their open shirt collars. Ten feet away from where she stood, a nervous-looking blond man traded cash for a little ziplock bag with a bored-looking guy in a cowboy hat; both men stepped back into the shadows of the alley as a black-and-white LAPD patrol car glided past, like a silent shark prowling through the late night traffic.

Liane and Billy were twenty feet further up the sidewalk, gawking at leather jackets in a storefront window. She took her eyes off the panorama of the street around her, and joined them at the window. "Nice stuff," she commented, looking at a tailored leather jacket with metal studs. The price tag said $249 . . . but it might as well have been a million dollars, she still couldn't afford it.

She leaned against the cold metal bars over the glass and thought about stealing some aspirin. Just the same as every night for the last few months, it felt like someone was pounding on her skull with a hammer. The noise from the traffic only made it worse. "Guys, okay if we stop someplace for some more aspirin?"

"Another headache?" Billy asked.

"It's nothing," Kayla lied.

"You've been having headaches every day for weeks now," Liane said. "Maybe we should take you to a doctor. What if this is something serious?"

"It's nothing, guys. I'll get some aspirin, it'll go away. There's a QuickStart down the street, we can stop there."

A red convertible slowed on the street next to them, the man in the driver's seat calling out to them. "Hey, chickies, want to party?"

Billy glared at the driver until he shrugged and looked away. The convertible pulled away back into the traffic.

"We could've just let him buy us some dinner and drinks," Liane said softly. "Nothing more than that." Liane had a hungry look in her eyes, the way she stared wistfully after the fancy red convertible.

Kayla thought about the man, and that he had a hungry look in his eyes, too. A different kind of hunger.

Billy shook his head. "He'd want something for his money, wouldn't he? And then we'd end up in a situation like last weekend with you and Nick."

Liane, already pale under the streetlights with her white-blond hair and very fair skin, turned even paler. That had been an awful night, one that Kayla thought they wouldn't survive. Nick, a local "businessman," had been watching Liane for a few days. When Kayla and Billy were busy buying Cokes from a street vendor, Nick told Liane that he wanted her to work for him. Billy and Kayla weren't his style . . . Billy was too mean-looking, with that knife-scar on his chin and that cold blue-eyed "Don't mess with me" look, a trick that he said he'd learned from his old man, who was currently up for armed robbery in Folsom. Not at all like the pretty boys on Melrose Avenue. And Kayla, with her long brown hair and green eyes that were too big for her face, knew she just wasn't cute enough for the chickenhawks, either.

Liane, on the other hand, was drop-dead gorgeous, blond and with the face of an angel. And she attracted men like a magnet. Especially slimeballs like Nick.

Maybe Billy telling Nick to go sit and spin wasn't the best idea, she thought. Billy and Nick had screamed at each other for fifteen minutes. Nick had stormed away, and they were walking down the street two hours later when he and some friends had pulled up in Nick's blue Chevy, waving a pistol at them. It'd been a fast run through the back streets of Hollywood, with Nick screaming curses in two languages at them, until they'd managed to lose him by climbing over several fences and hiding in a gardening shed in someone's backyard.

But, even after a night like that, she knew that getting out of that latest foster home *had* been a good idea. The lady who ran the place was nice enough, but her husband was slime, and he'd already started hitting on Liane, not even two days after she arrived there. True, every straight guy with hormones tried to hit on Liane, she was just too pretty for her own good, but this place was a foster home. It was supposed to be safe. Especially for someone like Liane, who was just a little too quiet, too easily spooked by people yelling, and scared of crowds and people standing too close to her.

Liane was quiet and shy, and it had surprised Kayla that the blonde girl had been the one who'd first talked about running away, about how she, Billy, and Kayla could go out on their own. It had started out easily enough, stealing enough money to take the bus from Orange County to downtown L.A. From there, they went to Hollywood, mostly because Liane wanted to see the Chinese Theater. It was Kayla who'd spotted the abandoned office building across the street from Mann's Chinese, and now Suite 230 (formerly an insurance agency, by the stationery they'd found in a closet) was their new home.

It wasn't bad: running water, though no showers or bathtubs, and plenty of old carpet padding to use for blankets. Kayla just wasn't certain how long all of this could keep working out for them, though—she knew they were balancing on the edge, with too many people like Nick waiting around to catch them if they fell.

Billy was the one who kept them together. Billy, who knew all about shoplifting and jimmying locks and using Sterno to heat up cans of chili. He treated them like his kid sisters, though sometimes Kayla caught him looking at Liane in a way that wasn't very brotherly. Kayla knew that she and Liane would never have made it on their own without him. *We're lucky he was at that foster home, too,* she thought. *I don't think I would've been brave enough to leave there without him. . . .*

Billy's words broke into her thoughts. "Hey, Kay, there's the QuickStart. Didn't you want some aspirin?"

"Yeah, sure." Though she was sure that it wouldn't help. Nothing seemed to help, not anymore. "You guys hang around up front, I'll get the pills."

The headaches weren't the worst of it; she could live with the pain, not a problem. It was the weird dizziness that hit her every so often, making her feel like she'd touched a live electrical wire. She was sick with something, she knew that, but it didn't pay to worry about it . . . there was no way she could go to a doctor, at least, not now.

They walked into the store, a brightly-lit building with rows of metal shelves, past a cheerful woman who was chatting with the store clerk, a quiet-looking young man with shoulder-length blond hair. Liane and Billy started looking through magazines near the front counter, and Kayla moved to the back of the store. In the last few weeks, they'd refined shoplifting to an art, running interference and distracting the people so one of them could walk out with enough food for dinner. It was a lot easier than other kinds of theft. Kayla smiled in spite of herself, remembering how Billy had climbed through an open apartment window only to find the occupant, a fat middle-aged man, up to his neck in bubbles in his bathtub with several rubber ducks floating around him. He'd yelled and Billy had practically fallen out the window, terrified but still unable to keep from laughing.

The three of them still laughed about that one, but the time when Billy had gone through an open house window and another guy had reached for a handgun next to his bed, that hadn't been so funny. Fortunately for him, the gun hadn't been loaded, and by the time the guy had managed to put some bullets in the revolver, Billy, Kayla, and Liane were already two blocks away and still running.

Since then, Billy had said that they'd have to get by without any more breaking-and-entering. Shoplifting, that was a good trick, though Kayla was getting very tired of pork-and-beans heated in the can, chili, and stew. Sometimes she caught herself fantasizing about fresh-cooked food, something that didn't come out of a can: baked potatoes, pancakes, or even bowls of oatmeal. Anything but canned spaghetti.

She found the brand of aspirin she was looking for and checked the overhead mirror to make sure the clerk wasn't watching—those mirrors worked both ways, if you knew what you were doing—and slipped the package into her jacket pocket, smiling to herself. It was a quiet night, all right, and once she took some pills to get rid of the headache, she'd be feeling fine. . . .

Gunshots shattered the silence.

Liane screamed a moment later, a sound that echoed through the store. Kayla didn't even think about it; she ran toward the sound of Liane's scream and skidded around the corner of the row of shelves, stopping short at the sight before her.

The woman was lying very still in a pool of

her own blood, sprawled across a small potted palm. The clerk's body wasn't in sight, but Kayla could see more blood sprayed across the wall behind the counter. A man wearing a long leather coat stood near the doorway and smiled at her, a military assault rifle clenched in his hands.

Not three feet away from her, Billy held Liane in his arms, both of them frozen with terror. The man brought the assault rifle up, aiming at the three of them. Kayla brought up her hands instinctively to shield her face.

Nothing happened.

He isn't going to kill us, Kayla thought with a faint wave of relief, and opened her eyes.

The man was staring at her. Directly at her, not at Billy, not at Liane. A split-second later, she realized why: her hands were on fire. No, not exactly fire . . . it was a blue light that flickered over her hands, lines of light that weaved and danced around her fingers.

She was too startled to do anything except stare at her hands and the pale blue light. A wave of dizziness hit her, and that strange feeling of hot power, like electricity running through her entire body—she could feel the hair on her forearms standing on end, her hands tingling faintly where the light touched her.

Oh my . . . oh my God . . .

The light faded away. She stared at her fingers, and through them, saw the gunman shaking his head slowly, as though he couldn't believe what he'd just seen.

Then she saw his hands tighten on the rifle and knew that in another split-second he'd shoot them anyhow. . . .

Kayla didn't even think about it; she dived for

him and that gun, sending both of them crashing into a rack of magazines. She tried to pull the gun out of his grip; he shoved her, hard, and she fell back against the blond woman's body, which gave way beneath her. She landed on the floor; her head hit hard against the linoleum. She blinked; the barrel of the gun was only inches from her face . . . she could see the man, smiling with delight, as his finger tightened on the trigger. . . .

Billy slammed into the gunman with a football tackle. The gun went off again, gunshots echoing through the small store. A bullet zinged past Kayla to impact the floor next to her.

She lay there for a moment, concentrating on breathing, then climbed unsteadily to her feet. Her legs were shaking so much she could barely stand as she moved to where Billy and the man were both lying motionless on the floor.

Billy was still alive, blood slowly staining through his shirt and jeans. She could see where the bullets had hit him, one in his leg, another in his shoulder. The shoulder wound was the worst, blood welling out in a wide stain down his side and onto the floor.

She wanted to scream, but knew there wasn't time for it. Billy was always the one who knew exactly what to do in a bad situation; she had to think the way he did, do something fast before all of his life spilled out onto the floor.

She tried to remember what first aid you were supposed to do for gunshot wounds. Applying pressure to stop the bleeding, that was the only thing she could think of. And shock—you had to cover them with a blanket or something so they'd stay warm. She didn't have a blanket, or anything to use on the wound . . . she pressed her hand against the ripped skin and shirt on Billy's shoulder. Blood flowed out around her fingers, more with every heartbeat.

This isn't working. . . .

She pressed harder. "It isn't working," she whispered. She looked up suddenly at Liane, still standing by the candy racks. "Go get help, damn it!" she yelled. Liane didn't move: she was standing silently, staring at Kayla . . . at Kayla's hands . . .

. . . at the tendrils of blue light, twisting around her fingertips. The light brightened as she looked at it, radiating out from her hands, moving in rippling circles over Billy's shoulder and chest. Suddenly she saw Billy's wound beneath her hands, through her hands, as though she was a ghost. No, it wasn't exactly seeing . . . it was *feeling*, knowing, sensing the tears through the skin and muscle, the pressure of the tiny bullet lodged against the bone . . . *so small, to do so much damage!* The bullet, a little squashed piece of metal, was buried beneath a layer of muscle—she reached the part of her mind that was sensing all of this deep into the wound and tugged at the bullet, carefully working it loose.

It slid into her hand before she realized it. With a shudder, she flung it under the magazine rack, then turned back to Billy. There was more blood now, flowing from an artery that had been nicked by the bullet's passage. She touched the wound with unsteady fingers, and the blue light intensified, so incandescent that she had to close her eyes.

The light still shone through her closed eyelids, impossibly bright. Now she could feel the cut artery sealing itself, the muscles knitting together beneath her fingertips. She could feel

the energy pouring out of her and into Billy,
into the damaged tissue. And she knew this
without seeing it, her eyes still tightly closed
against the brilliance of the light. Somehow she
knew how to help him, how to do whatever it
was that she was doing, and it felt terrific. It
felt better than anything she'd ever done before,
exhilarating and electric, as though she was
finally alive at last after being half-awake for
years. Then it was over; the light faded away,
leaving her dizzy and light-headed and as
exhausted as though she'd been running for
miles.

She opened her eyes to see what she'd done.

The bullet hole was gone. Billy's shirt was still
soaked with blood, but the wound had disappeared, only a dull pink line marking where it
had been. Her friend was still unconscious, but
she could feel the life returning to his body, that
the danger of immediate death was over. He was
still in pain from another bullet in his leg, but
even without looking at it, Kayla knew that she
could close that wound as well. As soon as she
took another couple seconds to catch her breath,
she would . . . she would . . .

Dizziness and nausea hit her like a fist, and
she fell back against the magazine rack, closing
her eyes and concentrating on breathing.

This isn't real, she thought. *People don't just
wake up one morning able to seal up bullet holes
in their friends just by wanting it to happen.
Something is going on here, something weirder
than anything I've ever heard of in my entire
life. . . .*

She heard a choked noise behind her and
turned. Liane was still standing there, visibly
trembling, making odd gasping sounds like she

couldn't get enough air to breathe. Without saying a word, she ran for the door, flinging it open. The noise of the street outside was deafening in the deathly silence of the store.

"Liane, wait!" Kayla shouted. Not even glancing back at her, Liane ran through the doorway and out into the street.

Kayla tried to get up and follow her, but another tide of dizziness washed over her. She slumped back against the magazine rack.

" . . . help me . . ." a weak voice whispered, very close to her. " . . . please . . ."

She looked around for the source of the voice, then realized, with a tiny start of fear, who it was. She stared at the gunman, lying on the blood-stained floor not quite three feet away from her. "W-what?"

"Heal me," he whispered, his face contorted with pain. "I know you can do it, I saw you help the boy. Please."

She edged away from him, shaking her head. He grabbed for her hand, pulling her close. "Please . . ." His face was very pale, his lip bleeding where he'd bitten it in pain. He placed her hand on his chest, rising and falling with each painful breath, against the torn flesh and warm wet blood.

He killed those two people, she thought. *And he nearly killed Billy. And he would've killed me and Liane, too, but now . . .*

Now his eyes were human again, not smiling inhumanly at something she couldn't see or understand. She could feel her hands tingling again, that strange feeling like something was going to happen.

I should help Billy, he's still hurting, his leg is still bleeding. I shouldn't help this guy, even if he is dying. . . . She could feel, somehow, the sensation that his life was fading away in front of her eyes.

This time she called it to her, that strange cold blue fire, and felt it wreathe around her hands and flow down through her fingertips. The man made a faint noise, something between a whimper and a moan, as the light coursed over his chest. She worked slowly and methodically, drawing the bullet out and sealing the wound shut. It was easier this time, in a way, though she could feel the exhaustion and dizziness pulling at her, a wave of darkness threatening at the edges of her mind. She fought it off for as long as she could, trying to concentrate on the man's wounds, but everything was moving too fast, whirling around her. . . .

No crowd had gathered in the convenience store parking lot yet. *Thank God for small favors*, Officer Dale Walker thought, drawing his service revolver and gesturing to his partner. She nodded, her pistol already out and ready, and edged closer to the door. He moved in quickly, gun held at waist height, covering the entrance to the QuickStart. Anne followed him in a moment later. He stepped over the bodies lying near the doorway, pushed the rifle away from the unconscious man in the long coat, then carefully bent to pick it up by the strap. Anne slipped past him, the petite red-haired woman checking through the rest of the store to make sure there was no one else in the building. He glanced behind the long counter: one motionless body, not a threat. She rejoined him at the entrance. "All clear, Dale," she reported, and hearing that there were no immediate dangers, he took a genuine look at the bodies for the first time.

"*Damn.*" The woman was obviously dead. The young man behind the counter must have died almost instantly—a bullet had caught him in the throat. He had a surprised look frozen on his face, a look he'd carry with him to the city morgue.

A few feet away, Anne Houston knelt next to the man in the leather coat, touching his throat for a pulse. Two kids were sprawled on the floor beside him. Walker swallowed painfully; the kids couldn't have been older than fifteen, maybe sixteen. Too young to be caught up in whatever had happened here tonight.

He crouched down next to the kids, checking them quickly. Both were covered with blood, and the boy . . . there was a wound in the boy's leg and a bullet hole in the boy's jacket, and a lot of blood stains, but no apparent wound there. *That doesn't make any sense,* he thought. *Maybe the kid moved after the first shot, fell into his own blood from the other wound, but it's unlikely. . . .*

He pushed that thought aside, concentrating on his work. The leg wound was bad but not life-threatening, and could wait until EMS arrived on the scene in a couple minutes. He turned to the girl, hearing the sirens as the ambulance pulled up in the parking lot outside.

As he leaned over her, the girl opened her eyes, blinking up at him. "You'll be all right," he said, smiling reassuringly. She looked up at him, dazed and uncomprehending.

"Dale," Anne Houston said, her voice sounding shaken, "This is too weird for words . . . the guy's covered with blood and there's a hole in his jacket, but there's no bullet hole in him!"

*   *   *

"Just shock," someone said directly above her. "I didn't find a head injury . . . she probably fainted during the attack."

Everything hurt. That was her first thought when she opened her eyes: her entire body felt like one big bruise, like she'd gone through the tumble-dry cycle on a clothes dryer. Someone was looking down at her, a tall man with graying brown hair, wearing the dark blue uniform of the LAPD.

"Thanks, Randall," he said to someone out of her sight. He smiled at her, his brown eyes crinkling at the corners, then looked up sharply as a woman shouted, "Dale, grab him!"

Kayla blinked and sat up, then wished she hadn't. Everything spun around her, and she felt like she was falling. Someone fell on top of her, and she screamed. It was the man in the leather coat, his face only inches from hers. "Got him, Anne," the police officer said, and hauled the man in the leather coat up against the magazine rack, twisting his arms behind him and slapping on a pair of handcuffs.

"Do you know this guy, kid?" the female officer asked.

Kayla found her voice. "I've never . . . never seen him before. But he . . . he killed those people. He would've killed all of us."

The gunman grinned at her, licking his lips. Whatever had been human in his eyes, for that brief moment when he'd pleaded with her to save his life, was gone again.

She tried to sit up, and everything went blurry again. When her head cleared, she saw two paramedics carefully moving Billy out of the store on a stretcher. The blonde woman's body was still lying by the counter, but someone had placed a blanket over her face. The policewoman was reading Miranda rights to the gunman, two other police officers holding the man by his handcuffed arms. The brown-haired policeman was next to her, watching her intently. "Do you feel up to a trip to the station, kid?"

She nodded, not trusting her voice.

"Good." He helped her stand up. Her knees were so wobbly, she had to hold onto his arm for support. "You're a tough kid," the cop continued. "You survive this, you'll survive anything."

Will I? she thought.

"She's magic!" the gunman shrieked suddenly, trying to wrest free from the policemen. He struggled briefly, staring at Kayla with insane eyes. Beneath the leather coat, his shirt was still wet with blood. "She healed me, she has the Devil's power! I saw it, she has the Devil in her!"

"Jesus, get him out of here," the policewoman said in an exasperated tone. The other officers complied, wrestling the man through the door.

"I'll take you to the station now," the brown-haired officer said. "Easy now, I know your legs aren't working too great just yet. We'll walk slowly, it's okay. . . ."

Easy for you to say, she thought resentfully. *You didn't just see these people get blown away in front of you, including your best friend almost dying, and then have that—whatever it was— blue light thing happen to you.*

They moved out through the doorway, and Kayla stopped short, momentarily blinded by bright lights.

There were several camera crews aiming cameras at her, and a huge crowd of people gathered on the sidewalk, held back by several police officers.

Kayla wondered if she ought to faint or throw up. Either seemed likely right now. . . .

"Just a little more," the policeman said in a gentle voice. His grip tightened on her arm, as though he realized that she was about to fall. Half-supporting her, they walked to a police car parked on the edge of the lot. The policeman helped her into the back seat; Kayla fumbled with the seat belt strap for a few seconds before the officer reached over to fasten it for her.

There was someone already seated in the car next to her, a beautiful Chicano girl with feathers knotted into her hair. The girl gave Kayla a curious look. "Why are they not taking you to the hospital?" she asked. "I saw you lying there, I thought you were dead."

"Please, witnesses can't talk," the policeman said from the driver's seat. "Neither of you can talk about what happened yet, okay?"

Okay by me, Kayla thought. *I don't want to talk about it, anyhow. I don't even want to think about it.*

The officer drove in silence through the brightly lit streets. Kayla leaned her face against the cold glass and tried not to think.

Billy was alive. She knew that much, from the moment that her entire world had faded back from bright blue lights and hot electricity into normal reality again. She'd saved his life, somehow, and the life of the guy in the leather coat.

I should have let that slimeball die, she thought, then shook her head. Even now, she knew she couldn't have done that. It didn't matter that the man was a murderer . . . even if he was slime, she couldn't just sit back and watch him die, not when she knew she could do something to help him.

Because she could. It didn't make any sense—none of this made any sense, really—but she could do it, whatever it was that she'd done. She could help people. A people-helper, that's what she was. The thought made her feel a little better, despite the awful headache and dizziness and pain.

Except . . . except that wasn't what the crazy man had called her. His words echoed in her mind: "She's magic. She has the Devil in her."

Oh God, Kayla thought. *I sure as hell hope not.*

Chapter Two

Kayla sat on the wooden chair, feeling the sweat drip down the inside of her shirt, wondering how much longer they'd have to sit in this room. "Can I have a glass of water?" she asked Officer Walker.

"Once the homicide detectives arrive, I'll get you something to drink," the policeman said. "Just be patient a little longer, Kayla."

"Okay," she said, trying to find a more comfortable way of sitting on the hard wooden chair. All of this would be much easier to deal with if the chairs in the police station were a little more comfortable, she thought. Instead, she was stuck in this empty room with Officer Walker, who was a nice guy but didn't want to talk very much. He'd said that to her when they arrived at the police station, that they'd have to wait in a separate room and not talk about what had happened at the convenience store until the homicide detectives from the Detective Headquarters Division arrived.

The Hispanic girl was seated on a chair by the door, looking as though she wished she was somewhere else. Kayla understood *exactly* how she felt.

The silence in the room was making her crazy, she decided. After all the noise of gunshots and screaming, the silence was more than she could handle. "Do you know who that guy was, Officer Walker?" Kayla asked.

"Kayla, I've already said that we can't talk about it, not until the detectives arrive. Please, no more questions."

She sat with her arms folded on her knees, curled up on the chair, until the door opened again. Two more police officers walked in, a blonde woman and a heavyset man. "So, Dale, what did you bring home today?"

Officer Walker stood up. "Consuela Rodriguez was the first person to arrive on the scene, and she called the police. Kayla here was in the store when it happened. She wasn't hurt; none of that blood is hers."

"I'll start with the kid," the woman said. She gestured for Kayla to follow her. Kayla did, wondering what was going to happen next.

They walked down the hallway to another office. The policewoman closed the door after them and turned to a small table with a coffee-pot, cans of soda, and paper cups. "Here, take a couple of paper towels; let's get some of that blood off you. Dale didn't even let you wash, did he? Would you like something to drink?"

"Anything with sugar in it," Kayla said, reaching for a can of Pepsi. She opened the bottle of aspirin that she'd lifted from the convenience store and swallowed several of the pills with some soda, then carefully wiped her face and hands with the paper towel.

The woman poured herself a cup of coffee

and glanced up at the clock on the wall. "One A.M. Well, this will certainly be a long night. Have a seat, young lady. I'm afraid you're going to be here for a while, and I can't let you talk to anyone else just yet, not even your parents. By the way, I don't think I introduced myself. I'm Detective Cable. You can call me Nichelle, if you'd like."

Kayla gingerly sat down on one of the chairs. Detective Cable set a small tape recorder on the table next to them and took out a small stack of paper forms and a pencil.

Then the questions began.

Forty-five minutes later, Kayla was trying to stay awake as she explained for a second time how she hadn't seen the gunman actually walk into the store, how she hadn't seen anyone outside the store who could've been with the gunman, and that she hadn't heard the gunman say anything until after the police arrived.

I wish Billy was here. He'd know what to say, how to handle this.

"All right," Cable said, stifling a yawn. "Let's go over what happened when your friend Billy was shot. You said you jumped the guy, he knocked you down and you fainted, and . . . ?"

" . . . and I woke up when Officer Walker was asking me if I was okay," she said, not saying anything about the entire "blue lights" situation. *They'll lock me up in a padded cell in five minutes if I start talking about that,* she thought.

To Kayla's relief, the policewoman switched off the tape recorder. "Thank you, Kayla," she said with a tired smile. "Thank you very much. Now all I need is for you to fill out some paperwork, and then I'll give you over to

Elizabet Winters, our resident psychology therapist, specializing in juvenile psychology. She'll want to talk to you a little, make sure that you're handling all of this okay. I know it's been an awful night for you, and you seem to be dealing with everything just fine, but we have to be certain. Elizabet will also call your parents and make sure you get home all right. I'm sure they're worried about you, and will want to know where you are." She set a form and a pen in front of Kayla, then walked over to pour herself another cup of coffee.

Call . . . my parents? Kayla thought in dismay. She looked down at the form and at the second line, where she was supposed to write in her address. *What am I supposed to do now?*

Maybe if I just fill it out quickly, then I can ask to go to the bathroom or something and get out of the building.

Then I'll find Liane, and we can find Billy at the hospital. He'll know what to do, he always does.

Good plan.

She wrote in carefully: 6925 Hollywood Boulevard. Hollywood, California.

The other questions were just as bad; she put down fake names for her parents, grandparents, school, and everything else.

Cable took the form from her, scanning it quickly. Kayla sat and waited, trying not to look nervous. The policewoman walked to the door with the form still in her hand. "I'll be back in a minute, Kayla," she said, and left the room.

Maybe I should try to get out of here now, Kayla thought, then decided against it. Somebody would probably stop her before she could get to the front door. No, waiting until the right moment, that was a better idea—wait until someone was taking her home, she could just walk away and then head back home, to Suite 230.

Home. Once upon a time, that had meant something better than an abandoned office building in downtown Hollywood. She thought about what the policewoman had said about calling her parents and fought back the sudden tears that threatened to escape from her eyes.

I wish you could call my folks, lady, she thought. *I just wish you could.*

Elizabet Winters set down the case folder, rubbing at her eyes with a tired hand. Too many blank pages left to fill out . . . the file on that last runaway child would keep her here for another hour, when all she wanted to do was go home and get some sleep. At least there'd been a happy ending to that story, unlike most of them. She and Lieutenant Simmons had escorted the boy to the LAX airport, where she'd seen him off on the midnight plane to Chicago, knowing that the boy's anxious parents were waiting for him on the other end of the line.

Sometimes these things worked out.

Sometimes they didn't. Elizabet didn't want to think about Marie, a lovely sixteen-year-old who'd been brought in to the station for child prostitution at least five times. The last time, they'd taken her to the county morgue instead, with five knife wounds in her. No suspects in that case yet, and Elizabet doubted they'd ever find any.

"Hey, Elizabet, you got a minute? I need some help."

Elizabet looked up, to see Nichelle Cable from Detective Headquarters Division. Nichelle looked just as tired as Elizabet felt. "What's up?"

"I have a girl who witnessed a double homicide tonight on Sunset Boulevard. I didn't think there was anything unusual about her until she gave me this." Nichelle held up the witness identification form and pointed at Line 2.

"So, she lives on Hollywood Boulevard? What's strange about that?" Elizabet asked.

"I wouldn't have thought anything was weird about it, except that when I was in high school, I worked in a particular movie theater for a few months. This girl gave me the address of Mann's Chinese Theater." Nichelle smiled. "I ran her name through the runaway database, and it came up cherries. Kayla Smith, state ward. She's been in Juvie twice for shoplifting and is currently reported missing from a foster home in Orange County. She ran away two months ago. God knows what she's been doing since." The homicide detective dropped the form on Elizabet's desk. "She's all yours, Elizabet."

"Thanks," Elizabet said with a wry smile. "Anything else I should know about this child?"

"She's bright and obviously thinks fast on her feet. Doesn't look like she does drugs, though she's wearing a half-trashed denim jacket that would cover any tracks. No terminal case of the sniffles or jitters, anyhow, so I doubt she's a crackhead. Maybe you can do something for this one."

"Maybe." Elizabet stuffed the case folder in her briefcase. "Is she in a holding room or one of the offices?"

"Simmons' office. There's still some fresh coffee in there, if you need it." Nichelle yawned and stretched, smiling tiredly. "I'm calling it a night. You might want to buzz Collins and get him ready to process this kid. I doubt anyone would want to drive her over to Juvie at this hour."

"You're probably right about that. Thanks for the coffee, Nichelle, I'll need it. Good night."

"Good luck," the policewoman said with a grin.

Elizabet picked up her briefcase and her jacket and headed over to Simmons' office. Ten feet away from the office door, she stopped, closing her eyes for a brief moment.

She knew.

She'd felt it earlier, an "incident" in the city, magical power like a flare going off, as someone called down magic with all the subtlety of a high-explosive rocket. She'd wanted to go investigate, but with the boy to escort to the airport, there had been no chance. But now . . .

It was this girl. She could feel it already, even though she couldn't see the girl through the closed office door. But even at this distance, the sensation of power sparked around her, tingling and alive. Whoever this girl was, she was a little powerhouse, and probably remarkably dangerous because of it.

Maybe she was the cause of the double homicide?

No . . . she could sense the child's power, and it burned clean and incandescent. The girl was bright with power and promise, with no taint of death around her. Instead, it was something else that she sensed, something that she only saw dimly sometimes when looking in the mirror, moments when she could see herself and her own magic glowing within her. . . .

The child has magic!

Elizabet opened the door and walked into the office. The girl looked up from where she was seated with her elbows propped on the table. She didn't look like much, just a street kid wearing jeans and a denim jacket over a stained T-shirt, long tangled brown hair, and large green eyes. Those eyes followed Elizabet as she draped her blue suit jacket over the back of the chair and then sat down across from her.

"I'm Elizabet Winters," she said. "Elizabet is a mistake on my birth certificate that I've lived with all these years. You're Kayla, right?" She extended her hand. The kid didn't move, just sat and watched her with those terrified eyes. Elizabet withdrew her hand, wondering how to handle this.

"Who are you?"

The girl's voice was surprisingly soft, Elizabet thought. "I'm a psych therapist working with the police department," she said. "Usually I help the relatives of victims of crime, or work with people who have been through a traumatic experience. Like what you went through tonight. Do you want to talk about that?"

Yes, I'd like to talk about it, but I also don't want to spend the rest of my life in a padded room, Kayla thought, looking at the woman across from her. Elizabet Winters was a beautiful black woman in her fifties, black and silver hair coiled up in a braid. She sat silently, apparently waiting for Kayla to say something.

What am I supposed to say? That some guy killed two people in front of me and shot my best friend, and I created this weird light show to get rid of the bullet holes? No way.

"I've—I've had a bad night," she said at last,

choosing her words carefully. "I'm okay, but I'd like to go home."

The older woman nodded. "That's a problem, unfortunately. Detective Cable wanted me to lock you up here for the night and maybe send you to Juvenile Hall in the morning, since it's a little impractical to take you back to the foster home in Orange County in the middle of the night."

"What?" Kayla sat upright in shock.

"I think I have another alternative," Elizabet continued, "since neither a midnight trip to Orange County or a night at Juvenile Hall seems to be the appropriate answer."

"Terrific," Kayla said, and slumped back down in her chair. "So are you going to send me back to Mr. and Mrs. Davis? I know it doesn't matter what I think, but I don't want to go."

"Obviously, or you wouldn't have run away from them." The black woman smiled. "Kayla, if you could do anything, what would you do?"

"I—I don't understand," she answered uncertainly.

"I'll rephrase this. Pretend for a minute that you don't have to go back to that foster home, or Juvie, or anything like that. If you could choose where you wanted to live, what you wanted to do, what would you choose?"

Who is this lady? Kayla wondered. *She isn't like any cop or social worker I've ever met before.* "I don't know. I guess . . . if I could have anything, I'd want to live with my parents again. But that won't ever happen, I know that." At Elizabet's questioning look, she added, "They disappeared when I was twelve years old. I was at school, Mom never showed up to take me home." The memory of that afternoon was still burned into her mind:

how she'd waited and waited at the school, then walked home, to find the police at her house. "Nobody knew how to find any of my relatives, so I ended up in a foster home." She thought about it for a few moments longer. "If I could do anything, I'd want to live with people that understood me. Good people, not like Mr. Davis. People who like to talk about real things, and treat people right, and . . . and read books. People who do more than sit around drinking beer and watching TV."

"You like to read?"

In spite of herself, Kayla blushed. "I love reading," she said, looking down at her sneakers. "Sometimes it's the only way to escape, get away from everything."

"Have you thought of going to college?" Elizabet asked.

"Yeah, sure, but there's a snowball's chance of that, you know? You have to graduate high school before they'll let you go to college."

"Maybe I can help you with that." The woman stood up, pulling on her blue jacket and picking up her briefcase. "Time to go, child."

"To Juvie?" Kayla's voice quavered, and she hated it for that. She clenched her fists, trying to keep her voice steady. "Is that where you're taking me?"

Elizabet Winters smiled. "No, I have another idea. I'll need to find Lieutenant Simmons first, but I doubt he'd have any objections."

Curious, Kayla followed Elizabet out of the office. Elizabet led her through the corridors and open office rooms of the police station.

"The lieutenant's downstairs with our new psychopath," one officer told Elizabet, and she led Kayla down a flight of stairs to a brightly lit row

of holding cells. A sandy-haired policeman stood
a few feet back from the rows of concrete-walled
rooms, from which Kayla could hear someone
screaming curses and obscenities. There was one
small iron-barred cell next to the larger holding
cells that had several prisoners in each, men that
were mostly sitting around quietly. In the smaller
cell was the man from the QuickStart, wearing a
stained white shirt and jeans instead of the long
black leather coat.

In spite of herself, she stared at the killer.
Another man, wearing jeans and a plaid shirt
and seated quietly on a bench in the next cell,
was watching her through the open bars. She
avoided his curious eyes, looking instead at the
man who'd tried to kill her.

There was something wrong with him, she
could tell, even at this distance. Something broken inside that made him crazy this way. Her
hands tingled, and she glanced down quickly,
making sure that her fingers weren't glowing
again. They weren't, fortunately. Kayla looked
back at the crazy man, wondering just how one
would fix something wrong inside somebody's
head; it wouldn't be like fixing a gunshot wound,
that was more like patching things back together.
No, this would be like reaching inside and
changing something. . . .

Elizabet began speaking in a quiet voice to
the policeman; with the lunatic screaming at the
top of his voice, Kayla couldn't hear what she
was saying.

"Hey, chickie." The gunman's voice suddenly
dropped to a whisper. "I know who you are, I
know what you did."

Kayla moved closer so she could hear him.
"What?"

"It's magic, did you know that? I've seen magic, and that's what you did."

Elizabet spoke sharply from behind her. "Kayla! Get away from—"

The man reached out and grabbed Kayla's arm, yanking her toward him with inhuman strength. "Devil!" he screamed. Kayla was pulled hard against the metal bars, struggling to get free. The man's other hand clamped onto her throat, tightening painfully.

Elizabet's hand was on the man's arm, trying to pull him away from Kayla. A split-second later, Kayla felt a shock of hot fire go through her hands, a sudden pain like a knife. The man yelped and leaped back, falling onto the floor of his cell.

Elizabet pulled her back from the cell, blocking the lieutenant's view of Kayla with her own body. Kayla glanced down, and saw why: a handful of blue sparks, flickering like fireflies on a Southern night, were fading from her own fingertips as she watched.

"Are you all right? Did he hurt you?" Elizabet asked urgently.

Kayla shook her head. "I'm okay, really." She looked at the man cowering in his cell, clutching his left arm. "Did he—?" She turned quickly to look at the police officer, hoping he hadn't seen anything.

"Good use of pressure points, Elizabet," Lieutenant Simmons said, motioning for them to stand further back from the cell. "I've seen Ms. Winters do things like that before," the police officer continued. "It's some Japanese martial art, isn't it?"

Elizabet's eyes never left Kayla's. "I know a few useful tricks, Jeff," she said.

"Yes." The police officer nodded. "In any case, Elizabet, my answer is yes. I don't see why you can't foster this girl for a few days until a judge figures out what to do for her. Just make sure the correct paperwork ends up on the captain's desk."

"That's what you were asking about?" Kayla asked, her eyes wide.

"Only if you don't mind, child. If you'd rather go elsewhere, we can make other arrangements," Elizabet said.

"No, that's okay by me." Kayla didn't know what else to say. She thought about being locked up in Juvie, and decided that it would be a lot easier to get away from this lady than the cops at Juvie. Because all she could think about right now was running away, running as far away from all of everything that had happened tonight, until she didn't have to think about it anymore.

Then she thought about a warm bed, and maybe a chance to take a shower, maybe even get some clean clothes. *I'll see what her place is like*, Kayla thought, *And then I'll decide. Maybe I'll want to stay there tonight, maybe I can steal some stuff that I can get some cash for . . .*

Maybe this lady is all right. I mean, she saw what just happened, and she didn't freak, or even say anything about it. Maybe she can answer some of these questions . . . maybe she can explain what in the hell is happening to me.

She followed Elizabet out of the holding cell area, making a wide berth around the crazy man's cell. When they were outside the police station, she couldn't hold back the questions any longer. "You saw, didn't you? Why didn't you tell the cop? I don't—"

"Not here," Elizabet said. "We'll talk at my house." They walked to one of the few cars left in the parking lot next to the station, an old white VW Rabbit convertible. "We can stop by Cedars Sinai Hospital and check on your friend Billy if you'd like," she offered.

"We don't have to. I know he's okay," Kayla said without thinking.

Elizabet smiled at her. "Yes, you would know that, wouldn't you? All right, then we'll just go straight to my house."

She knows! Kayla thought. *She knows exactly what happened!*

"Bitch!" the man screamed as the police lieutenant left the room. "She's an evil bitch, she's the Devil's daughter!"

Carlos Miguel Hernandez listened to the man's raving for another few minutes, then uncurled from his position on the jail cell's wooden bench and moved to the corner of his cell, as close as he could get to the other man. "Why do you say that little *puta* is the daughter of the Devil?" he asked conversationally. "She's just a child."

"I saw it, kid!" the man shrieked. "I saw it, I saw it!"

"Please, *amigo*, calm down. Tell me what you saw."

Carlos listened intently to the man's descriptions of the evening's events, and nodded thoughtfully. "Can you prove that this happened? Do you have proof?"

"I'll show you, kid, but you have to give it back to me, you have to promise!" the other man said shrilly.

"I promise, I promise," Carlos snapped

impatiently. "And do not call me kid," he added. "I'm nineteen years old, I'm a man."

For an answer, the man's hand reached out through the bars, holding out his shirt. Carlos pulled it into his cell and looked at it curiously.

"Look on the right side, you'll see the mark," the man said.

Carlos turned the shirt in his hands and saw the bullet hole. The bloodstains around the hole were fresh, not yet darkened to the red-brown color of old blood. He brought the shirt closer to his face and sniffed. Yes, fresh blood.

"I have a hole in my jacket, too," the man said. "But no bullet wound. She healed me, she's the Devil's daughter!"

"I believe you," Carlos said. "If you were still hurt, you would be in the security ward of a hospital, not here in county jail." *How remarkable*, he thought, *And how very useful. Though if that child is the Devil's daughter, it is a kind and gentle Devil who would save the life of someone trying to kill her.*

I want to see this miracle for myself, this child who heals friend and enemy alike.

"Do you know who she is?" Carlos asked. "Do you know where she lives?"

The other man mumbled a negative. Carlos pushed the shirt back through the bars of the cell into the other man's grasp and sat down on the bench to consider what he had learned.

She could be very useful indeed, this healing child. Tomorrow morning, he would stand in front of the judge and pay his fines to leave this place. After that, he could begin searching for this child. Somehow he did not doubt that he or one of his homeboys, the Tyrone Street Boys, would find her, one girl in all of the city of Los Angeles. He stretched out on the bench and listened in silence to the incoherent words of the man in the cell beside him. Tomorrow, he would find her. . . .

"Nice place," Kayla muttered, looking up at the darkened house. She glanced at Elizabet. "How much does the police department pay you, anyhow?"

"I also have a private practice," Elizabet said, unlocking the front door. "Besides, child, I bought this house fifteen years ago, before the rich folks decided that Laurel Canyon was the perfect place to build a fancy house. You'll see, it's not much on the inside."

Maybe you think so, Kayla thought, walking into the wood-paneled room, *But I can sure spot a few things that would get me some good bucks at Mel's Gun and Pawn.* She paused to look at a collection of crystal dolphins on a shelf in the hallway. *I wouldn't even think of hocking those— they'd probably break when I was carrying 'em out. But the VCR, that looks like it's new, and it's one of the better brands . . . that could be worth something. . . .*

A moment later, she noticed something else: the house was *quiet.* Not just from noise, but from the jangling pressure she'd felt for the last months, the sensation that the world was tightening down on her and making her crazy. Her headache faded as she looked around in surprise. *Totally weird.*

"I'm getting something to drink from the fridge. Would you like anything?"

"A glass of milk would be great," Kayla said, and Elizabet walked away. Kayla studied one of the crystal dolphins; it seemed to float in midair, caught forever in a leap out of the water. Only the tip of its tail touched the cut-glass water, the dolphin sculpture delicately balanced on that point.

"Do you like that one?" Elizabet asked, walking up behind her with two glasses of milk. "I like to think of it as a representation of life, balanced perfectly at a single moment."

Kayla took the offered glass from Elizabet's hand. "Thanks." She sipped the milk, then looked wistfully in the direction of Elizabet's kitchen.

"Of course, you must be hungry, child. I probably have some sandwich fixings in the fridge. I'll show you where everything is."

Kayla followed her into the kitchen, and as Elizabet took out a plate and silverware from the cupboards, she asked, "Why did you say, 'of course'?"

Elizabet was silent for a moment. "Make yourself whatever you'd like to eat, then we'll sit down and talk."

"Yeah, sure." Kayla decided not to be polite about the fact that she felt like she hadn't eaten in weeks, and made a huge sandwich out of a whole wheat roll and several different kinds of cheeses. She sat down across from Elizabet at the kitchen table, alternating quick bites of the sandwich with swallows of milk. The older woman watched without speaking as Kayla finished the sandwich. "So, what did you want to talk about?" she asked hesitantly, uncomfortable with Elizabet's long silence.

"We have a few things to discuss," Elizabet said thoughtfully. "Like what happened to you earlier this evening."

"You read Officer Cable's report," Kayla

offered. "It has everything in it. Did you want to know about something else?"

Elizabet lifted her hand; white-gold light flickered over her fingers, glittering in the cold light of the kitchen.

"This is what we have to talk about," Elizabet said, the light brightening around her hand as she spoke. "This is magic."

Chapter Three

"I don't want to talk about it," Kayla said. Her eyes darted to the door out of the kitchen; she was certain that Elizabet couldn't run as fast as she could, especially if Kayla had a head start. Maybe she could get out of this house and away from this crazy woman, make it back to Hollywood before the police could catch up with her.

"You're not going to run anywhere, not in your current condition," the woman said, watching her closely. "I think you nearly killed yourself tonight, and it'll take time to recover from that."

"I didn't . . . how did you know about that?" Kayla demanded.

:Trust me, child, I know.:

Kayla stood up quickly, and her chair tilted and clattered to the floor. She backed to the door. "Stop that!" she shouted, her voice very loud in the small kitchen.

"I didn't say anything," Elizabet said mildly. She glanced at her hands; as if an afterthought, the sparkling lights faded away. *:But you heard me, didn't you?:*

Kayla whirled, looking around the room for

the source of the words. This time she was certain of it; Elizabet's lips hadn't moved. "It's a trick, isn't it?" she said, her hand reaching behind her for the doorknob. "You're playing tricks with your voice."

:*You know I'm not. Why won't you listen to me?*:

"Get out of my head!" Kayla covered her face with her hands, unable to stop the tears and hating herself for crying. "Stop it!"

"I'm sorry, Kayla. I didn't mean to frighten you." Elizabet's voice was gentle. "But I wanted to prove something to you."

"What's that?" She looked up angrily.

"That you still have a lot to learn."

Carlos breathed deeply of the cool early morning air outside the police station, smiling despite the taint of automobile exhaust and street garbage. "It's good to be out, Manny," he said.

His brother Manuel grinned at him. "I'm glad to see you outside the *cárcel*. But it was a little expensive, paying for your three speeding tickets." His grin broadened. "Maybe next time I'll let you stay longer, until you learn to appreciate me more, eh?"

Carlos laughed and swatted cheerfully at Manuel. They walked together to the waiting car, Carlos' customized old Chevrolet. *At least the policía didn't take my car,* he thought. *That would've been much worse than spending a night in a jail cell next to a madman.*

Ramon was seated at the wheel, and he smiled and nodded respectfully to his eldest brother as Carlos slid into the seat behind him. "Mother will be glad to see you home," Ramon said by way of greeting. "She was very sad to hear that you'd been arrested again."

"Mama is saying that county jail is like your home away from home, Carlos," Manuel joked.

"Heh, they haven't arrested me for at least a year!"

"Until last night," Ramon observed from the front seat.

"Ramon doesn't mind, since he could make time with Roberta at the party last night." Manuel smiled, then his smile faded at the cold look Carlos gave to Ramon.

"Is this true?"

The young man shook his head. "Roberta is your girl, Carlos, and everyone knows that. Maybe someday I'll meet a girl that I like, someone who isn't already in love with my handsome oldest brother." He grinned. "Maybe she won't even like you! Wouldn't that be a wonderful joke!"

"Heh." Carlos sat back in the seat, glancing out the window at the city. Ramon was driving carefully, even sedately, probably not wanting any more trouble than they'd already had. Soon they'd be on the 101 Freeway and out of Hollywood, which was good. He would never have admitted it to his brothers, but he had been afraid after being arrested in Hollywood. Outside of Van Nuys and the San Fernando Valley, and away from his own *barrio*, any other city gang boy could've tried to make points by cutting or killing him. That would've started a war, which he didn't want at this point—everything was going too well for his homeboys, and he didn't want anything that could cause trouble now. Especially not now, with what he'd heard from the madman in the jail.

"I have some work for you, Manuel," he said. "There is a young girl I want to find. I only saw her for a few moments, and I don't know where she lives. . . ."

"Isn't Roberta enough for you, Carlos?" Manuel asked. "How many other women do you need?"

Carlos considered hitting his brother, then decided against it. Manuel would always be a joker, no matter how many times Carlos bruised his fists against him. "This girl is different, Manny. She was at the jail and is staying with a black woman who might be a policewoman. The girl's first name is Kayla, I don't know her family name. The black woman's name is Elizabet Winters. You will find out where she lives today."

"What, today?" Manuel's voice held surprise and a hint of laughter. "You'll give me one day to find this girl in the entire city of Los Angeles? That's very generous of you, brother!"

"Why do you want this girl so much?" Ramon wanted to know.

Carlos thought about it for a moment, then decided to tell them. They were his brothers, after all, and there was no one in the world he could trust more than them. "She may be a *bruja*, a witch," he said at last. "At least, that is what a crazy man in jail told me. If we find her, I will be able to know for certain." He smiled. "If she is a witch, she could be useful to me. To the homeboys. We've had trouble with those *bastardos* from the city, trying to take over the drug selling near our *barrio*. With a *bruja*, maybe they would be more afraid of us."

"I think Carlos just wants another woman, a girl who is a *bruja* in bed," Manuel said. "I can't wait to tell Roberta that she isn't enough for him anymore!"

"Carlos, what if this girl doesn't want you?" Ramon asked.

"What do you mean?"Carlos said, surprised by the question. "She'll come with us, whether she wants to or not. She's just a girl."

"But that's—"

"That's what? Survival, that's what it is! Ramie, it's us against them, our family against the T-Men, the *bastardos* that would ruin our business. You know that!"

Ramon glanced at him. "Carlos, I don't like this. You know I've never liked what we're doing, but this is even worse. It's changing you, changing all of us, making us into . . . into something I don't like."

"So, what else are you going to do?" Carlos asked. "The money's good, I know you like that. Are you going to work at McDonald's for a handful of dollars a day?"

Ramon shook his head, his eyes on the traffic ahead of them. "I . . . I talked to Luisa this morning. She says they might have work for me at the store. I could do that during the day, go back to school at night. . . ."

"Heh, you couldn't even finish high school!" Carlos laughed.

"I couldn't, because you made me quit! You made me quit and help you sell drugs!" Ramon said angrily.

Carlos glanced at Manuel, who was being very quiet in the seat next to him. He leaned forward, speaking quietly to Ramon. "Ramie, Ramie, I need you. We've built a business, but I can't hold it all alone. Not with those *bastardos* from downtown trying to cut into our territory.

Do you forget, Rey's in the hospital because of them? They want our territory, and who knows what they might try next? No, you can't go back to school now, I need you too much. Our family needs you too much."

"But you know, I want more than this. . . . I want to finish high school, become a lawyer. . . ."

"A laywer, that's good!" Manuel laughed. "Then you can keep Carlos out of jail when they arrest him for selling rock!"

Carlos gave him a dirty look, then turned back to Ramon. "We'll go find this *bruja*, Ramie. If she's real, if she can do what that crazy man said, then she'll make the difference for us. Then you can do whatever you want, Ramie. You can go back to school, become a lawyer, do anything."

Ramon didn't answer. Carlos thought about saying something more, trying to find other words to convince his baby brother, then decided against it. Today Ramon was saying that he didn't want to help, but he wouldn't walk away from the *familia*, Carlos knew that. And if Manuel didn't believe him about the *bruja*, that was fine, too. When they found the girl, his brothers would change their minds.

Because he'd seen the magic himself. Oh, he'd heard his mother's stories of *magia* and *tierra del las hadas*, the land of the faerie people, but he'd never believed them.

Until last night, when he'd seen the sparks of witchlight on the girl's hands, blue and bright in the harsh light of the jail cell. And the shirt with the bullet hole in it; he'd felt *something* when he touched it, a strange sensation he couldn't identify. He knew the crazy man's story was true, even if no one else believed it, not even the *policía*.

He would find the girl, the little *bruja*. Even
in a city as large as Los Angeles, it was only a
matter of time before they found her.

"It's called magic," Elizabet said, pouring
another cup of tea. "And you have enough for
three, child. More than anyone I've ever met, to
be honest."

Kayla yawned again, and glanced at the
kitchen clock. *Six A.M. I wonder if this lady
ever goes to sleep?* "I don't believe in magic,"
Kayla said stubbornly. It was the third time
she'd said that in the last five minutes, and she
wasn't really certain whether she believed it
anymore. Especially after what had happened
tonight.

"You keep saying that, but the evidence is
before your eyes. You healed the man in the jail
cell . . . yes, I could tell that just by looking at
him," she said in response to Kayla's wide-eyed
look. "I expect you healed your hurt friend who
was mentioned in the police report, though it
seems you didn't do a complete healing on him,
since he's in the hospital right now."

"I'm not a healer. I don't believe in magic,"
Kayla repeated, rubbing her eyes.

:*How can you keep saying that, Kayla, when
you know it isn't true?*:

"Stop that!" Kayla shouted, furious. "I hate it
when you do that!"

Elizabet put her hand over her mouth, and a
moment later Kayla realized why: she was stifling
her laughter.

"Don't laugh at me!" Kayla yelled. "And stop
saying things without opening your mouth. It
isn't natural," she concluded.

"Who's to say what's natural and what isn't?"

Elizabet leaned forward across the table. "I believe everyone has a touch of it, a little magic. But only a very few people ever develop it into anything useful and predictable. And I've never met anyone like you before."

"I'm nothing special," Kayla said, looking down at her hands. The same hands that had held that weird light . . .

"No. At the moment, I'd call you remarkably dangerous, not special."

"Dangerous?"

"That man in the cell—you could've killed him, if you'd wanted to. Did you want to?" Elizabet was looking at her intently.

Kayla shook her head. "No. If I wanted him to die, I could've just let him bleed to death in the store. I just wanted him to let go of me. I don't . . . I don't want to kill anybody. Ever."

"I'm glad to hear that." Elizabet folded her hands on the table, looking down. To Kayla, she looked suddenly nervous, which was very different from the impression she'd given all evening of a tough, self-confident lady. "I'm not quite certain how to say this, Kayla . . . but I want you to consider staying here. As my student."

"What?" Kayla wasn't certain she'd heard her correctly.

"Oh, I'm sure I can find a foster home for you in this area. The local schools are fairly good, and I can arrange tutoring for you in academic subjects, if you need to make up for lost time. But what I'd like to do is teach you about magic. You're the first person I've met that has the potential to learn magic . . . no, more than just the potential to learn magic. You have the potential to easily surpass me and become someone who could make a major difference in this world, for many people."

"You're kidding, right?"

"I've never been more serious about anything in my life. You need to learn how to use this magic. Because it's not going to go away, not now that you've used it once. And until you learn how to control it, your magic is incredibly dangerous, to you and everyone around you. Believe me, it's true. You have to learn to control the magic, not let the magic control you." Elizabet looked up at the kitchen clock. "My, look at the time. I forget that not everyone is used to working the night shift. We'll talk more about this after you've slept. I'll set you up in the guest bedroom."

"Okay." Getting some sleep did sound like a great idea. Maybe all of this would make more sense in the morning . . . or maybe she'd be lucky and it would all turn out to be an awful dream. That would be great, waking up in Suite 230 next to Billy and Liane; they'd all laugh about her weird dream and then go scrounge some breakfast on the street.

She was so tired, she didn't resist when Elizabet tucked her into bed after she'd changed into a granny nightgown that was four sizes too big for her. The bed was warm and soft, much nicer than sleeping on a pile of carpet padding in a drafty office building. She was asleep a few seconds after Elizabet switched off the bedroom light.

Elizabet Winters walked quietly back to the kitchen and poured herself another cup of tea. *This child isn't quite what I expected in a student,* she thought wryly.

Her grandmother had been her own teacher, after Elizabet had discovered her odd gifts. Gram, who'd been born only a few years before the end of the Civil War, a wrinkled old woman with a talent for making sure that her grandchildren never suffered from any illness for more than a day. One day she'd been ill with the influenza and *seen* Gram use that magic to help her. From that day onward, she'd learned everything she could from her grandmother.

After Gram had passed away when Elizabet was twenty years old, she'd continued studying on her own. Reading, researching, trying to learn everything she could. But never revealing her talents, no. Because Gram had warned her about that above all else . . . that even if she could prove that her abilities were real, it was too dangerous to show them to the world. So she'd studied alone, always hoping to find others who understood.

And she'd hoped to find a student someday. Elizabet had watched her nieces and nephews closely, looking for any sign of the family gift. Eventually, she'd decided, one of the children would show the talent, and Elizabet would pass on the learning to a student the same way Gram had taught her.

She'd never dreamed that her student would be a scrawny, underfed, unwashed runaway white girl.

Well, she could live with it. Everything but the girl's ethnic background could be cured with good meals, rest, and a thorough scrubbing. And the fact that the child was white wasn't a problem for her, though Gram would probably have carried on for hours about how *her* lessons were meant for good, solid people of color, people who knew how to respect an old woman's African wisdom and would use her teachings in the right way.

She hoped Kayla would use her teachings "in the right way." That was the danger. She didn't know how much of the street life had rubbed into the girl; was she a junkie? a whore? a thief or a dealer? Elizabet would have to find this out, and soon.

I should get some sleep as well. Tomorrow, I'll see what I can learn from this girl, before I begin to teach her anything.

Kayla rolled over in bed, pulling the blankets over her head. It was too bright, too early . . .

"I've called the hospital. They'll have visiting hours later this afternoon. Do you want to go see your friend?"

"Uhn," Kayla said incoherently from under the blankets, then sat up slowly, rubbing her eyes at the light streaming in through the open window. "I mean, yes, I'd like to go see Billy." *This lady looks like she's been awake for hours. Doesn't she ever sleep?*

"I washed your clothes for you. They're folded over the chair. There's enough time for you to take a bath, if you'd like."

"Thank you." Kayla climbed out of bed and grabbed the handful of clothing from the chair. She remembered the location of the bathroom from the previous night and smiled at the sight of the large bathtub. *That* was something she'd missed, living in Suite 230—a chance to really get clean. Scrubbing down while standing next to the sink just didn't work that great. She found a bottle of nice-smelling herbal shampoo on the tiled counter and a towel that Elizabet had left her, and got to the serious work of removing several weeks of built-up grime.

Clean clothes were a nice change, too. She combed her hair, struggling with the tangles, and smiled at her reflection in the mirror. This was a Kayla who looked very different, happy and well-rested and clean, no more smudge marks on her face or tangled and dirty hair.

A couple minutes later, she joined Elizabet in the kitchen. "Breakfast?" the black woman asked, and Kayla nodded politely.

They ate in silence, until Kayla set down her fork to ask the question that had been bothering her all morning: "How do you do . . . that speaking thing?" she asked, tapping her forehead.

Elizabet laughed. "I don't really know. My Gram could do it, and one day I was able to do it as well. We'll see if you can learn it, too."

"Sure beats using the telephone," Kayla said around a mouthful of scrambled eggs. "Once you get used to it," she added.

"You have to be discreet about that kind of thing, though," Elizabet said. "Gram taught me that, telling me a story about how some folks tried to burn her out of her house in Georgia, back in the thirties. That's the first thing I'd like to teach you, how to help people without them realizing it. So you can stay out of trouble, child."

"I'd—I'd like that," Kayla said hesitantly, and was rewarded by another of Elizabet's warm smiles.

"Well, we'd better start moving," the woman said, standing up and carrying the dirty plates to the kitchen sink. "We have a lot to do today."

She wasn't kidding about that, as Kayla found out over the next few hours. The first stop was at a shopping mall in West Hollywood, where

Elizabet wielded a credit card like a medieval knight with a sword, buying Kayla a new pair of jeans, several T-shirts and sweatshirts, underwear and socks, and a new pair of high-top sneakers. The new sneakers squeaked on the linoleum floor as they walked through the mall.

Kayla was uncertain how to react to all of this generosity on Elizabet's part, but that didn't stop her from looking wistfully at a pair of silver hoop earrings in one window display. She had the plain steel stud earrings that the lady in the shop had used to pierce her ears last year, but she'd never owned another pair of earrings. Elizabet only laughed, out came the credit card again, and Kayla left the shop with her stud earrings in her pocket and the new silver hoop earrings dangling from her ears.

Their next stop was Cedars Sinai Hospital, only a few blocks away from the shopping mall. Elizabet parked the convertible in the garage. Kayla followed her into the lobby of the hospital, and stopped just inside the entrance as a wave of dizziness and nausea hit her like a fist. "Elizabet—" she managed to say, as everything whirled around her. The older woman caught her as she nearly stumbled and helped her to a nearby chair.

"Take a few deep breaths, child," she said quietly.

Kayla buried her face in her hands, afraid she was going to faint. Beyond the dizziness, she thought she could hear voices: someone cursing in Spanish as a pain ripped through her, the wail of a newborn baby, a boy screaming as a doctor set his broken arm, the unending pain of an old man breathing through a respirator.

"I hadn't thought about this," Elizabet murmured, chafing Kayla's hands with her own. "Just

keep breathing and try to push all of that away
from you—it's not happening to you, it's someone else's life, someone else's pain."

"I think—" Kayla said, gulping for air and
wishing she hadn't eaten anything for breakfast
"—I think I'm going to be sick." She pulled away
from Elizabet and ran for the women's bathroom,
which fortunately was only twenty feet away.

Elizabet was waiting for her in the bathroom,
standing by the counter, when she emerged
again. Kayla accepted the wet paper towel from
her and wiped her face, then rinsed her mouth
out with water from the sink.

"I think I'm okay now. It was just an awful
shock, that's all." Kayla dried her face with
another paper towel. "I want to go see Billy."

The woman at the front desk directed them to
Room 416 in the children's ward, where Billy
was staying.

Walking through the children's ward was
harder than she'd thought it would be, with
sudden pain and shock pummeling at her from
behind every closed door, striking without
warning. She walked stiffly beside Elizabet,
tense and wary, waiting for each new assault on
her senses.

Elizabet placed her hand on Kayla's shoulder
as they walked down the corridor, a warm touch.
A wave of calm flowed over her, holding the
shrieking pain at bay. Kayla stopped, looking up
at Elizabet in surprise.

"It's an old trick," Elizabet said, and then she
smiled. "I'll teach it to you sometime."

"I'll hold you to that promise," Kayla said as
they stopped in front of Room 416. "Damn," she
said without thinking about it.

"What?" Elizabet asked.

"He's asleep. We probably shouldn't wake him up." She pushed through the door anyhow, wanting to see how he looked.

Billy was lying on his back, breathing steadily. An IV needle ran to his left arm, clear fluid dripping into the plastic line. He looked very young, asleep and in a hospital gown, not at all like the tough guy that had taken care of Kayla and Liane for so many weeks.

Even from the door, she could sense the steady beating of his heart, the torn muscle slowly knitting itself back together in his leg. Kayla backed out of the room and closed the door quietly behind her. "He's okay," she said. "I'd like to come back here later, though, when he's awake. And I want to ask the nurses if Liane's been here. I haven't seen her since . . . since what happened last night, and she's probably scared out of her wits."

The nurse, when asked, only shook her head. No one other than Kayla and Elizabet had even called to check on Billy Johnson, except for an officer from the Detective Headquarters Division.

"Liane . . . that's your other friend, who ran away from the foster home with you and Billy?" Elizabet asked. "I think we should call the police to go pick her up, Kayla. It wasn't safe for the three of you, living on the streets together—it's far more dangerous for her, now that she's alone."

"You're right," Kayla admitted, and told her about Suite 230, the abandoned office building where they'd been living. She felt like a traitor, telling Elizabet about their secret hideaway, but just the thought of Liane alone, without Billy to protect her from people like Nick, was terrifying.

I just hope she's okay. . . .

Kayla was silent on the drive back to Elizabet's house, thinking about Liane and life on the streets. It had been so easy for her to get used to the idea of living in a house instead of a trashed office building, to hot showers and clean clothes and good food. Sure, they'd survived just fine on their own, but it wasn't anything she wanted to go back to. At least, not now.

Besides, she couldn't go back to what they'd been. She was different now, with this strange magic simmering inside her, twisting her mind with pain and power.

The sun was setting, turning the hills to shadowy outlines, as Elizabet drove into the driveway of her house. In the house, she went to the guest bedroom and sprawled out on the bed. In the other room, she could hear Elizabet dialing the telephone, talking to someone about Liane. Elizabet walked in the bedroom and sat down on the bed next to Kayla, watching her thoughtfully. "Want to talk about it?" she asked at last.

Kayla clenched the blanket in her fingers. "I hate this," she said. "I feel sick all the time, and people keep calling me 'witch' and worse, and I wish it would all go away."

"You know it won't." Elizabet shook her head. "No, all you can do now is learn how to live with this." She glanced at her watch. "I need to head off to work shortly, Kayla. You're welcome to go through my library while I'm gone, or watch tapes on the VCR. I'd suggest you call it an early night, though; you do still look exhausted from everything that happened last night. Is there anything you might need?"

"More milk," Kayla said promptly. "I finished almost all of it this morning."

Elizabet smiled. "I'd better make a complete shopping run on my way home—you seem to be working hard to clean out my refrigerator."

"I—I can eat less," Kayla said, suddenly alarmed. *I don't want her to send me to Juvie!*

The woman laughed. "No, that's not a problem. I guess I'll see you in the morning, child."

"Good night," Kayla said awkwardly, watching as Elizabet gathered up her blazer and briefcase and walked out to her car. She stood at the open door for a few minutes after Elizabet's car disappeared down the hill, then closed the front door and turned back to look at the room. *She must really trust me, to leave me here all alone.*

If I really wanted to, I could clean this place out before she gets back, be back in Hollywood in another two hours.

Back in Suite 230, eating canned chili and stolen sodas, just her alone now, unless she could find Liane somehow. No Billy to take care of them, keep the slimeballs like Nick away . . .

No. I don't want to do that.

She wandered to the bookshelf and took down an old hardcover book, something about dragons. In the guest bedroom, she made a small nest of pillows and blankets and curled up inside, opening to the first page of the book.

"Carlos, she's leaving. Without the girl."

Carlos sat up and stretched, looking out the car window. The black woman drove past in her convertible, obviously alone. "Good. Go tell the others, Ramon. We're going up to the house."

Kayla looked up from the book, hearing the

sound of breaking wood. There was a sudden crash from the hallway; she was off the bed and through the door a half-second later. The first thing she saw was one of the glass dolphins, lying shattered on the floor. The fact that she was surrounded by a group of young men, all wearing jeans, plaid shirts, and bandannas, registered a split-second later.

"What's going on here?" she asked, and then she saw the switchblade in one man's hand. Kayla couldn't hear anything beyond the pounding of her own blood.

The man holding the knife smiled at her. He was very handsome, Kayla thought as he moved toward her. A dark-haired, dark-eyed Hispanic man, maybe twenty years old, very handsome and completely terrifying. "This is the girl, the *bruja*," he said to the others, gazing into her eyes.

Kayla backed up toward the window, into the arms of one of the other young men. She twisted to look at him, the youngest of all of the strange men. He held her by the shoulders, but she could feel the nervousness in him, the tension in his hands.

"How do you know that she's for real?" one of the other young men asked.

"I'll prove it to you, Ramie," the handsome man said, standing very close to Kayla. The knife glittered in his hand; she watched that hand, afraid to breathe. There was a strange small smile on his face. Then he lowered his hand, and Kayla breathed a sigh of relief.

The pain hit her an instant later, a shock that took her breath away. She thought she heard someone shout, but she wasn't certain—everything was happening too fast. She saw the man pull the switchblade free, wiping the blood off on his jeans, and then she was falling, the world going white around her, everything blurry and very bright.

"*Madre de Dios*, Carlos, you didn't have to do that!" someone said from above her.

"She'll heal herself," the handsome man said, and she could hear the laughter behind his voice. "Or she won't, in which case she doesn't matter to us."

Bastard, she thought, the wooden floor rough against her cheek. The pain was falling on her in waves, each wave higher than the last. Kayla closed her eyes, feeling the warm blood against her skin, and wondered what dying would be like.

Through her closed eyes, she saw the light brightening. Her hands, and then her entire body, now felt like they were on fire, burning from within. She opened her eyes to see all of the men staring at her, at the patterns of blue light that coursed over her body.

She caught at the light in her hands, holding it against her middle, aiming it at the pain. The light poured into the emptiness of the knife wound, drawing out the pain and closing it back up again. A moment later the light was gone, except for a few bright sparks that flickered over her hands before finally fading away to nothingness.

Everyone was still staring at her.

The man they'd called Carlos knelt beside her. She tried to pull away, but was too weak and exhausted to move. He lifted her shirt, looking for the knife wound. A moment later he stood up, a satisfied look on his face.

"Ramon, carry her to the car," he directed. The youngest man nodded, easily lifting her up and moving toward the door. Kayla tried to pull free, struggling weakly. *No, this can't be happening to me!*

Kayla's last glimpse was of the shards of the broken glass dolphin on the floor, as the door closed behind them.

Chapter Four

Elizabet turned on the Volkswagen's radio, listening to the light jazz that was playing on KWAV. The traffic wasn't bad at all, as she headed down Laurel Canyon into Hollywood. At 9 A.M. on a weekday morning, it would've been another story, with cars backed up all the way to Van Nuys. But now, it was quiet enough that Elizabet could let her mind drift as she drove down the narrow, winding road.

Kayla. She was still uncertain about the girl, very uncertain whether she'd still be at the house when Elizabet returned after work. It wouldn't surprise her to find that the child had left and taken all the valuables she could carry. She hoped the girl had better sense than that; Kayla was a danger to herself and everyone around her right now, with that bright pool of magic simmering inside her. Serious magic, more than Elizabet had ever seen in one person before, and of course the child had no idea how to use or control it. . . .

Thinking about Kayla's magic, it was several seconds before she noticed the sensation of power in the hills behind her, a magical flare that was suddenly too bright to ignore.

"KAYLA!"

The girl was doing something with her magic, Elizabet couldn't quite tell what. In half a second, she made a snap decision and yanked the steering wheel hard, the Volkswagen skidding in a sharp 180-degree spin. Car horns blared, and she thought she could hear someone shouting at her, as she floored the accelerator and drove at top speed back toward her house.

She could feel the rising levels of power and a sense of desperation. *Something's wrong . . . something's very wrong. . . .* Elizabet hit the brakes as she came up behind a large truck, moving slowly up the road. She wanted to scream in frustration, but instead watched carefully for a break in the traffic on the other side of the road and made a quick illegal crossover of the double yellow line to get ahead of the truck. But that had wasted valuable seconds, and already she could feel the magical power fading, dying away. . . .

They shoved her into the back seat of one of their cars. She lay on the seat, trying to catch her breath and pull free from the dizziness that made it impossible for her to think straight, let alone run or fight. To make things worse, her head was pounding again, the same awful headache.

When she could sit up, they were already driving over the top of the crest of Laurel Canyon. In the last moments of fading sunlight, the lights of the San Fernando Valley were flickering into life, like a million bright jewels scattered over the valley and surrounding hills.

She leaned her head against the window, wincing every time the car bounced over one of the many potholes in the road.

"Are you all right?" a soft Chicano-accented voice asked, startling her enough that she opened her eyes. "Are you still in pain?"

It was the young man now driving the car. In her dizziness and pain, she hadn't noticed who was in the vehicle with her. She shook her head, not wanting to answer. The young man spoke again, saying something in Spanish to the man in the front seat next to him. They talked for a few minutes in that musical language, then it was silent in the car again.

They drove down from the last hill, into the flat urban maze of the San Fernando Valley. Kayla thought about leaping out of the car and making a run for it as the Chevy paused at a stop light, then thought better of it. *I don't think I can walk real well right now, let alone outrun these guys. I'll have to wait, find a better opportunity to run like hell. . . .*

God, why are they doing this? Kidnaping me. I can't believe this nightmare is really happening to me, I can't believe it. . . .

The young man parked the car in front of an old apartment building, on a quiet street with young children playing among the dead cars and garbage cans. The other man had to pull her from the car; her legs didn't seem to be working right yet, and she would've fallen but for his hands holding her up. Leaning on his arm, she managed to stay on her feet. The two men walked her into the apartment building and up three flights of stairs.

Kayla was certain she was going to die by the time they reached the top of the stairs; her insides felt like they were on fire, every movement ripping pain through her. The young man unlocked the door of an apartment and helped her walk through.

Inside, the living room was sparsely furnished with an old sofa and kitchen table, rock star posters on the walls, a television on a low table across the room. Someone had left a radio on, playing Spanish pop songs.

Down a short hallway was a bedroom. The men let her fall onto the large bed in the corner of the room. She just lay there for a few minutes amid the rumpled sheets and blankets, remembering what it felt like to breathe without pain. Several minutes later, she felt like she could sit up again without dying. She still felt awful, but at least it wasn't as bad as it had been.

The young man was standing at the doorway, watching her. *Why did they bring me here, what do they want with me?* She stared at her feet, not speaking, then glanced up at him.

He was still standing there, just looking at her. He wasn't as handsome as the older guy, who was breathtaking in a Hollywood star kind of way, like a twenty-year-old Richard Gere with wavy black hair. *And a real bastard, too.* This younger guy's black hair was very curly, looking like he'd never really succeeded in combing it down. His dark eyes were thoughtful when he spoke. "Rest now, *querida.* Carlos and the others will be here soon."

He started for the door, then stopped. Walking across the room, he unplugged the telephone on the wooden dresser and took it with him, closing the door behind him. Kayla lay back on the bed, thinking: *I don't want to rest. I want to get the hell out of here. . . .* Her eyes closed, and she drifted off to sleep to the sound of the Spanish music playing from the other room.

The Volkswagen's brakes squealed as Elizabet pulled up in the driveway. She was out of the car a split-second later, heading for the front door.

The door was slightly ajar, and Elizabet saw the ripped wood where someone had forced the lock and felt a chill run through her. Very quietly, she slowly pushed the door open.

She listened, hearing nothing but the faint sound of traffic from down the hill, and stepped into the room. The first thing she saw was the broken glass sculpture on the floor. She skirted it carefully, looking around the living room.

There was no sign of Kayla.

She walked to the open guest bedroom door and saw the pile of pillows and blankets, and the abandoned book. She turned back to the living room and saw the blood on the floor near the window.

Fighting the impulse to panic, Elizabet knelt beside the pool of wet blood. Someone had been badly hurt here, or possibly died; she tried to hold back the terror, forcing herself to concentrate. She held her hands out over the blood staining the wooden floor and closed her eyes.

Another person's emotions flickered through her mind, flashes of pain and terror. Kayla, lying here on the floor, her life bleeding away. Then the bright fire of magic and more terror. Images of faces, a darkly handsome man in his twenties, and being lifted, carried away somewhere.

She's survived it, Elizabet thought with a wave

of relief. *Whatever they did to her, she survived it. And then they—whoever "they" are—they took her away.*

She straightened and crossed to the phone, dialing with shaking hands. "Detective Cable, please." She waited for an endless several seconds, until she heard the police officer's voice answer on the other end of the connection. "Nichelle, this is Elizabet. Someone's kidnaped Kayla. I don't know exactly what's happened but she's gone. . . ."

She was standing in a park with Elizabet, in a meadow bright with early morning sunlight and colorfully costumed people. All of the people were strange, wearing glistening metal armor and odd clothing. And there was something else about them, something she knew but couldn't quite remember, about who they were and what they were doing here. It was something important, she knew that, she just couldn't remember exactly what it was. . . .

A group of musicians were standing together on the damp grass, playing strange melodies. It was a kind of music she'd never heard before, wild and haunting.

Elizabet was with her, which meant that everything was all right, she was supposed to be here.

:Of course we're supposed to be here,: Elizabet said silently. *:It's what the An Caillach Beara told us, that we needed to be here. That we needed to meet these people at the Whoopie Donuts shop at precisely 7:15 A.M. That if we weren't here, something awful was going to happen to all of Los Angeles. That it might happen anyhow, but if we were here, there was a better chance that it wouldn't.:*

:Why can't people read the future as something more concrete than a lot of "What ifs?": Kayla asked. *:I mean, you'd think that the ogress would be able to read the future like the* Sunday L.A. Times *sports page, wouldn't you? I hate all that mystical bullshit.:*

"Shhh, child," Elizabet said aloud. "They're starting now."

Something really strange was happening, that was for sure. She could feel it, the gathering of power like a rising wind, a hurricane building from a deceptive calm—and the long-haired guy with the flute, he was the center of all of it, silently calling the forces of nature to this spot. She could see it reaching from him, touching all the magic around them and drawing it in, creating something from nothingness, a focus point of simmering magic. . . .

"Carlos, I don't want her here!"

The loud female voice broke through Kayla's dream, startling her awake. She opened her eyes sleepily to see two people standing in the doorway. One was a young woman with long dark hair and full red lips accented by bright lipstick. Those lips pouted as she looked at Kayla. The other was the handsome guy, Carlos. *The guy who tried to kill me*, she remembered.

The young man spoke in a placating tone, but Kayla could hear the steel underneath it. "Roberta, *querida*, she has to stay somewhere. It's only for a few days, until we find a permanent place for her."

"But there's no room for her! You have to take her somewhere else. . . ."

They were ignoring her. They were standing right in front of her, arguing, and it was like she wasn't there at all. Kayla's initial terror gave way to anger. "Look, I don't know who you are, but—" she began.

Both the man and the woman continued to ignore her completely. "Roberta," Carlos said, "No more arguing about this, please. She stays here for tonight, and that's final. I'll try to find another place for her tomorrow." The man glanced at Kayla for the first time. "If you're hungry, Luisa is cooking dinner for everyone."

The two walked away, the woman still trying to argue. Kayla looked out the window, wondering whether she ought to jump. *Better to wait until I can get out of here without risking breaking my neck,* she thought, and realized with a start that she *was* hungry. And her head wasn't hurting anymore, though her gut still ached—a faint reminder of the knife wound. What she did feel was exhausted, with every muscle in her body aching like someone had pounded on her for several hours with a brick. And hungry. Very hungry. The smell of hot food wafted through the open door, enough to make her want to ignore her fear of these people, and whatever it was that they were going to do with her, enough to brave the world outside the bedroom.

She stood up a little unsteadily, then walked out to the living room, now overflowing with men and women and loud rock music. Most of them were helping themselves to the plates of food laid out on the counter, while a couple of the younger kids sat playing video games in front of the television. She felt like a stranger at a wedding, surrounded by people she didn't know, in a place she didn't want to be. Most of them seemed to be ignoring her, too—maybe she could just go to the door and walk right out of this place? She glanced at the door, where a big man in a plaid shirt and green bandanna, dressed like so many of the other guys, was standing guard. He met her gaze squarely. No, she wasn't going to be able to walk past that guy, at least, not very easily. . . .

But I'm tough, I can handle this. These guys won't see me cry, that's for sure. I've been in bad situations before, like a couple of those awful foster homes. And I survived on the street just fine; no bastards made me cry then. So now these crazy people have kidnaped me, I don't know why. But I'll survive it. I'll get out of this, they'll see.

"Are you hungry?" a voice asked from beside her.

She turned to see the young man, the driver who had brought her to this awful place. She looked down at her sneakers and nodded.

"I'll get you some dinner." He elbowed his way past a couple of the others and quickly filled a plate with a large burrito and several tamales. Some of the people were looking at her strangely; the young man said something fast in Spanish. Kayla caught the word "brooha" mixed in with other words too fast and foreign to understand.

"Here." He handed the plate to her. "Do you want a soda? Maybe a beer?" He tilted his head to look at her, and a grin flashed across his face, like a burst of sunlight from behind a cloud. "You *can* talk, can't you?"

"I can talk," she said, not looking up at him.

"How old are you, *querida?*"

"Fifteen," she said, surprised by the question.

"I'm seventeen," he said. "I didn't think Carlos' *bruja* would be so young."

"What—what's a brooha?" she asked.

He smiled. "A witch, a magician. Someone who can do what you did tonight." He shook his head, as though he still couldn't believe what he'd seen. "I never dreamed that could be possible, until I saw the magic in your hands. Carlos was right, we need you here." He gestured at her with the glass in his hand. "So, what do you want to drink?"

"Soda's fine, thanks," Kayla whispered, glancing at the door. Everyone seemed to be ignoring her except this kid and the guy at the door; maybe she could take a seat by the door and just slip out when the door guard was getting his dinner or something. It would take her a while to steal some money for bus fare, but eventually she'd be back at Elizabet's. . . .

"Who's this, Ramon, your new girlfriend?" a short boy with greased black hair asked.

To Kayla's surprise, the young man blushed. "No, Carlos found her—she's the *bruja* he was talking about. Her name is . . ." He stopped and looked at her, smiling a little. "I'm afraid I don't know your name, *querida*."

"Kayla," she said. "Kayla Smith."

"Ah. A pretty name, Kayla. I'm Ramon Hernandez. That's Carlos over there, my brother. Roberta's his girlfriend, she and her sister Luisa live here, and two of their cousins . . ." He continued on a mind-numbing list of names, rattling off information about everyone in the apartment. She bit into one of the tamales and pretended to listen, keeping an eye on the front door. Maybe later she'd have a chance. . . .

The tamale was hot, spicy, and very oily. Kayla took one bite and decided she wasn't that hungry after all and set the plate down on the closest table. The young man watched her with an odd expression in his eyes. He seemed about to say something, then turned away to talk in rapid-fire Spanish with one of the other men.

"Roberta, please, I don't want to argue this anymore. . . ."

Don't those two ever stop? Kayla wondered, as Carlos and Roberta's argument increased in volume to the point where she could hear it over the other conversation in the room. The two of them were walking toward her. Kayla looked around quickly for a place to hide.

"Just let her stay here a few days, and I promise I'll do anything you want, buy you some new clothes, jewelry, whatever." They stopped in front of Kayla, who felt all the eyes in the room moving to her.

Roberta gave Kayla a long, hate-filled look, then suddenly smiled. Kayla decided instantly that she didn't like that smile at all.

"I want her earrings," Roberta said.

Kayla stared at her in shock. She had to be kidding—the earrings were hers, Elizabet had bought them for her just a few hours ago. It wasn't like they were expensive, or even unusual. And they were *hers.* "'Berta, you have lots of jewelry; I buy you more all the time. . . ." Carlos said.

"I want her earrings, Carlos," the woman insisted.

Carlos glanced at Kayla. "Take off your earrings, girl," he said.

Anger overrode the terror that had haunted her since these people had forced their way into Elizabet's house, stabbed her, and then carried her off like a piece of meat. "Like hell, you bastard!"

The man's hand clamped down painfully on her arm. "Take off the earrings. Now."

Kayla started to protest and then saw the look in his eyes. It reminded her of the look he'd had at Elizabet's house, the same tiny smile that had been on his face . . . just before he tried to kill her. It was a smile that said that he was enjoying this, and whatever was going to happen next.

Her hands shaking, Kayla removed the silver earrings. She held them in her hand for a moment, then tossed them onto the floor. They rattled on the worn linoleum. "Here, take 'em, they're yours," she said tightly.

Carlos' eyes narrowed even more dangerously. "Pick them up and give them to Roberta."

"The little bitch can pick them up herself—"

"Pick them up and give them to Roberta," he said in a voice like ice.

Kayla knelt and picked up the silver loops, handing them to Roberta. With all the dignity she could muster, she walked down the hall to the bedroom.

She sprawled facedown on the bed, trying not to cry. She couldn't stop the first few tears and angrily wiped them away. *I don't know what's going on here, I don't know what they're going to do with me, but I'll be damned before I let them see me cry!*

"Kayla?"

She rolled over to see Ramon at the doorway. "What do you want? I don't have any more jewelry to give away, sorry . . . how 'bout my sneakers? They're new too, Elizabet just bought them for me. . . ." She saw that he was holding the plate that she'd left on the living room table. "Go away, I'm not hungry."

He sat down at the end of the bed, setting the plate down next to her; Kayla edged back, closer to the wall. "I know it's difficult for you," he said awkwardly. "I know you don't want to be here. But you'll see, it'll get better. You'll be happy here, one of the homegirls. You have to understand, it's hard for Carlos and the rest of us, too. We're not used to anything like this, bringing someone like you here to our *barrio.* . . ."

"You mean, you don't go around kidnaping people all the time?"

He smiled. "No, not usually. Though there is a great family tradition of kidnaping our brides . . . of course Carlos is so handsome, he'd never have to do that. The women just fall at his feet, all the time." He looked down at his hands, clenched in his lap, then back up at her with those dark eyes. "We need you, *querida.* We need you to help us with your magic. Carlos should have told you why we need you, then you'd understand. It's a matter of life and death for us: if we lose, they'll kill us all. That's why we brought you here."

"Carlos should have told me this, instead of trying to kill me! He stabbed me, remember? I could've died!" Kayla's gut twisted, remembering. It still ached where the knife wound had been, a dull counterpoint to the exhaustion and secret terrors.

She saw the troubled look in his eyes before he hid it behind a smile. "But you healed yourself, didn't you? Carlos just wanted to prove that you could do it. You're fine now, it didn't do any real harm to you . . ."

"What if he'd been wrong? What if he'd picked the wrong house, stabbed the wrong kid?"

"But that didn't happen." Ramon shook his head. "It all worked out fine."

"Listen, please, I just want to go home, all I want to do is go home . . . can't you let me go?" She felt the tears threatening again, and bit her lip to hold them back. *I just want to be gone, be out of here, go back to Elizabet's. . . .*

"What, you don't want to be here with all of these handsome homeboys? Like me, Ramon, the handsomest of them all?" He brushed back his hair with one hand, giving her his most appealing look. In spite of herself, Kayla smiled.

"It'll be all right, *querida*," Ramon said reassuringly. "You'll see, everything will be all right." He picked up the plate of food and held it out to her. Reluctantly, she took it from him. "Eat some dinner, you'll feel better," he said. "Maybe tomorrow Carlos will let me take you out into *mi barrio*, show you our home. And I'll explain why we need you here."

He left the room, and Kayla lay staring at the ceiling for a long time. Her thoughts were moving too fast, racing through her mind, all the words blurring together.

They were going to keep her here, maybe forever. That thought hurt more than everything else. They'd keep her a prisoner here for the rest of her life, if they thought they could get away with it.

She crossed to the door and listened. It was silent in the hallway beyond. Maybe everyone had left the apartment, and she could just sneak out, get to a telephone and call Elizabet. . . .

Quietly, she opened the door. A man she didn't recognize was seated on a folding chair by the bedroom door. He watched her silently as she walked to the bathroom. Inside, she checked the window. It was the same situation as the bedroom, no way to climb down and too far to jump. She splashed some cold water on her face and walked past him again into the bedroom.

With the door carefully closed against the watchful eyes of the man in the hallway, she lay down on the bed and wondered how in the hell she was going to get herself out of this situation.

I want to go back to Elizabet's, she thought. *I want to go home, I want to go home . . .*

:Kayla, can you hear me? Kayla, child, where are you?:

She sat upright in bed. "Elizabet?"

:Where are you? Tell me where you are . . . :

The words tumbled from her, she didn't care if anyone outside the bedroom could hear. "Elizabet, they've locked me up in an apartment, I'm somewhere in the Valley, please, you have to get me out of here!"

:Kayla, where are you? Can you hear me?:

"Yes, I can! Please, Elizabet, they're going to keep me here forever, you have to help me! I can't get out, they won't let me leave, I'm locked in here—"

:Kayla, can you hear me? Kayla . . . :

Elizabet's voice was fainter now, moving further away.

"No! Elizabet, I'm here, please, help me! Don't go, don't leave me here! Elizabet!"

:Kayla, where are you—:

Elizabet's voice faded to silence, too distant to hear. Kayla curled up on the bed, one fist pressed against her mouth to keep her from sobbing out loud. "Elizabet, please, don't leave me here, please . . ."

The bedroom door opened, her impassive guard looking at her silently before closing the door again. She thought about trying to get past him and escape, maybe hit him with something and make a break for the door.

The first step, she thought, *is to get organized.*

Make a plan. She angrily brushed the tears out of her eyes and began exploring the bedroom, opening every drawer in the dresser to look for anything useful. The top drawer was filled with pretty lingerie, all lace and silk. Beneath that were two drawers with jeans and folded blouses. Nothing useful.

The fourth drawer wasn't much better. It mostly held women's shoes: one pair of fancy heels and a couple pairs of cheap woven leather shoes. The jackpot was inside one of the shoe boxes: no shoes, just a small mirror, several razor blades, and a small bag of white powder. Kayla carefully picked up one of the razor blades, replacing everything else exactly the way it had been.

It's not much, but now I have a weapon, she thought, hiding it under the mattress of the bed. She checked the closet next, riffling through the dresses on plastic hangers and several cardboard boxes. She was hoping to find some extra bedsheets, envisioning herself tying sheets together to climb down from the window like a movie heroine. But the boxes only had some towels and notebooks written in Spanish inside. The sheets that were already on the bed wouldn't get her very far, though maybe if she ripped them into strips and braided a rope out of that . . .

Tomorrow. I'll do it tomorrow. She was tired, even after taking the nap earlier. Too tired to deal with anything right now. All of this craziness, and getting hurt, it felt like it had taken something major out of her. Kayla took the plainest nightgown she could find out of the dresser and changed out of her clothes.

In the bed, she tried to imagine a handsome

hero arriving to rescue her—some handsome, blond guy with a flashy smile and lots of dimples. Wasn't that what all fairy-tale heroes were supposed to look like? And a white horse, he needed a white horse. He'd show up below her tower window—in this case, a third story apartment window—and climb up to rescue her. That's the way the stories always worked.

This time, I think I'll have to rescue myself.

I'll do it, she thought, drifting off to sleep again. *I'm tougher and smarter than they are. I'll figure a way out of this. They won't keep me here forever, no way. . . .*

Chapter Five

"Carlos, she's wearing one of my nightgowns!"

Oh God, Kayla thought, burying her face in the pillows. *It's the Dragon Lady again.* It was too late to pretend to be asleep, and besides, no one could sleep with that lady's shrill voice screaming in their ear. She sat up, pulling the covers more tightly around her.

Roberta was still going on about the *puta* who was wearing her clothes, with Carlos standing there taking it all in. She wondered why he put up with her. Sure, the woman was pretty, but that voice!

"Why are you wearing her nightgown, girl?" Carlos asked mildly, as Roberta paused to inhale between sentences.

"Because I don't have anything of my own!" Kayla said furiously. "And what I've got is covered with blood!" It was true; her jeans, draped over a chair, looked like someone had painted them with blood. *Her* blood.

"Ramon!" Carlos called through the open bedroom door. The younger man appeared a few seconds later. He was wearing a black leather jacket over yet another plaid shirt, which Kayla thought looked rather good on him.

"I want you to take the girl to buy some clothes," Carlos continued, taking a large wad of money from his pocket and peeling off several bills. "Get her anything she needs. Roberta, we can't let her go out wearing her own clothes now, there's too much blood on them. The *policía* might see her, then there'd be trouble. Let her wear something of yours just for today, all right?"

Roberta gave Kayla a sullen look and said something fast in Spanish. From the expression on her face, Kayla decided she was glad she didn't understand that particular phrase. Carlos gave her a very sharp look, and Roberta visibly flinched. "She can wear my clothes to go shopping," she said in a flat voice.

Carlos handed Ramon a handful of bills. Ramon looked at the money, then at his brother. "I don't know, Carlos, she doesn't have any clothes at all, and this isn't very much money. . . ." Ramon gave Kayla a wink. Carlos hesitated, then fished in his pocket for more money. Kayla blinked as Carlos gave Ramon several hundred-dollar bills. "Just try to bring back some change, heh?" Carlos grumbled. "I hope you're worth it, girl," he said, giving a direct look.

"Well, you could just let me leave, then I wouldn't cost you anything at all," she retorted.

He laughed and clapped her on the shoulder. "I think I'll like having you around, after a few weeks of getting used to it," he said, then glanced at Roberta's sour face. "Maybe it'll take longer than a few weeks," he added morosely. Carlos walked toward the door. "Get dressed now, and Ramon will take you shopping. Make him buy you a hamburger or something, too. He said you didn't eat any dinner last night."

Kayla watched silently as the three left the room. It didn't make any sense. Were Carlos and Ramon trying to be . . . nice? . . . to her? Kidnapers weren't supposed to be *nice* to the people they kidnaped. They were supposed to treat them awfully, threatening to kill them, maybe starving them or keeping them tied up. At least, that's the way it was in the movies.

What they *never* did was offer to take you out for shopping and a hamburger.

It just didn't make sense.

She turned to the closet and dresser and thought about which of Roberta's clothes she was going to borrow for the day. The best, she decided. She found a lovely matching black skirt and blouse, decorated with red ribbons. It looked a little odd with her sneakers, but Roberta's shoes didn't fit her feet—they were too small. She found a hairbrush on the dresser and brushed her hair until it crackled against her fingers.

Ramon was waiting for her in the living room. There was no sign of Carlos or Roberta, which Kayla thought was unfortunate, since she really wanted to see the look on Roberta's face when she saw Kayla wearing her nicest clothes. Two dark-haired young women were in the kitchen, talking to each other in Spanish.

"You look very pretty, *querida*," Ramon said, opening the front door for her.

"Thanks, I guess," she said, as they walked down the stairs. Two of the young men she recognized from last night were waiting for them, leaning against a car. "Don't you guys wear anything but plaid shirts?" she asked.

Ramon laughed and said something in Spanish
to the two men. They smiled at her. Kayla
smiled back, but wished she knew why they
thought what she'd said was funny.

She climbed into the back seat of the car next
to Ramon and sat silently as they drove away from
the apartment building. She looked out the
window, trying to memorize the route in case she
had a chance to run away later. A few minutes
later, they parked in a lot on Van Nuys Boulevard.
The street was already busy, with slow-moving cars
driving past the stores and the Van Nuys
courthouse and police station.

The police station!

Kayla glanced longingly down the street at the
large white building, wondering if she ought to
take a chance and run for it now. If she could
just get close enough to call for help . . .

Ramon took her arm, leading her down the
street. The two other guys walked beside them.
The taller of the two hitched up his jacket, and
Kayla glimpsed a small handgun tucked into the
back of his jeans.

"Ramon, he's—"

"Shhh, Kayla, I know." Ramon glanced around
nervously. "Jose is just being careful," he said.
"We've had some trouble here lately; we have to
be very careful now."

They walked past one of those inexpensive
haircutting shops, and Kayla saw a glimpse of
herself in the store window, the long curly brown
hair falling over her shoulders and into her eyes.
She caught Ramon's hand. "Can I get a haircut?"

He looked at her curiously. "But your hair is
very pretty. Why do you want to cut it?"

"Come on, Carlos gave you lots of bucks.
Can't I get a haircut, too?"

She walked into the store, before he could say
no, and up to the counter.

"So, what would you like? A trim?" The blond
young woman behind the counter looked very
bored.

"Shampoo and haircut," Kayla said, as Ramon
and the two guys joined her at the counter. The
blonde took her back to the sinks where she
scrubbed Kayla's hair with some strange fruit-
scented shampoo, then sat her down in one of
the barber's chairs.

"How much do you want me to take off?"

Kayla thought about it for a moment. "How
'bout everything?" she asked.

"What?"

"I want it real short. Like, a couple inches in
the front, kinda shaved along the sides. All
punked out. You know, something really
different."

"Hey, it's your life, sweetheart," the blonde
said, and started cutting. Ramon and their two
silent escorts sat down by the door to wait.
Twenty minutes later, after a long one-sided conversation in which the woman talked about her
ambition to work as a hairdresser for an under-
taker, because the money was good and the
clients never complained about her work, the
haircut was finished. Kayla looked at herself in
the mirror and grinned.

"I don't like it," Ramon said as he paid the
woman and they left the shop. "Too short. A
woman should have long hair."

"Well, *this* one doesn't," Kayla said, feeling
better than she had since this entire awful experience had started. *I look like Annie Lennox
now,* she thought with glee. *Except that she's
blond. Well, maybe I can try that next.* "How

'bout a pair of leather pants?" she asked Ramon
as they walked past a store with mannequins in
skintight black and red leather in the window.
"It would look great with my haircut."

"Absolutely not," Ramon said in a tone that
didn't allow room for arguing.

"Oh, you're no fun," she said, still looking at
the clothing in the window. A heavy weight
landed on her shoulders, and she saw that
Ramon had draped his black leather jacket over
her. "What?"

"For you, *vida mia,* since you want some
leather clothes." As Kayla stared at the jacket in
shock, Ramon turned away quickly and started
walking down the street.

Jose said something in Spanish, and the other
man laughed. Kayla followed Ramon down the
street, wishing the men had spoken in English
so she could understand them.

*Then again, maybe I'm better off not knowing
what these guys are saying about me. . . .*

She caught up with Ramon in front of a
department store. "Hey, take your jacket back, I
don't want it!"

"You don't?" He looked at her, surprised. "But
I thought you wanted a leather jacket."

"Yes, but . . . but I can't accept this from
you!" She held it out to him.

"Why not?"

"Because . . ." She found herself blushing, and
willed herself to stop. "Because I don't know
what you want in exchange for it."

He stared at her blankly, then grinned. "Oh,
I see. No, not to worry . . . you're too young
for me. I like older women, like Roberta. The
jacket is a gift, nothing more. Like the rest of
the clothes we'll buy for you today." He pointed

at a pretty white blouse in the window. "Would you like one of those, Kayla? It would look very nice on you, I think."

"Yeah, sure," she said, feeling strangely shy. "Thanks for the jacket, Ramon."

He smiled, not looking at her. "I'm glad you like it. Come on, we need to buy you some more clothes."

All I seem to be doing this week is nearly getting killed and buying clothes, Kayla thought as she looked through the racks of women's clothes in the store. Jose took up a position by the door, glancing out at the street every few seconds, as Ramon and the other man—Fernando, his name was—took clothes down from the racks and shelves and held them out for Kayla to inspect.

Ramon was weighted down with an armful of clothing by the time they were finished and ready to pay for it all. Kayla stood looking at a display of earrings by the cash register as they waited for the clerk to tally up their purchases. Now she was wearing a pair of new jeans, a skin-tight black shirt sewn with silvery threads, and the leather jacket.

"You should buy some new earrings," Ramon said, watching her look at the earrings.

Kayla contemplated her reflection in a small mirror. "No, I don't think so." She picked up two metal safety pins from the shop counter, and fastened them in her ears. "There. That looks better with the leather jacket, I think."

"Carlos won't like it," Ramon said definitively.

"Well, that's another great reason to wear them," Kayla said. "Anything that pisses off Carlos is fine in my book." Ramon gave her a doubtful look, but didn't argue. "Hey, how 'bout some lunch?" she asked. "I didn't eat any

breakfast, y'know. Or any dinner," she added
after a moment.

Ramon gestured to Fernando and said something quickly in Spanish. Fernando nodded,
picked up the bags of Kayla's clothing, and
headed for the door. "He'll meet us at Fastburger," Ramon said.

As they walked down the street, Jose walking
watchfully ahead of them, Kayla glanced again at
where Jose's gun was hidden. "You didn't tell me
why Jose is carrying a gun," she said to Ramon,
quietly enough that none of the other pedestri-
ans could hear them.

"It's because we've had some trouble here
lately," Ramon said after a long pause. "Bad
trouble."

"Is it with the police, or another street gang?"

"How did you know that we're a gang?"

"I figured it out for myself," she said, a little
sarcastically. "The bandannas and identical plaid
shirts kinda give it away, you know.

"We don't think of ourselves like that," Ramon
said. "I mean, I'm a homeboy, and this is *mi
barrio*. We all hang out together, go to parties
and all that, maybe make a little money together,
but we're not really a gang. It's those *bastardos*
from the city, they're the real gang. The T-Men.
They're trying to move in here and sell drugs,
take our money away from us."

"You sell drugs?" Kayla asked.

He shrugged. "They want our neighborhood.
They already did this to another gang, the guys
that live over by Fulton Street. Killed maybe
ten of their guys; the rest are too scared to
even go out on the street now. They just got
started with us, a few weeks ago. So far, they've
hurt one of our guys real bad. Reynaldo is still

in the hospital. We got even, Carlos stabbed one of their guys, so now it's a war."

"Carlos is really good at stabbing people," Kayla said, rubbing her gut, which still ached a little as she walked. "Did he study how to do that in high school or what?"

"You could make a real difference," Ramon continued, as if she hadn't spoken. "A *bruja,* a real witch, to use against them . . . maybe you could change them all into frogs or something, eh?"

"If I could, I'd start with your brother," Kayla said under her breath.

"What did you say?" Ramon wanted to know.

"I doubt I can change anybody into a frog," Kayla said, a little louder. "I don't think it exactly works that way. I mean, I don't know how it works, this is all as weird to me as it is to you. I never knew that magic was real until two days ago."

"I didn't believe in it, until I saw you—" Ramon grabbed her suddenly by the arm, looking back at the street. Kayla twisted to see what he was looking at; a white Mercedes convertible was driving very slowly along the street, maybe thirty feet away. Inside were four young black men wearing blue sweatshirts and baseball caps, all watching Ramon, Kayla, and Jose.

Ramon pushed Kayla ahead of him. "Walk faster," he said quietly. The white convertible accelerated past them, one of the guys turning to look back at Kayla and Ramon. The car disappeared around the corner. Ramon spoke quickly to Jose in Spanish; the other man nodded and took off at a run in the direction of the parking lot.

"Keep walking," Ramon said. "The Fastburger

is up ahead, another block or so. Just keep walking."

This is my best chance, she suddenly realized. *Jose and Fernando aren't here, Ramon doesn't have a gun—I think—now it's just the two of us walking along the street . . .* "Ramon, look!" she said, pointing across the street.

"What?" he asked.

Kayla shoved him, hard enough that he fell against a trash can, and took off running. The police station was only two blocks away . . . she could make it, she knew she could make it. . . .

She risked a glance backward to see Ramon staggering to his feet, then starting to run after her. "Kayla!"

She felt like she was flying, her feet barely touching the pavement. Her gut hurt, but she ignored it, concentrating on running as fast as she could. Another block, only another block . . . she could see the glass doors of the courthouse, the men and women in business suits walking in and out of the building . . . almost there, almost there . . .

A car screamed to a stop on the street next to her. The white convertible.

Oh, shit!

Kayla dived for the closest doorway, a bookstore. The startled proprietor stepped back as she ran past him, going straight for the back door. A moment later, she was out in the back alley, looking up and down the narrow street. *Which way to go, which way . . . ?* She could see the street off to her left—another left turn, run across the intersection, and she'd be in front of the police station. Her gut began aching again as she gasped for breath, putting everything she had into running.

The white convertible turned into the alley
ahead of her, blocking her path. She stumbled
to a stop, looking for another direction to run.
She yanked at the back door of the closest
store, but it was locked. Before she could run
to another door, the young men were out of
the car and surrounding her. She tried to dive
past them; someone caught her by the arm and
spun her around. She fell against the wall,
sliding in the garbage and mud. She saw the
pistol in one guy's hand, saw him pull back the
hammer with his thumb.

Oh God, he's going to kill me, he's going to—

Fernando's car screamed to a stop at the end
of the alley. Jose was leaning halfway through
the window, firing his pistol. The other guys
dived for cover, pulling out handguns and shoot-
ing wildly. Kayla crouched with her back pressed
against the wall as Fernando's car crashed into
the front of the Mercedes with a sickening
crunch of metal, shoving it backward.

Ramon leaped out of the car, grabbing Kayla by
the arm and yanking her back toward Fernando's
car. The car's engine shrieked with the strain as
Fernando reversed direction, accelerating
backwards out of the alley. Ramon pushed her into
the back seat of the moving car, pulling himself in
after her. "Go, go!" Ramon shouted, shoving Kayla
down and firing his handgun through the open car
window. The car skidded backwards into the street,
then raced forward in a hard turn, leaving the
Mercedes behind in the alley.

At the next intersection, Fernando turned left,
driving very fast through the residential streets.
Ramon stared out through the back window for
several blocks, then turned to Kayla. "Are you all
right?"

She nodded, too scared to speak. A hot pain hit her; every nerve in her arm was screaming at her, as the blood dripped down over her fingers. She looked at her own arms in shock; no, it wasn't her, she wasn't hurt at all.

"Jose, *mi hermano!*" Ramon's horrified voice startled her. She looked up to see Jose pressing a handkerchief to his arm. The cloth was already bright with blood, a widening stain of red.

Jose said something in Spanish, his voice weak. His lips were tight, and he was very pale. Kayla fought the impulse to touch him—she knew he must be in incredible pain already, and her touch couldn't help . . . wouldn't help . . .

A blue spark flickered over her palm, then another. Her hands moved forward as if by themselves, drawn to that pain that she could feel, the pain that was calling out to her. Her hands brushed against Jose's face, his skin cold and damp to her touch. She could feel the magic welling inside her like an irresistible tide, higher and higher . . . she closed her eyes, caught up in something she couldn't understand. Beneath her hands, she could feel the magic coursing into him, flowing down to the source of the pain and washing it away.

She opened her eyes to see Ramon staring at her. His dark eyes were wide with surprise and something she didn't understand. He raised his hand to touch her face. . . .

His hand paused, a fingertip's distance from her cheek, but close enough that she could feel the warmth of it. She felt as though she was within his thoughts, caught up in his astonishment and delight. She couldn't tell her thoughts from his, everything was too close and strange and tinted with the bright glow of the magic.

:¿Querida, que tipo de magica es eso?: he asked silently, and she could feel his joy like a tangible thing, singing inside her mind. It was overwhelming, too many thoughts and emotions that weren't hers, catching her up and spinning her around faster and faster until she couldn't think or feel for herself. She felt like she was falling, lost within his mind and the magic.

"Oh my," she said, and fainted.

Someone was carrying her. That was her first thought. Her second thought was that everything hurt. She shivered, pulling closer to whoever it was who was carrying her.

There were voices above her, speaking quickly in Spanish and English. One loud voice overrode the others. She recognized Carlos' strident tones without even needing to open her eyes. "What happened, Ramon?" he demanded.

Ramon's voice. "I don't know. Jose was hurt and she helped him, and then she fainted—"

"Is she going to die?"

No, I'm not going to die, I just want to, Kayla thought, feeling as though every inch of her was on fire. Then she was lying on something soft; she felt someone gently take off her sneakers and leather jacket. She opened her eyes to see Roberta, a concerned look in her dark eyes, pulling a blanket over her. To her annoyance, Kayla saw that Roberta was wearing the silver hoop earrings.

Bitch, Kayla thought, and would have said that aloud to her, but for some reason her voice wasn't working quite right. "She's awake," Roberta said to someone out of her sight.

Carlos' face appeared above her. "What happened?"

She could feel the intensity of his thoughts, his love for his brother mixed in with terror over their near escape. There was something else, a distant memory of believing that Ramon was going to die, and the furious frustration of being able to do nothing to stop it. She saw herself through his eyes, a fear of losing something of value, something that he desperately needed. Not a person, but a *thing*, something to be guarded and used carefully.

Kayla tried to push it all away, not wanting to know any more, but she could still sense Carlos, the heat of his thoughts only a few feet away. And Roberta, a seething pool of different emotions: love, hatred, fear, and even concern for the girl lying on the bed in front of her.

And beyond both of them, a sensation of a dark pool, a place of warm emotion that lifted her up and sang within the confusion of her mind. She saw herself through Ramon's eyes, a beautiful girl with bright green eyes and the magic coiling and dancing around her hands.

No, I don't want this, she thought fuzzily, trying to focus on Ramon's face, which was too blurry for her to see. *I don't want you to care about me, I want to hate you, I just want to get away, run a thousand miles from here.*

Somebody, please, get me out of here!

Elizabet blinked, trying to keep her eyes open. She'd been at the police station for too many hours, waiting to hear the lab reports from what they'd found at her house. Too many hours without sleep, ever since she'd come home and found the pool of wet blood on her living room floor. . . .

Searching with the police, they'd found some

physical evidence, but there was no way to know anything until the lab reports returned. Searching magically, she had found nothing. Kayla had vanished into the city without a trace.

Something brushed against her thoughts, a distant sense of magic. Then she heard the echo of a young girl's voice, a cry of desperation and pain: "Somebody, please, get me out of here!"

Kayla!

She closed her eyes, hoping that no one else in the police station would notice her odd behavior, and cast her mind out in widening circles, searching.

There! She found it almost immediately, the residue of major magic, somewhere in the San Fernando Valley; traces of magic fading away even as she reached out to track it, disappearing into the eddying, drifting thoughts of one million Valley residents. Damn!

"Elizabet?"

She opened to her eyes, startled out of her near-trance. Nichelle Cable was standing by her desk, a folder tucked under her arm. "Are you okay?"

Elizabet nodded. "Just . . . just very tired. Do you have anything new?"

Nichelle shook her head. "Fibers and prints came up negative, except for that print on the broken dolphin which is, unfortunately, a match to your left thumb. I'm sorry, Elizabet."

"Anything new on a connection between the double homicide and this kidnaping?" Elizabet asked.

"William Kennison III is a nutcase. Long history of mental instability. He was fired from his job earlier that day, apparently went home and loaded his assault rifle, then went hunting for his boss. Couldn't find the boss, so he went after those people in the convenience store. He doesn't have any connection to the kidnaping that we can find; he's just a dead end." The homicide detective smiled grimly. "At least we got a full confession out of him this morning, so even if your missing kid never turns up, we have this guy nailed down tight."

"But he has no connection to Kayla's kidnaping." Elizabet clenched her fists in her lap.

"Maybe your kid will turn up on her own," Nichelle said. "I mean, we don't have much evidence that this was a kidnaping, except for the fact that there was blood on your living room floor. Maybe the blood was from an accident of some kind, and she called her friends to help her out. Maybe she just went off with friends. If she ends up back on the street, we'll find her again eventually."

I know that Kayla was taken against her will, Nichelle, but if I tell you how I know that, you'll think I'm insane. Elizabet unclenched her fists and said, "Thank you for your help on this, Nichelle. I appreciate it."

"I'm sorry it turned out this way," Nichelle said. "I'll let you know if anything else turns up. Here's the lab folder, by the way. If any of this gives you ideas, let me know. The rest of us are drawing a blank right now."

Elizabet opened the folder and leafed through the printed pages. The blood was Type A Positive, which matched Kayla's medical records. No sign of the weapon that had caused the wounds; the perpetrators must have taken it with them. Some mud on the floor corresponded to a partial footprint in the flowerbed beside Elizabet's front door. Not enough to make any identification, though, or even a guess as to shoe size. Some hairs that were identified as Elizabet's.

In short, nothing.

She left the folder on Nichelle's desk and slowly walked out to her car. There was nothing in that folder that the police could use to track down the kidnapers. If anyone was going to find Kayla, it would be by luck or magic.

I'll keep trying, Elizabet thought. *Every time she uses magic, it leaves a trace that I can follow. I'll keep searching until I find her.*

She's out there somewhere . . . I know she is. . . .

An awful thought occurred to her then, chilling her blood: *I can sense her, know what she's doing, that she's out there somewhere . . .*

What if someone else is tracking her?

Chapter Six

"Are you certain of it?" Nataniel asked.

The dark-haired young woman, dressed in a black mini-skirt and silk blouse, who looked to be maybe twenty years old but was closer to two hundred, nodded seriously. "As certain as I can be. There's a new magic in Los Angeles. I felt it two days ago, and again, yesterday afternoon. It's young, strong, and glows like the lights on the Strip."

"Are you sure it's not one of the local elves?"

"They're all dead or Dreaming, even Prince Terenil. No, this one's human. Not a Bard, but still dangerous. I say we kill it before it becomes a genuine danger to us."

"You would say that, Shari." Nataniel turned away from her, looking out of the window at the lights below, at the brightness that turned night into day on the Las Vegas Strip. Even here, in his office on the top floor of the hotel, he could feel the vibrancy of life from the street below, the heat of human emotions. He savored the taste of it; this was his realm, this high tower and all within it. But it was not enough, it would never be enough. He always wanted more, always. "No. You won't kill it, Shari. You'll track it, report what you find, and then we'll make arrangements to capture it and bring it here."

"Why?" Sharanya's fine, dark eyebrows drew together in puzzlement.

He kept the hint of irritation out of his voice. "Because it could be useful to us, Shari. Because I want it. Isn't that enough?"

"Of course, my lord." She bowed elegantly, but not before he saw the anger in her blue eyes. *Have I deprived you of a choice Hunt, my dear?* he wondered. *Is that what you wanted, to hunt down this human mage and kill it?*

"What of Perenor, the Seelie Lord? If he finds it first, you know he'll kill it."

A good question. He considered it thoughtfully. "Perenor is not of our Court, but he has been a valuable ally to us. I would dislike seeing our business relationship damaged because of this. Does he know of this new source of magic?"

Shari shrugged. "He's not blind or stupid. This one burns like a flare in the sky. He's probably hunting for it already. He might kill it before we can track it down."

Nataniel steepled his fingers together. "That would be unfortunate. So . . . we'll recruit him to our side. I have other coin to pay him with, other than a human mage's blood. Do you think he'll be able to track it that quickly?"

She shook her head. "It will take him some time. A human Bard, as you know, is obvious all of the time. This talent, however, seems to come and go. I can only follow the human when it is using magic, which makes finding it a rather difficult proposition."

"Then you'd best get started. You still have time to catch the 2:15 flight to Los Angeles . . . call me tonight with your report." He smiled slightly as he saw her face go pale; flying in a jet aircraft, while not physically dangerous to their kind, was close enough proximity to a great deal of Cold Iron to make for a very uncomfortable trip. From the look on Shari's face, Nataniel could see she knew this was her punishment, but also that she wouldn't dare to defy him on this. *At least, not yet.*

She bowed again and left the office. Nataniel sat back in his leather chair, propping his feet on his desk. This was an unexpected but marvelous opportunity. He'd had a notion for some time about using a human mage for an unusual experiment. A young, untrained mage would be perfect. It was not that he needed any more magical power . . . after all, he was already the most talented mage he knew, short of that drunken and Dreaming wreck of a Prince, Terenil, in Los Angeles. He suspected that he could take even Lord Perenor in a fight, though that opportunity had never presented itself. But eventually, when Perenor was no longer useful to him . . .

You could never have too much, that was Nataniel's philosophy. True, he was the Prince of this Unseelie Court, as well as a very rich owner of some of the best businesses and property in Las Vegas. Not to mention a powerful mage and skilled swordsman, with more human money and political influence than he could spend. But you could always want more. Always.

She was standing on a grassy hillside, seeing the stars above, the moonlight shining down

*upon her. Someone stood beside her, a guy with
long dark hair and wild eyes. To her eyes, he
glowed like a torch, bright with life and power.
Around them swirled the creatures of night, living shadows that flickered and laughed silently.
She held back a scream, feeling their hatred and
their hunger. They wanted her, and the guy, in a
way that chilled her blood. It took everything
she had just to stand there, when she could feel
them drifting closer and closer to her, reaching
out to rip her apart . . .*

She opened her eyes, sweating and shaking. It
was too warm in the apartment, even though all
she was wearing was a nightgown and sleeping
under a single sheet. She remembered Roberta
helping her change into the nightgown, after . . .
after . . . She remembered Ramon carrying her
up the stairs, and Roberta . . . Roberta sitting
next to her. Vague images flitted through her
mind: a damp washcloth on her sweating face,
Roberta rinsing the washcloth in a bowl of water.
The taste of warm soup in her mouth, as
Roberta held another spoonful to Kayla's lips,
urging her to eat.

And the nightmares: dreams of awful shadowy
winged monsters that chased her through a
deserted city, a man with cold blue eyes who
walked toward her with a glittering sword—a
sword?—in his hands and raised the weapon to
strike . . .

Maybe I've been a little sick, she thought,
looking around the room. Someone had left a
carved wooden cross on the table next to the
bed, and there was an old black telephone next
to it.

A telephone!

Kayla sat up too quickly; everything whirled

around her, too bright and too fast. She fell back, closing her eyes and hoping that she wasn't going to throw up.

After a few seconds, she tried sitting up again, this time very slowly. She picked up the phone receiver and dialed 411 for Information.

"What city, please?"

"I'd like a home phone number," she said to the operator. "Elizabet Winters . . . she lives on Laurel Canyon, it's either Hollywood or maybe Van Nuys, I don't know. . . ."

"Please hold for the number."

"Yeah, thanks." Kayla listened to the mechanical voice reciting the phone number and repeated it to herself over and over as she dialed. *Come on, Elizabet, answer the phone, answer the* . . .

"Hello?"

Kayla wanted to cry with relief. "Oh God, Elizabet, it's me, please, you have to help me . . ."

"Kayla!" Elizabet's voice was sharp. "Tell me where you are. The street address, if you have it."

"I don't know, I'm somewhere in Van Nuys, an apartment building, maybe a couple miles from the courthouse. Wait, they wrote the phone number on the phone—it's area code eight-one-eight, seven-six-one . . ."

A hand reached past her and pulled the plastic plug from the telephone, breaking the connection. Kayla looked up with a sick feeling in her stomach. It was one of the nameless guys in plaid shirts. He took the phone receiver from her nerveless hand and left the room with the telephone under his arm.

Kayla lay back on the bed, hot tears of frustration stinging at her eyes. She had to get out of here, somehow. Somehow . . .

*   *   *

She awakened again to darkness and the smell
of smoke. A few feet away, she saw the glow of
a burning cigarette, just bright enough to illuminate Carlos' face. He was sitting on a folding
chair and watching her.

She stared back at him as he slowly bent to
crush the cigarette in a metal ashtray on the
floor. "Are you well, girl?" he asked.

Kayla's throat was too dry; her voice squeaked
on her reply. "I'm okay."

He shook his head. "You were very sick, and no
one knew why. Do you know why you were sick?"

"I—I don't know."

"Mmmm." He gazed at her. "Why did you
heal Jose?" he asked suddenly.

Kayla pulled the sheet tighter over her. "He
was hurt. I didn't want to see him hurting."

"But he's one of us. One of the people who
are making you stay here."

Kayla shook her head. "He was in pain. I
couldn't help but feel it. So I had to—had to—"

"Good." Carlos smiled. "So you have to heal
someone in pain, whether or not you like them?
That's good." He stood up and walked to the
door. "Get well, little *bruja*," he said, his hand
on the doorknob. "Already we need your help.
Ramon was hurt last night in a fight. He's out in
the living room right now."

"Ramon? But—"

Carlos smiled at her, a flash of whiteness in
the darkened room, and closed the bedroom
door behind him. Kayla sat quietly for a long
moment, then got out of the bed. Her legs wob-
bled slightly, and she grabbed the night table for
support.

When her legs steadied, she began searching the room for something to wear. After a few minutes, she found the bag of clothes that Ramon had bought for her, lying on the floor near the foot of the bed. She dressed quickly in a pair of jeans and the white blouse, then left the bedroom.

In the living room, she saw Carlos and Ramon sitting on the couch, talking in Spanish. Ramon looked up as she walked into the room and smiled. "Good morning, *querida.*"

"Carlos said you were hurt," she said. "What happened?"

Ramon shrugged. "I didn't move fast enough, so one of those city boys cut my shoulder with a knife. It's nothing."

"Take off your shirt and I'll see what I can do about it," she said.

Carlos stood up and walked to the door. "I have to meet Roberta at the pharmacy," he said with an odd little smile. "I will call you later, Ramon."

Kayla helped Ramon remove his long-sleeved shirt, and winced at the sight of the long cut across his shoulder. She went to the bathroom to search for anything she could use, and returned a moment later with a plastic bottle and several washcloths in her hands.

"It's nothing, *querida,* only a scratch . . ."

"Hold still, this won't hurt," she said, tilting the bottle of medicinal alcohol to dampen the wadded washcloth. She put the cap back on the bottle and set it to one side, looking thoughtfully at Ramon's shoulder. Ramon watched her with a look of trepidation in his eyes, especially as she put on her best "soap opera physician" look and said, "Don't worry, I know what I'm doing."

She wiped his bared shoulder, and the long, shallow cut, with the wet washcloth. It really wasn't a bad cut, but it needed to be tended properly. . . .

"Madre de Dios!" Ramon leaped up, knocking her and the bottle of alcohol onto the floor. "That hurts!"

"Don't do that, you'll just make it worse!" Kayla protested as he grabbed his shirt off the back of the couch and rubbed his shoulder with it.

"But it hurts!"

"Okay, I'll just wash it with soap and water," she said. She walked a little unsteadily to the sink and squeezed some dishwashing soap onto a washcloth, wetting it under the faucet.

"Are you okay, *querida?*" Ramon asked, a concerned look in his eyes.

"Just a little dizzy." She leaned against the sink for a couple seconds, until her head cleared. "I've only been out of bed for less than ten minutes, so I'm doing okay, I guess."

"You were very sick," Ramon observed, as she walked back with the wet washcloth. "I wanted to take you to the hospital, but Carlos said that we couldn't. I'm glad you're okay now."

She carefully dabbed at the wound with the corner of the soapy towel, then wiped it dry with another cloth. "There. It's clean now. I'll see if I can do anything more for it. . . ."

She had never *called* the magic to her before—it had always happened on its own, never by her will. She thought about how to do that now, imagining the hot fire running over her hands, the bright blue sparks dancing.

Nothing happened.

She concentrated then, focusing on the cut on Ramon's muscular shoulder, marring his tanned skin. She could feel it, the dull ache of pain, and reached to it. . . .

Everything went white for a long moment, and she felt like she was falling, falling . . .

She blinked, looking up into Ramon's eyes. He was holding her . . . how had she ended up half-sprawled across his lap? She blinked again.

"Are you okay?" Ramon asked, concerned. "I saw the magic fire in your hands, then it faded away and you fainted."

"I feel awful," Kayla said from her awkward position in his lap.

"Maybe it's the magic? Maybe that's what happened, the magic is making you sick?"

"Let me up," Kayla said, trying to sit up and falling back onto his lap. She was acutely aware of his bare arms holding her. All she was wearing was a light cotton blouse and jeans, but it suddenly was too warm in the small living room.

"Rest for a moment, *querida*, until the sickness passes," he said gently.

"I'm okay, really!" She gave up trying to sit up; he wouldn't let her, so she just let herself lie back against him. "Ramon, I never—" she began awkwardly, then started again. "Listen, you saved my life, back there in the alley. I just wanted to say thank you for that."

"You're welcome," he said gravely, then grinned. "Though I have to admit, I was thinking more of how Carlos was going to kill me when I came home, if anything had happened to you. I'm glad you weren't hurt."

"Yeah, me too." She shifted slightly, so she could look at him better. He was very handsome, she decided, though not as handsome as Carlos. Then again, he wasn't a bastard like Carlos, either. There was a funny little scar on his cheek, an old cut mark. Impulsively, she leaned forward and kissed him there.

Ramon jerked back as if he'd been burned. "Kayla!"

She laughed at the shocked expression on his face. "Ramon, I was just saying thank you," she said. "I mean, if I really wanted to kiss you, I'd do this . . ." She leaned forward again, kissing him on the mouth.

His arms suddenly tightened around her, pulling her closer against him. Then he pushed her away abruptly. "No, it's too soon, we can't . . . *Madre de Dios*, this isn't fair!" he wailed, looking upward.

Kayla caught his hand with hers, holding it against her cheek. "Why not?" she asked.

"Because . . . because . . ."

The sound of running footsteps on the stairs outside the apartment made them both look up. Carlos burst back into the room, the apartment door banging loudly against the wall.

Carlos asked something in Spanish, and Ramon looked quickly from Kayla to his brother, his eyes wild. He answered in Spanish and pulled his hand free from Kayla's. They spoke in rapid-fire Spanish for another few seconds, then Ramon turned to her and spoke quietly. "Kayla, Carlos wants to know . . . are you a virgin?"

"What?" She felt herself blushing. "What does he care?" *And why does he want to know?* Sudden fear tightened around her throat. *My God, what's he planning to do?*

"He says it's important. Are you a virgin?"

Kayla bit her lip, looking down at her bare feet, and decided that maybe truth was the best answer right now. *I hope.* "Well . . . yes."

Carlos said something in Spanish to Ramon, who stood up and replied angrily in the same language. For a moment, Kayla thought Ramon was about to punch Carlos. Then he sat back down again, his hands clenched into fists.

Carlos gave Kayla a stern look. "Listen to me, girl," he said in tones like ice. "I was talking with my grandmother. She said that in the legends, sex and magic are very closely linked. If you really are a virgin, we're going to make sure that you stay that way. I will make sure there are always two people with you, to protect you and your . . ."

Carlos looked away briefly, and Kayla thought she saw him flush slightly with embarrassment. "Jose is married, he would be good for this," Carlos continued, picking up the telephone receiver. He dialed the phone and spoke into it in Spanish. Every few seconds, his eyes flickered to Ramon, who was now seated stiffly on the couch, as far away from Kayla as he could be.

Damn, Kayla thought. *Damn, damn, damn . . .*

That evening, Kayla sat at the edge of a circle of chattering women in the living room of Roberta's apartment, feeling about as miserable as she could. No one seemed to speak anything but Spanish, and while she was learning to pick out a few words here and there, she didn't understand most of what was being said. She knew they were talking about one of the women's little baby, though, just by the way everyone kept pointing and gesturing at the kid. The baby was cute, a little round-faced kid with tufts of black hair who made all these funny cooing and giggling noises. She would've enjoyed playing with the kid, but the women had given her cold looks when she tried to get closer to the baby.

Ramon had left the apartment, a few minutes after that awful scene with Carlos. Carlos had waited until Jose and another equally silent young man had shown up, then left as well. Jose and the other guy had sat around reading the newspaper and talking between themselves in Spanish, while Kayla sat in the bedroom, slowly going stir-crazy. Then Roberta and all of these women had shown up, filling the apartment with loud conversation and the smell of spicy hot chocolate. At least that had been good . . . thinking about it, Kayla went to the kitchen to refill her mug with the rich chocolate drink. And Jose had left after a few minutes, probably figuring that Kayla would be safe, surrounded by all of those older women and one sullen-faced young man sitting near the front door.

In the kitchen, Roberta and another girl were talking in Spanish. Kayla slipped past them to ladle more chocolate into her mug. As she left the kitchen, she saw Roberta say something to the other girl, who laughed.

The hell with you, Kayla thought. She sat down in her chair and leaned against the window, looking out. She could see the mountains in the distance, dusted with a light cap of snow. In the street below, some kids were playing with a football, tossing it back and forth.

"Kayla?"

She looked up as Roberta sat down next to her. "What do you want?" she asked.

"I wanted to give these back to you." Her hand closed over Kayla's, dropping something into her palm. Kayla looked down to see her

silver earrings lying in her hand. "I'm sorry I
was so angry. I thought you were Carlos' new
girl, and I was very jealous. He explained everything to me, and I wanted to say something to
you, but then you were so sick . . ."

"Th-thanks." Kayla's fingers reached up to
unfasten the safety pins in her ears and replaced
them with the silver rings. "Thanks a lot."

"Why are you sitting here by yourself?"
Roberta asked. "Don't you want to talk with
anyone?"

Kayla shrugged. "I can't speak Spanish."

A quick smile brightened Roberta's face, and
for the first time, Kayla understood why Carlos
might find this girl attractive. "And they don't
speak any English. Well, there's someone here
that doesn't speak any language yet at all. . . ."
She gestured for one of the women to give her
the baby, which she placed in Kayla's arms. "Do
you like babies? I saw you looking at her
earlier. Her name is Juanita, and she's two
months old."

Kayla gingerly held the baby in her arms. Juanita
giggled and drooled on Kayla's shirt. "She's really
cute," Kayla said, looking into the baby's large
brown eyes. Those eyes looked back at her very
solemnly, then her mouth curved into a big,
toothless grin.

"She likes you," Roberta said, smiling.

A shrill voice shouted in angry Spanish from
across the room. Kayla looked up as the baby's
mother hurried towards her. Roberta intercepted
her, talking quickly in Spanish, with occasional
glances and gestures at Kayla and the baby.

"What is she saying?" Kayla asked.

"She doesn't know who you are, so she doesn't
want you holding the baby. I'm telling her that

you're a *bruja,* and that you healed Jose's
gunshot wound. She doesn't believe me."

More of the women joined into the argument,
voices clamoring loudly in Spanish. Kayla shrank
back in her chair, holding the baby close against
her, as the argument became more and more
heated. Roberta was able to yell louder than any
of them, Kayla noticed.

As the argument continued, Kayla decided to
play with the baby and pretend to ignore it all.
Juanita had a good grip, she discovered, as the
baby clutched at her fingers. Though she was
best at drooling . . . *probably because she
doesn't have any teeth yet,* Kayla thought.

"I'll take the baby now," Roberta said, and
Kayla realized that all the arguing had stopped,
and that everyone was looking at her now, some
with curiosity, others with distrust.

"Okay," she said, lifting the baby into Roberta's
arms. "She's a great kid."

"She's my cousin," Roberta said fondly, rubbing her finger against the baby's cheek. "You
need to do some magic now," she added.

"What?"

"I said that you'd show them some magic,
show them how you healed Jose, so they'd see
that I wasn't lying. You have to do magic now."

"Roberta, I don't know if I can—"

"Just try, okay?"

It was getting easier, she realized, as she
called the fire to her hands. There was no dizziness or headaches, only the sheer joy of it,
feeling the tendrils of power weave around her
fingertips. The blue light was very bright in the
small living room. She let it die away a couple
of seconds later.

There was a stunned silence in the room,

then all of the women began talking at once. One of them, a quiet girl with long dark hair, hesitantly touched Kayla's hands, as if expecting them to burn her. Another woman placed her hand on Kayla's chin and tilted her face upward, studying her eyes . . . for something? Kayla didn't know. Juanita's mother took her baby from Roberta and gave her back to Kayla to hold. Then she gestured for Kayla to sit next to her, in the circle of folding chairs. Kayla smiled and joined her there, listening to the musical flow of Spanish around her as Juanita did her best to eat Kayla's shirt.

One of the women addressed her directly in Spanish; Kayla smiled and shook her head. The woman called to Roberta, who sat down next to them. "She wants to know if you can help her husband, the way you helped Jose," Roberta translated for Kayla.

"What's wrong with her husband?" Kayla asked.

"Cancer. He came home from the hospital three days ago, after another surgery. They don't think he's going to live much longer."

"I don't know," Kayla said. "I mean, this is as new to me as all of you guys. A few days ago, I couldn't do any of this at all. Maybe I can do it, maybe I can't. I still have to learn how to do this. I just don't know."

Roberta spoke with the woman in Spanish, then in English to Kayla. "She says that any help would be good. She says that you're still young, maybe you can learn quickly."

"Maybe." The naked hope in the woman's face frightened Kayla, hurting her as much as someone's physical pain. She looked down at the baby in her arms, not knowing what to say.

The telephone rang, a shrill sound from the kitchen. Roberta rose to answer it. A few seconds later, Roberta spoke quickly in Spanish to the young man at the door, who nodded and ran out of the apartment a moment later. Roberta spoke to Kayla in English. "Quickly, put your shoes on, we must go."

"What's going on?"

"Some of the boys have been hurt. Hurry, hurry!"

Kayla gave Juanita back to her mother and ran to the bedroom, pulling on her tennis shoes and grabbing her leather jacket. Roberta ran with her down to the street, where the young homeboy was already waiting with the car, engine running. "Come on, come on!" he urged them as they piled into the car.

"Who was hurt?" Kayla asked Roberta.

"I don't know!" Roberta's hands twisted in her lap. "Carlos didn't say who, just that some of them had been hurt. I don't know, I don't know. . . ."

Chapter Seven

The car pulled up in front of a row of warehouses, in an older, industrial area of Van Nuys. The street was deserted, dimly lit by distant streetlights, the shadows hiding everything but the outline of large buildings. The driver motioned at them to stay in the car and moved carefully toward one of the warehouse doors, drawing an automatic pistol from beneath his jacket. He glanced inside, then waved to them to join him.

Roberta was out of the car a split-second later, running to the door. Kayla followed her and stopped short at the entrance to the warehouse.

It was like a vision of hell. There was blood everywhere, unmoving bodies lying on the floor and across the wooden boxes, some wearing the bright blue of the black city boys, others in the plaid and bandannas of the homeboys. Several homeboys moved among the dead and wounded. Carlos was on the other side of the warehouse, holding Roberta in his arms and speaking quietly to her. She didn't see Ramon among the wounded or dying, and a wave of relief went through her.

She stared at the carnage, and suddenly the smell of it hit her as hard as physical pain; she clutched at the doorpost for support, mentally trying to shove all that terror and agony away from her. It flooded down on her mind, threatening to crush her beneath the pain.

She held it back, fought to overcome it. As the pain receded enough for her to move, she went without thinking to the closest wounded young man. She recognized Fernando, lying sprawled across a wooden crate, blood trickling down from his mouth and chest. She placed her hands on his face, his blood wet and warm against her fingers, and called the magic to her.

She felt a fierce joy, feeling the power coursing through her, sliding down into Fernando's pain. She found the source of it, the bullet lodged in his lung, and drew it out with her thoughts, sealing up the wound behind it. She could feel the life returning to him, as the pain faded away from within her mind, to be replaced by dizziness and exhaustion.

Kayla paused long enough to catch her breath and forced herself to move to the next man, who was curled on the floor, clutching his leg and whimpering in pain. A bullet had shattered his leg, leaving white fragments of bone sticking out through the shredded denim of his blood-soaked jeans. He nodded weakly at her as she touched him, forcing the pain away from his mind. She coaxed the bone back into place, forcing the broken pieces to knit back together again.

Exhaustion burned through her mind and body when she was done, dragging her down into the shadows. She knelt by another man, lying facedown on the floor, and carefully turned him over. It was Jose, a look of shocked horror on his face.

She stared at him, trying to touch him with her magic and finding . . . nothing. Only a dark emptiness, a nothingness where he had been. She bit her lip, unable to keep the tears from her eyes.

"Why aren't you helping him?" She turned to see Carlos standing close behind her. He was pale and shaking, a crying Roberta clinging to his arm. "Help him, *bruja!*"

"I can't. He's dead."

"Heal him!" His face was streaked with tears as he shouted at her. "You little bitch, help him!"

"There's nothing there, he's gone, there's nothing left to help!"

Roberta tugged Carlos away from Jose's body, whispering something in Spanish to him. Kayla quickly turned to another wounded guy, a kid that looked younger than herself, one of the black boys. His eyes were wild with pain, but he smiled. "Hey, pretty lady," he whispered.

"You'll be all right," she whispered back. She saw where he'd been shot, one gaping wound in his chest, another in his shoulder. It was bad, but she knew she could heal him, it wasn't any worse than Fernando with the bullet in his lung. She set her hands, shaking with exhaustion, on his chest, and began to concentrate . . .

Someone grabbed her arm and yanked her up, just as she felt the first stirrings of the magic beginning within her. "No, not that one!" Carlos said roughly. His eyes burned with anger. "He's not one of ours."

"I don't give a shit! He's hurt, I can help him!"

"You'll heal Miguel next, *bruja!*"

Kayla pulled her arm free of his grasp. "Like hell, you bastard!"

The force of his hand slapping her across the face knocked her to the floor. Stunned, she landed close to the hurt black kid, nearly on top of him.

The boy looked at her with pain-filled eyes as she wiped the blood from her mouth. "S'alright, pretty lady . . ." he whispered. The glow of his body, the sensation that he was alive and close to her, faded away a moment later. His eyes were still staring at her, but they were empty, no longer seeing her or anything else.

Kayla stared at the boy's lifeless body; she sobbed and turned on Carlos. "Damn you!" she screamed. "I could've saved him!" Her hand brushed against something cold, metallic: a semi-automatic pistol lying next to the boy's body. She grabbed it and brought it up, aiming it at Carlos.

He stood very still, watching her.

She blinked back tears, trying to hold the pistol steady. Carlos didn't move. Kayla could see Roberta's horrified face beyond Carlos; one of the homeboys drawing a pistol, but hesitating, not certain whether to shoot her or not.

"So, are you going to kill me?" Carlos asked calmly, as if he was asking the time of day.

Her hands were shaking; she couldn't stop it. She thought about pulling the trigger, sending a bullet ripping through Carlos' chest, through his lungs or heart, shattering everything in its path. She saw him lying on the floor with the blood trickling from his mouth as he died. Another dead body, no life singing in it, nothing that she could touch. And it would be because of her, because she had done it to him.

Her finger tightened on the trigger.

And stopped.

She couldn't do it. She couldn't kill him.

She stood there, shaking, as Carlos moved toward her. With a muttered curse, he took the gun out of her hand. He shoved it under his belt and hauled her to her feet. She was barely able to walk; he manhandled her across the floor and dropped her next to another wounded homeboy. Blinded with tears, she felt the magic reaching out to the guy, drawn to his pain. When she was finished healing him, Carlos shoved her to another fallen body, to heal another wounded kid.

And another. And another.

It turned into an endless blur of pain. She was caught up in the magic, unable to stop or break free. Agony and exhaustion and terror pulled her down, and she felt as though her own life was draining out with each healing, leaving her unable to move or think. Through the haze of pain, she felt Carlos lifting her again, setting her down next to another hurt homeboy. Then the magic took her again, sending her into another wave of pain as she healed again and again.

She lay on the floor, not aware of anything but the sensation of the cold concrete against her face, trying to keep breathing. It was more and more difficult, just breathing in and out. She could still feel the magic in her hands, but it was sputtering and dying, fading away. She felt her heart falter once, skipping a beat, and then another. Everything hurt, more pain than she had ever dreamed could exist, and all she wanted to do was let go of it all, slide down beneath the shadows lurking around her. But there was someone else lying on the floor next to her, a young man. She couldn't remember his name, but he'd been one of her guards at Roberta's apartment. He'd been shot in the shoulder and was moaning quietly with the pain.

She reached out to help him, and someone grabbed her by the shoulders, pulling her away from him. Someone was arguing over her, loud voices in Spanish. She recognized the voices but couldn't remember who they were. She was so tired, so very tired. . . .

"Her hands are so cold. Sit up, *querida*, open your eyes." She recognized Ramon's voice, and the sensation of him being close to her, the warmth of his thoughts around her. She reached for him like a dying person for water, somehow drawing on his strength in her desperation. She could feel her own heartbeat steadying, growing stronger with every second, and the electric sensation of power moving through her, wiping the exhaustion and dizziness away. Then she felt Ramon's arms sliding away from her, followed by a loud thump a moment later, a sound like a body hitting the floor.

She lay there for a moment, still just a little dizzy, then her head cleared suddenly and she opened her eyes.

Ramon was sprawled on the floor next to her, unconscious. She held his hand and tried to figure out what had happened.

"What did you do to him?"

It was Carlos, glaring down at her. "Nothing," she said, glaring back at him. "I don't know what happened. He just passed out."

Carlos crouched down beside his brother, touching Ramon's forehead and calling to him in Spanish. "He isn't waking up," he said to Kayla, giving her another accusatory look.

"Look, I don't know why he passed out! But there doesn't seem to be anything wrong with him, he's just tired. I don't understand it, okay?" *He passed out, and I feel fine—no, I feel better than fine. I feel like I'm not totally exhausted for the first time in days. . . .*

"Carlos, *la policía!*" One of the other homeboys came running in through the warehouse door. "A patrol car just went by on Oxnard Street! I don't know if they're coming back here or not."

"Don't panic, Luis. Tell the others that we have to leave now." Carlos turned back to Kayla. "You'll heal Manuel as soon as we're out of here. Walk with me now to the car." He lifted Ramon gently in his arms and started for the doorway.

Carlos set Ramon down on the back seat. Ramon was a little pale, but otherwise looked to be fine. His heartbeat was strong; Carlos couldn't understand why he had fainted, but it probably had something to do with the *bruja's* magic. The *bruja* herself, sitting next to Ramon, really looked awful, her face completely bloodless and soaked in sweat, but he assumed that her own magic would take care of her, as it had before. If it didn't, that was unfortunate. None of them knew anything about sorceresses or magic, so she was on her own.

He called Luis and Juan to join him at the car. They were lucky that this warehouse was so far away from anything but a few other businesses, there was no one here to call the *policía*. There wasn't much else here; the reason they'd come here earlier in the evening was to move all of the supplies to another location. Luis worked at this place during the day and had found good places to hide the small crates of their drugs, the weed and crack that the homeboys used and sold in the *barrio*. When Luis said that a T-Men boy had followed him to work, Carlos had decided to move everything to another location. Which was why all the homeboys were in this place at one time, when the T-Men had shown up with their assault rifles and Uzis.

It wasn't as bad as it could have been. Jose was dead, but he was the only one. Manuel's shoulder was still bleeding, the *bruja* hadn't managed to do anything for him yet, but his brother was up and walking around, so it couldn't be too bad. It was Jose's death that made Carlos want to cry inside, but there were four dead T-Men lying on the floor, which made him feel a little better.

There would be more dead T-Men because of this, he knew. As soon as his people were ready for it, they'd go into the city and make them pay. The bastards would pay for Jose's death, for the fact that Carlos had to leave Jose lying there on the concrete like a dead dog, for the *policía* to find. They'd pay.

Sharanya sat quietly on the balcony of Nataniel's Santa Monica townhouse, listening to Lord Perenor's speech about the dangers of human magic and trying not to look too bored. *This is so tedious,* she thought. *Are all High Court Seelie elves like this idiot, unable to get to the point in less than twenty minutes of conversation?*

A lord of the Unseelie Court would have gutted this Seelie idiot before he was halfway through this speech.

" . . . which is why we can't let any of them live. We should hunt this new mage down and kill him now." Perenor concluded his speech and looked at her expectantly.

"Somehow, I can't understand your fears of human magic, my lord," Shari said. "After all, isn't your own daughter half-human?"

The daughter in question was standing at the far edge of the balcony, gazing out at the darkened beach. It occurred to Shari that Ria Llewellyn was standing as far away as she could, and still be within hearing range of the conversation. Shari had disliked Ria Llewellyn from the moment they'd met, when the blond and elegant half-elven woman had looked at Shari like something she'd found under a rock. *I wonder how long you'd survive in the Unseelie Court, darling?* Shari thought. *They'd probably have you for breakfast within ten minutes.*

Ria spoke without looking at Shari or Perenor. "My mother is human, yes. But I don't think the fact that this new mage is human or elven really matters at all. The question is whether or not he's a danger to us. And I think he's not." She gave Shari a calculating look. "I can't imagine a human, even a mage, as a danger to any of us. Certainly the Unseelie can handle any challenges, can't they?"

Maybe you'll find that out for yourself someday, Ria. "Of course we can," Shari said, smiling. "But capturing this human without killing it might prove a little more difficult. Nataniel wants it alive; he believes this human could be useful to us. If we need any assistance, it would be for that purpose."

"You think you could use a human mage? But you can't trust humans at all, they're—" Perenor began, and was interrupted by Ria.

"No, Father," Ria said tartly. "I've learned that you can't trust *anyone*, humans or elves, and especially the Unseelie. I didn't ask for this meeting with Sharanya, and I'm wondering if we're going to do anything but talk about some insignificant human mage tonight. You told me that the Unseelie wanted to discuss a business proposition with me. Something to do with a loan of over twenty million dollars? Chasing down a human mage isn't my idea of a multi-million dollar business proposition. If we have nothing else to discuss, then I have my own business to attend to, elsewhere."

My, what a prickly bitch. Maybe she would survive the Court after all. Better to play this carefully; we need that money. These Seelie fools can't know yet that Nataniel's being investigated for counterfeiting. I told him to be more careful with conjuring cash, but my lord didn't listen. Our next sources of financing must be impeccably clean, or the Feds will be onto us in an instant. "Nataniel and I know what a successful businesswoman you are, Ria," Shari said silkily. "That's why I asked Perenor to arrange this meeting—to discuss a joint venture with your Llewellyn Corporation."

"What, dealing drugs? That's not an interest of mine."

Shari bit back a quick retort, speaking in a quieter tone. "Don't tell me that you suffer from ethics? There's very good money in narcotics, and I'd heard that you were a smart businesswoman, interested in making a good profit rather than any foolish human ethics."

"Ethics?" Ria shook her head. "No, I don't have any problems with ethics. The question is risk versus benefit. I assume you've heard of

RICO? The Racketeer-Influenced and Corrupt Organizations Act? The one that allows the government to seize any assets that were acquired illegally? I have a multi-million-dollar, completely legal, business. Any legal difficulties with my investment money would reflect back onto the Llewellyn Corporation and could result in a Federal seizure of assets. I won't risk it. Tell me about a profitable and legal investment, and I'll consider that. But not drugs, no thank you."

Shari considered that for a moment. "We can offer excellent terms for your legal risks and some good layering to separate your investment from your operations. Perhaps investing in a third-party venture? Such as an air cargo company?" *Damn her, we need the money to invest in the new aircraft fleet, or it'll be another year before we expand into Northern California. We'll lose our competitive edge to the local humans, which will mean a long battle to win it back, a lot of wasted effort, and spilled human blood. We need that money now.*

"Still too dangerous. Even if you hide the direct ownership linkages, what happens to that air cargo company's profit line when the Feds confiscate the aircraft?" Ria said, then smiled suddenly. "Of course, Nataniel keeps his limited partnership ownership of that Las Vegas hotel entirely separate from his other businesses, doesn't he? Perhaps in exchange for a percentage in that business, I could be persuaded to invest in the hotel. That would free up some of your operating capital for these other . . . ventures."

Shari pretended to consider that for a moment, but she was seething inside. *She's done her homework, this one. Nataniel was a fool for saying that we could control her easily, that she's just her father's pawn. But this may be the only route we can go. If only my lord Nataniel hadn't told me that we need her aid, I'd teach this little human bitch some proper respect for the Unseelie Court. . . .* "I'll suggest it to him," Shari said. "In the meantime, I think—" She stopped, listening intently. Not to any audible sound, but something far away, a distant echo that resonated in her bones. It was the noise of magic, someone working a major sorcery. She recognized it instantly: it was the human mage.

"I can sense it too, Shari. It's in the San Fernando Valley," Ria said quietly. "Studio City, I think, or maybe Van Nuys."

Shari stood up. "I'll need to go track it down immediately. If you'll excuse me . . ." She saw the glint in Perenor's eyes, a thinly disguised hunger.

"Would you like my company, Sharanya?" Perenor said, but she could hear the eagerness beneath his cultured tones. "This could be dangerous for you. I know you have considerable talents, but you might want some extra protection."

He enjoys killing them, she realized. *It's like a game for him, more than anything else. This is closest we have to the Great Hunt now that we live among the humans, chasing down these pitiful human mages. Such a pity that Nataniel ordered me to bring this human back alive—I would enjoy killing it, if I could.*

And Perenor is a handsome man, for a Seelie, as handsome as Nataniel. I wonder what he would be like, flushed in the success of a Great Hunt, glorying in his kill? Perhaps I'll find that out for myself, someday. "My lord, your company would be welcome, but I must caution you:

Nataniel ordered me to capture this mage alive, and he would be very displeased if it were to die unexpectedly."

"I understand," Perenor said, though she could hear the frustration in his voice. *Maybe I can channel that frustration into another arena,* Shari thought with a silent laugh. *We'll see how skilled you really are, my lord Perenor.*

"Enjoy yourselves," Ria Llewellyn said, reaching for her purse and silk jacket. "I have some real work to do, if you don't mind. I'm sure we'll talk later about these investments, Shari. Call me when you two are . . . finished."

Shari flushed slightly, realizing that her thoughts must have been transparent as glass to the woman. *Someday you'll learn respect for your betters, half-breed bitch,* Shari thought, and smiled a cordial farewell to Ria Llewellyn. *But until then, I suppose I'll have to amuse myself in other ways.* . . . She extended her arm to Perenor, who gave her a courtly bow before escorting her from the townhouse.

Elizabet hesitated at the warehouse door, looking around the deserted street before touching the half-open door. She could still feel the residue of magic within, now slowly fading. It had been enough magic to startle her from her preoccupation with a backlog of juvenile-related files and bring her here, to this industrial zone. She wasn't certain what she'd find inside, but guessed that she had better be careful. She pushed the door further open with her foot, not wanting to leave any fingerprints on the smooth metal doorknob.

"Oh, God!"

She stared in horror. The warehouse floor was

splattered with blood and worse, bullet holes in
the wooden boxes and walls. Five young men
were lying motionless on the floor . . . she
moved to the closest blood-spattered boy and
searched for a pulse on his carotid artery.

He was dead.

So were the other boys. From the tempera-
ture of the first boy's skin, Elizabet knew it had
happened at least an hour before, maybe longer.
She leaned against one of the shattered crates,
breathing deeply. These boys were dead . . .
there was nothing more she could do for them.
But from the magic she could still feel rippling
through this place, she knew that Kayla had
been here, and that the girl had healed someone, or more than one person. She cringed at
the thought of Kayla doing a multiple healing.
*The girl is powerful, true, a hundred times more
than myself. But if laying hands on one person is
enough to make me nearly faint, what would
healing several people at one time do to Kayla?*

*First things first. Survey the damage, learn
everything you can, and then draw your
conclusions. Don't jump to conclusions; conclusions
can be deadly. There's no margin for error here,
not now.*

She walked through the warehouse, being
careful not to disturb the blood marks on the
floor. Yes, there had been more wounded people
here, by the looks of it—at least a dozen, all
told. And the traces of magic . . . six places
where she could sense magic, still glowing faintly
against the concrete of the floor.

*Six healings? That would've killed me for cer-
tain, and I don't think even Kayla could've
survived that.*

No, she was sure that she would've known if

Kayla had died here. There would have been *something*, some sign of it.

She heard the sound of a car pulling up outside the warehouse and moved quickly toward the office at the back of the building. Inside the darkened office, she saw another door leading to the outside. But she could hear footsteps on the concrete outside. She pressed herself back against the wall, out of sight of the large glass window that looked out onto the warehouse.

"My, what a mess." The voice was feminine and distinctly sardonic.

"They're all dead," a male voice said.

Elizabet risked a glance through the open glass window, wanting to see who was talking so cavalierly over the bodies of those dead boys.

The pair looked normal enough. An older silver-haired man in a gray business suit, and a young dark-haired woman in a black miniskirt, blouse, and fashionable jacket, talking calmly as they stood amid the bodies and blood. It was that calm that frightened Elizabet as she ducked back into hiding, and something else that took a minute to register.

Their ears. Their long, curved, *pointed* ears.

She knew what they were. Elves. The Faerie Folk. Even as the shock hit her, she knew that it was true. Gram had talked of them once, when she was already in the nursing home, about how she'd danced with elves on a warm Georgia summer night. Tall, graceful, inhumanly beautiful elves, who had whirled her around in a wild midnight dance before vanishing away again at sunrise. Elizabet hadn't thought anything of it at the time, thinking it was only a dying woman's fever dreams.

The elves Gram had met were happy,

benevolent creatures. This pair was more alien
than that, with their obvious indifference to the
dead boys on the floor. She didn't know why
they were here, but guessed that it wasn't a
social call. If she could get out of here without
them realizing that she was here at all. . . .

She edged as close as she could to the open
window, listening intently.

"Any sign of the human mage?" Elizabet
thought she could hear disappointment in that
quiet male voice.

"Not unless the mage is one of these dead idiots on the floor, my dear Perenor," the girl said.
"No, I think our mage has fled again. It's been
damn difficult to track that creature down. Once
it stops using magic, I can't follow it at all. . . ."

Kayla! They're hunting Kayla, these elves!

"It's only a matter of time until you find it,
Sharanya. I have complete confidence in you,
m'lady."

Elizabet glanced at the closed door and wondered if she could open it without the Fay
noticing her. She could crawl to the door out of
view of the window, that wasn't a problem, but
then she'd have to stand up and unlock the
door. . . .

She crouched down and crawled across the
cluttered office, straightening very slowly when
she reached the door. Now she was in full sight,
though the office was dark enough, and she
knew it would be difficult to see her. Her hand
fumbled for the deadbolts on the door.

"Look at this, Shari. They're all wearing simi-
larly colored shirts."

"Yes, they are. . . ." Elizabet watched as the
girl knelt by one of the dead bodies.

"Do you recognize him?" the man asked.

"No. But I recognize the color of that sweat-shirt. He's a part of a gang, one that buys drugs from Nataniel. They're from the Inner City . . . I wonder why he's here, so far from home."

The man extended a graceful hand to help the girl back to her feet. "A street gang war?"

A street gang? That doesn't make any sense. Why would Kayla be involved with a street gang? Unless it's something the girl didn't tell me before, that she's a gangbanger. . . .

"Quite possibly. That's something I can find out, easily enough. That'll be our next stop, I think . . . I'd like to find out who these children are, and why our little mage is involved with a street gang." Her head cocked suddenly. "Perenor, did you hear something?"

Elizabet froze next to the door, not daring to move. *I'm not here*, she thought, imagining her-self as invisible, part of the wall. *I'm not here, I'm not here . . .*

"Is there someone else in here?" the man asked. "I thought I heard something. . . ."

They know I'm here!

Elizabet took a deep breath, and another, and then flung the door open and leaped through.

There was a noise behind her, like a sudden thunderstorm, and the crackle of electricity. Elizabet slammed the warehouse door shut behind her, letting go of the doorknob an instant before it melted into slag. There was the sound of a muffled curse a moment later, and the door rattled but didn't open. "The other door!" she heard the man's voice say, but she was already running for her car.

She fumbled with the keys, wasting a precious second or two to unlock the door, then slid into the driver's seat and jammed the key into the ignition.

She accelerated away from the warehouse, glancing back in the mirror to see the two figures emerging from the far side of the building, staring after her as she drove away. Two minutes later, driving down Oxnard Street toward the 101 Freeway, she finally remembered to breathe again.

Elves who were looking for Kayla. Dead boys from a street gang. *What in the hell is that girl involved in?*

She had been afraid that someone other than herself was looking for Kayla.

Now she knew.

Chapter Eight

Kayla sat silently in the back seat as Carlos drove the car through the city. They weren't going back to Roberta's apartment—this was a different destination, somewhere further north. Ramon, still unconscious, lay close to her on the back seat. She held his hand, glancing out at the lights of the city as they drove past.

Manuel, the guy with the wounded shoulder, was in the front seat next to Carlos. Even from a few feet away, Kayla could tell that it hurt a great deal, though the bleeding had stopped beneath the shirt he'd wadded up against the wound, under his jacket. Some tiny part of her wanted to touch him and heal that pain, but she held herself back from it. *Not now,* she thought. *And not ever again, if I can manage that.* The image of the kid dying in front of her wouldn't leave her thoughts, burned into her mind. *I'm never doing anything for Carlos or his homeboys again, ever.*

Except maybe Ramon. Her hand brushed his curly hair back from his forehead. She thought he looked a little better now, less pale. It was hard to tell in the dim glow from the streetlights.

Carlos parked the car in front of an old house on a quiet street. "I'll be back in a minute for Ramon," he said to Kayla. He got out and walked to the passenger side of the car, helping the other guy out of the car.

Kayla thought about taking off at a run while Carlos walked the other guy to the door of the house. Then she thought about the pistol in Carlos' belt—would he hesitate to shoot her? Maybe, maybe not.

Carlos returned a minute later to sling Ramon over his shoulder and carry him out like a sack of potatoes. Kayla followed uncertainly.

Inside the house, a heavyset middle-aged woman was crying and talking angrily in Spanish as she looked under the improvised bandage on the guy's shoulder. She wailed even louder as Carlos set Ramon down on the couch. He turned back to Kayla. "You can do your magic on him now, *bruja.*"

"No," Kayla said, hoping her voice didn't sound as scared as she was. "I won't."

He blinked, as if he thought he hadn't heard her correctly. "What?"

"I said, I'm not going to heal him."

He nodded. "You must still be tired from everything you did earlier. That's all right, you can heal him later."

"I'm not going to heal him at all."

"You'll heal him, girl!"

"No, I won't!"

Carlos raised his hand, and Kayla was certain he was going to hit her again. "Carlos," Ramon called weakly from the couch. "Carlos, how did we get here?"

Carlos let his hand fall as he smiled at Ramon, a look of caring and concern replacing the anger on his face. "You're all right, Ramie?"

"I think so, but everything still hurts," Ramon said ruefully, and glanced at Kayla. "I remember that the *bruja* was doing a healing, and I thought something was wrong so I went to her, and then everything went black. I'm all right, Mama," he said to the woman fussing over him in Spanish. "Manuel's the one who was hurt, not me."

Mama? This lady is Ramon's mother?

Ramon turned to Kayla. "I heard what you said, Kayla. Will you heal my brother Manuel? Please? For me?" His face was still very pale; the whiteness made the small scar stand out on his cheek even more, contrasting with his dark eyes.

She nodded. "Sure," she said.

Manuel took off his jacket and removed the wadded shirt from the wound. The wound wasn't bad, more bloody than anything else. The bullet had scraped through the upper muscle on his shoulder; Kayla didn't know the name of it, but she traced it with her magic beneath his skin, seeing how it connected to the other muscles . . . with a start, she pulled herself back to the matter at hand. This healing was easy, compared to what she had done before. Within half a minute it was done, Manuel gingerly touching the closed wound that had been open and bleeding a moment before.

"She obeys you, but not me," Carlos observed from the side.

"Thank you, *querida*," Ramon said. Their mother was alternately staring at Kayla and Manuel's healed shoulder, then muttered something in Spanish and left the room.

"She says you must be the Devil's daughter," Carlos said with a laugh.

Kayla considered hitting Carlos, then decided it would be more trouble than it was worth. She walked past him to the bathroom that she could see down the hallway. In the bathroom, she scrubbed the blood from her hands and tried to wash the blood marks from her shirt, without much success. Everything she owned seemed to be bloodstained now, or would be soon, the way things were going.

"We'll stay here tonight," Carlos said to her, standing in the open bathroom doorway. "Mama has set up the spare bedroom for you. You'll find everything you need."

Kayla ignored him, concentrating on scrubbing her hands. There was blood under her fingernails which wouldn't come out. She reached for a washcloth to clean them.

Carlos moved closer to her; he caught her face in his hand and forced her to look at him. "What is wrong with you, *bruja*? First you threaten to shoot me, now you won't talk to me. You did well tonight. You should be proud of yourself. So why are you angry at me?"

Kayla pulled away from him. "Because you let that kid die, you bastard!"

"But he was one of the T-Men," Carlos said, as if that explained everything.

"He was a human being! He had a life, family and friends! I could've saved his life! He smiled at me before he died. . . ."

Carlos shook his head angrily. "He was one of those scum that are trying to kill us all! They started this, not us! And now Jose is dead because of them!"

"But you could stop it! It doesn't have to be this way. . . ."

"Is there any chance you two could stop arguing long enough for me to get some sleep, please?" Ramon asked, leaning against the doorjamb.

"We'll talk later," Carlos said, glancing at Kayla.

"No, I want to talk now!"

"Maybe we should, Carlos," Ramon said. "I think there is a lot that needs to be said between us." He walked unsteadily back to the couch and patted a place for Kayla next to him. Kayla sat down, watching Carlos warily. Manuel, sitting near the window, took one glance at the dark looks on everyone's faces and left the room quickly.

"She's angry at me because of the black boy who died," Carlos said without preamble.

"Do you think that's the *only* reason I'm angry at you? Just because you kidnaped me, keep me locked up inside all the time, don't let me call anyone or go anywhere, and force me to do magic, that doesn't count for anything? Not to mention the fact that you stabbed me in Elizabet's house . . . that isn't anything to get angry about, is it?"

"I can understand that you would be angry about my cutting you that night, even though you healed yourself," Carlos said slowly. "But the rest of this . . . we need you. Don't you understand that? Tonight you proved how much we need you, you and your magic. . . ."

Kayla pounded her fist against the couch. "God, I hate this! All of you treat me like a walking first aid kit instead of a human being! And the magic—I hate it, it makes me feel sick all the time. I hate it!"

"But you saved Fernando's life," Carlos

protested. "And Luis, and Manny, and the others. Surely that's worth a little pain, isn't it?"

"Next time," Kayla said, glaring at Carlos, "try calling 911. 'Cause I'm never doing anything for you, ever again!" Carlos looked like he was about to say something foul, when Ramon interjected, "We owe her, brother. How many lives did she save tonight? We owe her for that."

Carlos nodded grudgingly. "So, what do you want?" he asked Kayla.

"I want to go home," she said. *Home, back to Elizabet, please, that's all I want. . . .*

Carlos shook his head. "No."

Kayla felt tears starting in her eyes. "Please, I just want to go home. Can't you let me do that? Please?"

"No, absolutely not." Carlos' mouth was set in a firm line.

"Why not?" Ramon asked suddenly. "Hasn't she done enough for us already?"

"But what about next time?" Carlos said, standing up. He paced the room as he spoke. "Who will die because she isn't here to help them? No, she stays. We need her, now more than ever. Four of those *bastardos* died tonight, don't you remember? They'll be after us, even more than before."

Ramon said something terse and short in Spanish.

Carlos' eyes widened; he answered in the same language. They argued in Spanish for another few seconds, then Carlos turned to Kayla, speaking angrily. "You've done this, you've turned my own brother against me!" He glared at Ramon. "And you! All you want is to sleep with the little *bruja*! Do you care nothing about our people, our *barrio*?" He added something else in Spanish, spitting out the words, and Ramon suddenly lunged for him, hands reaching for his throat.

Kayla jumped back as the two men fell to the floor, Carlos trying to keep Ramon from strangling him. Ramon landed one solid punch on Carlos' face before Carlos shoved him away. The younger man fell back against the couch, started to get to his feet again, and fainted.

She had started toward Ramon when Carlos' voice stopped her. "Don't touch my brother, you little *puta*," Carlos snarled. "Stay far away from him."

Kayla backed away toward the hallway, frightened by the look in Carlos' eyes. When he turned away to lift Ramon back onto the couch, she fled down the hallway.

She found the spare bedroom, a pair of worn pajamas and a towel set out neatly upon on the bed. Kayla flung herself down on the bed, unable to keep from crying. She heard the sound of Carlos' footsteps in the hallway, another bedroom door closing. It suddenly occurred to her that no one was watching her, no one was guarding her. She could get out of here, this might be her only chance. She should run, run fast and far . . .

She closed her eyes, desperately wanting to rest for just a moment, and then she would run, then she would . . .

"Wake up, *bruja*, time to go." Carlos' hand shook her out of a pleasant dream, where she was walking with Elizabet along a pier, with the seagulls banking past overhead. . . . She blinked and sat up, rubbing her eyes. Carlos was already dressed, though it was still dark outside, not really morning yet. "Mama's cooking breakfast," he added, leaving the room.

Kayla got up, wishing she could've changed out of her clothes before falling asleep, or at least taken off her shoes, and followed the smell of cooking food out to the kitchen. She tiptoed through the living room, where Ramon was still asleep on the couch, and into the kitchen where Ramon's mama was busy working at the stove.

The Hispanic woman glanced at Kayla and then filled a plate for her, gesturing at several glasses of orange juice on the counter and an open drawer of cutlery. Kayla didn't know the name of whatever it was that she was eating, but she didn't care. It tasted wonderful, made with potatoes and eggs and sausages, all mixed together with salsa on flour tortillas. She finished the plate of food quickly and realized just how hungry she'd been. Not just hungry, but starving, as if she hadn't eaten in days. Maybe she could ransack the kitchen for something else . . . ?

The woman dumped another serving onto Kayla's plate and said something quietly in Spanish. Carlos, standing and eating on the other side of the kitchen, said, "She says thank you for healing Manuel last night."

"What, I'm not the daughter of the Devil anymore?" Kayla said around a mouthful of eggs and sausage.

Carlos laughed, and spoke to his mother in Spanish. The older woman gave Kayla a frowning look and another comment before turning back to the sizzling pan on the stove.

"She says what you did was a miracle, and God's work. But you still shouldn't make fun of the Devil. He could hear you."

"I wouldn't be surprised, I think he's eating

breakfast right next to me," Kayla said under her breath. She shoveled more of the terrific food into her mouth, then set the empty plate in the sink and headed back to the bathroom. She wanted to wash her face, maybe brush her teeth . . .

Ramon was still asleep on the couch, curled up against the faded pillows. Like Kayla, he'd slept in his clothes, though someone had removed his shoes and set them on the floor beside the couch. Asleep, Ramon looked a little less like his brother Carlos.

She stood looking down at him for a long moment before she realized that Carlos was standing next to her. "You like him, don't you?" he asked quietly.

"He treats me like a human being, which is more than you've ever done," Kayla whispered.

"I'm . . . I'm sorry," Carlos said after an awkward pause. "I don't know how to treat you at all. I want you to be happy, I want you to want to stay with us. Make your home with us, be one of us. But I don't know how to make you feel that way. And even if you're not happy, we need you too much. You saw what those *bastardos* did last night; it's a war between us now. . . ."

Kayla stared down at Ramon's sleeping face, not knowing what to say.

"I know you don't understand now, but maybe someday you will." Carlos knelt next to Ramon, resting his hand on his shoulder. "Wake up, Ramie, it's time to go," he said gently.

Ramon smiled sleepily at her and Carlos, and stretched. *"Buenos días,"* he said, yawning. Then his eyes widened. "Carlos, your face!"

"What? What's wrong with my face?" Carlos asked.

Kayla looked closely at Carlos for the first time that morning and saw the darkened bruise around his left eye where Ramon had punched him. "Oh, my," she said weakly, as Ramon started to laugh. Carlos glared at them.

Manuel emerged from the bathroom, still toweling his hair dry, and looked at them curiously. Then, a moment later, asked: "Eh, Carlos, what's wrong with your face?"

Carlos gave the three of them a sour look and stomped away to the bathroom to look at his blackened eye. He muttered under his breath in Spanish for the entire drive back to Roberta's apartment, giving Kayla, Ramon, and Manuel foul looks every few minutes as he drove through the light early morning traffic.

Shari checked the address written in her notebook and considered the house in front of her. It was old, with peeling white paint and several cars parked out front. One car was a lovely white Mercedes convertible with custom leather seats, which also had a badly crunched front fender.

That's Razz's car. This must be the place. She glanced at her Rolex watch, a human affectation, to check the time. *I'm an hour early, it's not even 8 A.M. yet, but no matter. I want to be finished with this quickly and back in Las Vegas by tomorrow.*

She walked up to the front door, sidestepping the broken glass on the walkway, and rang the doorbell.

A young black man opened the door and glared at her. "What you want, mama?"

"I'm here to see Razz Johnson. Escort me to him, if you would be so kind." She glimpsed a handgun tucked into the waistband of his jeans, half-hidden by his blue sweatshirt. Even at this distance, the proximity of Cold Iron made her twitch. "Hurry up, boy, he's expecting me."

Another youth appeared behind the other, looking at her curiously. "Hey, it's Nate's babe. You here to get sky-ed? Like, bringin' us some more rock an' flake?"

"I have a meeting with Razz," she repeated. "Would you please escort me to him?" *These fools know nothing of Courtly courtesy, or even common courtesy,* she thought, irritated. *Where does Nataniel find these children? At least they're good for generating income, Nataniel said that this one group sells nearly a million dollars a month of various pharmaceuticals. Not bad, for street thug amateurs.*

The youth opened the door for her, and she followed him past several boys playing at a green-clothed billiards table and others lounging around on the chairs, all watching her with interest.

Yes, look at me, she thought. *Can any of you see what I am, beneath the glamour of magic that hides my elfin nature? No, all you see is a beautiful human woman. Fools.*

They walked down a short hallway to an improvised office. Razz was sprawled out on a couch, looking through a car magazine. He looked up as she entered the room. "Shari, right? Want some fresh rock? We got some hot shit here. Word." He gestured at the table between them, which had several pipes and filled plastic bags set out upon it.

"No, thank you." She looked at the drugs with thinly concealed distaste. Most humans were annoying enough when they were sober;

intoxicated, they were usually insufferable. She hoped that Razz had enough brain cells left intact for her to conduct the necessary business.

"It's the flake your man sells to us," Razz added. "He's all right, my man, righteous. Not like some scrambling dealers, chalking their shit and acting all clocked out. So, mama, what can the Razzman do for you?"

"Nate sent me to Los Angeles on a particular errand," she said, choosing her words carefully. "I'm trying to find someone. And I think that person may be linked to what happened last night at a warehouse in Van Nuys, that involved some of your boys. Do you know what happened there?"

Razz sat up suddenly, giving her a narrowed look. "Damn straight I know what happened there, lady. Those bastard homies, they killed four of my guys. Those fucking Tyrone Street homeboys, Carlos Hernandez's gang. They all live in Van Nuys, been selling shit in _our_ territory. We went out there to teach 'em a lesson last night."

"Your territory? Isn't your territory entirely on this side of the hills?" Shari inquired.

"Used to be. We're expanding our business, y'know? Like a corporation, doing that hostile takeover shit. These guys wouldn't take a hint, so we went out there to reason with them, like. It didn't go down too well." He gave her an odd look. "You didn't know that we were moving into other areas, mama? Nate was the man who suggested it, helped us scan the plan. He wants us to expand our turf so we can sell more rock for him. I bite his style, he's hot shit."

Oh, did he? That's something that dear Nataniel neglected to mention to me at all. I

wonder why he's doing that? A little dangerous,
I would think—the odds are high that these boys
would get themselves killed, and then we'd have
to find new buyers for our supplies. Interesting
that Nataniel would consider that a worthwhile
effort.

But he's right, if they succeed, it means a sub-
stantially larger profit for Nataniel. And why
should we care if any of these worthless humans
die in the effort? "Did any of your boys see anything unusual there last night? Anything you
couldn't explain?"

"Like what, mama?" Razz asked.

She thought about trying to explain magic to
this human idiot and decided against it. "I need
to go talk with these homeboys. I assume your
people can direct me to their base of
operations?"

"Lady, we took *out* their base last night. That
warehouse was where they cut their rock and
wash the shake. I can tell you where some of
them live, though. We've been doing surveillance
on them, y'know? Like a real military operation."

A real military operation. What an amusing
thought. "Good. Let's go, then."

"What, right now?"

"Of course." She stood, tapping her foot impatiently. "You said over the phone that you owe
Nate for everything he's done for you. This is a
minor favor I'm asking of you, to take me into
this gang's territory."

Razz shook his head. "No way, mama. Not
that I'm dissin' you, but no can do till you tell
me what's going down. We wiped their asses last
night—you think we're just gonna walk in there
and smoke shit with them? They'll ice our
asses."

Shari thought about that for a moment. Razz couldn't use the information, couldn't even figure out who the mage was, probably. "All right, then. There's someone in the gang that I need to see. Someone unusual . . . someone who has the gift of magic."

"Magic?" Razz grinned, showing two gold teeth. "You been smoking too much rock, mama. You sky-ed. No such shit as magic."

"You don't need to believe me," Shari said quietly. "But you'll take me there. You do owe Nate that much."

Razz shrugged. "Yeah, I'm loyal to The Man, but we're not going in there without some serious firepower. I'll call the bros in for this." He walked into the main room. Shari followed him, listening as he explained what they were going to do to the crowd near the pool table.

"Why are you listening to this white bitch, Razz?" one of his boys asked. "Who gives a shit what she wants us to do? She's not The Man, she's just his babe."

Shari considered the problem from a tactical viewpoint. She couldn't damage Razz's control of his group, since a change of command could endanger Nataniel's investments in this gang. Of course, an insult to her was also an insult to Nataniel, her liege lord. An interesting problem.

"I work for Nate," she said, the human nickname feeling awkward on her tongue, "who has kept you supplied in drugs, guns, and bribe money for the police for the last two years. Besides—"

She had learned about human physiology on Nataniel's orders, after he'd brought her here to this human world from the Unseelie Court. She chose the exact attack and moved quickly to strike with her foot. Yes, perfect. The idiot crumpled on the spot, falling to his knees, clutching himself and gasping in pain.

"—no one calls me a bitch." She glanced at Razz, who was staring at her in shock. She smiled to herself; if she'd *really* wanted to impress this leader of fools, she would have used magic to incinerate him. This way, perhaps his follower had a chance to learn from his mistake.

"I assume we won't need this idiot for this trip into the Valley," she said, pushing the semiconscious boy out of her way with her foot. "Shall we leave, Razz?"

He nodded, ordering his followers out to their cars.

"Carlos, what happened to your eye?" Roberta asked as they walked into the apartment. Carlos gave her a sullen look and stalked past her, heading for the telephone. Kayla stifled a laugh.

"The entire *barrio* is talking about you now, after what happened last night," Roberta said to Kayla. "I wanted to thank you for healing Fernando."

"Fernando?"

"He's my brother," Roberta said simply. "Everyone has been bringing gifts for you," she added, a little shyly.

There was a pile of stuff on the table next to the couch. Kayla sat down to look at it: some chocolate and other candy, some cassette tapes, and a tall stack of paperback books.

Kayla picked up the book on the top of the stack, a fantasy novel with a horse on the cover, looking at it with interest. "Thanks." She plunked herself down on the couch, glancing up occasionally as Carlos, Ramon, and Roberta discussed something in Spanish, and dove into the book.

The book was great fun, a story about a girl who ran away from home with the help of a magical white horse. Kayla smiled at that, wishing there had been a magical white horse to help *her* get away from the foster home. No, she and Billy and Liane had taken the RTD bus. A hell of a lot less romantic, and not nearly as much fun.

She didn't realize how caught up she was in the story until the next time she looked up, when she saw that she was alone in the room. No, there was someone seated by the door, one of the homeboys she didn't know or recognize. He was sitting quietly, just watching her.

She looked out the window, hearing the sound of someone banging a hammer against something metal. There was Fernando, half-invisible under the hood of his car, pounding on something inside the engine. *He must be doing fine,* she thought. *I guess I did a better job on fixing his busted chest than I thought.*

Roberta was talking with Fernando as he worked, carrying baby Juanita on her hip. Ramon was a few feet away, playing catch with some of the younger kids.

"Can I go downstairs?" she asked the man.

He said something in Spanish, smiling at her.

"Uh . . . go downstairs?" She pointed out the open window. "Can I?" She looked down again and thought her heart was going to stop: she saw the white Mercedes with the trashed front fender, followed closely by several other cars, gliding down the street toward the apartment building.

"RAMON!" she yelled at the top of her voice.

He looked up, then turned in the direction she was pointing. A moment later he shouted something in Spanish and everyone, even the young children, all scattered for cover.

"Come on!" She ran for the door, not caring whether the homeboy understood or followed. Kayla vaulted down the three flights of stairs, hearing the clatter of her guard's footsteps behind her. She was out of the apartment building a moment later, looking around the street to get her bearings.

The Mercedes and the rest of the convoy had parked across the street, and a woman was getting out of the back seat of the white Mercedes. Kayla blinked once, uncertain what she was seeing, then stared.

This woman was beautiful, dressed like a model from a magazine, dark-haired and with vivid blue eyes. No . . . inhumanly beautiful, that's what she was—no real person could look like that. And she was bright with magic, Kayla realized, brighter than anyone she'd ever seen, practically glowing around the edges with power. She couldn't be a real person, not and look like that. . . .

But no real person had ears like this lady. *Pointed* ears, right out of Star Trek or one of her nightmares. . . .

And no real person had eyes like hers, either, blue as gemstones and slitted like a cat's.

The woman saw Kayla staring at her, and smiled.

:Do you see me for what I am, girl?: The cool feminine voice said within Kayla's mind. *:That's very good, because I can see you, as well. . . . :*

Chapter Nine

Kayla looked around quickly for somewhere to run, but the only obvious direction was back up the stairs, which wouldn't get her very far.

:*Don't run, girl. I won't hurt you.*: The voice spoke quietly in her mind. :*Just stand still, be calm. Let me look at you.*: The woman with the pointed ears walked closer to her, looking at her curiously.

"You're younger than I would've expected," the woman said aloud. "How old are you, girl . . . seventeen? Eighteen?"

"Fifteen," Kayla tried to say, but her voice wasn't working quite right. For the first time in her life, she understood what the expression about someone's "throat being tight with fear" really meant—she couldn't quite manage to say the word out loud.

"Fifteen," the woman repeated thoughtfully, as though Kayla had spoken. "That's very young, for one of your kind. I begin to see Nataniel's reasoning at last." She smiled. "My name is Shari, girl. I've traveled a long way to meet you."

Behind Shari, she could see the T-Men getting

out of their cars. Some already had handguns
ready, and one was carrying what looked like a
submachine gun. Kayla swallowed awkwardly.

"We're not here for a fight," Shari said loudly.
"I need to talk with Carlos Hernandez. Where is
he?"

"He's not here," Ramon said. He walked
forward from behind a parked van, matching
gazes with the strange woman. Kayla wanted to
scream. *No, Ramon, please, don't get yourself
killed, not over me. . . .*

"We need to talk," Shari said. "Tell him that I
work for Nate Shea. He probably will recognize
the name—Nate is one of the major drug suppli-
ers for downtown L.A. We don't supply the
Tyrone Street Boys, but he should know the
name. I need to talk to him . . ."—her eyes
drifted to Kayla, who felt like a rabbit caught
out in front of a hawk—" . . . and that child as
well. We'll wait in the car until Carlos arrives."
She turned and walked back across the street, as
elegant as a princess.

"'Berta," Ramon called quietly, and Roberta
edged forward from the side of the building. She
looked like she was close to tears, holding
Juanita protectively in her arms. "Go upstairs
and call Carlos," Ramon instructed Roberta.
"And don't come back down here, no matter
what happens."

"Ramie, they might kill you!"

"I know, I know. Just go now, quickly. Kayla,
you go with her."

"I want to stay with you!" Kayla protested.

Ramon gave her a sad smile. "Please, *querida.*
You are a brave girl, but you shouldn't be here.
Go upstairs now, please."

Kayla glanced at the woman—she could see

her face, serene and inhuman, through the window of the white Mercedes. "Okay. Okay, I'll go up." She walked with Roberta to the entrance of the apartment building and up the three flights of stairs. Roberta set baby Juanita down on the couch and picked up the phone, dialing quickly. She spoke into it for a few minutes in Spanish, then hung up. As she picked up Juanita again, Kayla could see the tears in her eyes.

"Hey, it'll be okay," Kayla said, wondering if her words sounded as empty to Roberta as they did to her.

Roberta held the baby very close to her, tears falling down her face and soaking into the baby's shirt. Kayla sat next to her on the couch, not certain what to do. Hesitantly, she put her arm around Roberta's shoulders. "It'll be all right, you'll see."

The young woman shook her head, not answering.

The next half hour was the longest of Kayla's life, as she wondered who was going to come through the door next. Ramon and Carlos, to tell them that everything was okay? The woman and the T-Men, planning to kill them?

That woman, Shari . . . Kayla still couldn't believe what she'd seen. She knew the woman wasn't a normal human being, but what else could she be? It didn't make any sense. There just weren't people with pointy ears walking around in Los Angeles—she couldn't be real. Except that she was downstairs in the street right now, sitting in a white Mercedes.

She wanted to ask Roberta about it, but Roberta was obviously not interested in conversation. She sat nervously on the couch, waiting for something to happen.

Eventually there was a knock at the door, and
when she saw that Roberta wasn't going to get
up to answer it, Kayla walked over and opened
the door. It was the homeboy who had been
guarding Kayla. He spoke to Roberta in Spanish.

"You need to go with him," she said. "Carlos
is downstairs, talking with the woman, and they
need you there as well."

Kayla followed him down to the street. Carlos
and Ramon were standing on the sidewalk, talking with the woman. "*Bruja*," Carlos said, "this
woman has questions for you."

"Tell me about your magic, girl," Shari said.

Feeling very self-conscious, Kayla explained
what had happened to her in the last two weeks,
ending with walking into the warehouse after the
gunfight last night and what had happened
there. The woman nodded as she finished, and
spoke quietly. "I believe I may have a solution to
the problems between the T-Men and the
Tyrone Street Boys. Nate is interested in you,
girl. I believe he could end this war by paying
off the T-Men, convincing them to pursue other
ventures . . . if you will agree to work for him.
He could make this financially lucrative for Carlos Hernandez and his Tyrone Street Boys, as
well."

"I'd be willing to help both groups, anybody
who needs it," Kayla said. "Just so they stop killing each other. That's all I'm asking." She
glanced at Ramon. "I don't want anyone else to
get killed, y'know?"

"We'll think about it, after you leave," Carlos
said. His lips were very tight, and he was watching the guys in the parked cars very closely.

"That would be fine." The woman removed a
business card from her purse. "Call me later

today, if you would. I'll talk to Nate immediately to work out the details."

Carlos took the card from her. She walked back to the white Mercedes. A few minutes later, the convoy of cars left, following the Mercedes. Carlos stood watching until the last car disappeared around the corner. "Upstairs," he said abruptly. "We have to talk about this now."

"Didn't you guys see it?" Kayla asked, running up the stairs behind Carlos and Ramon. "Didn't you see it?"

"See what, *querida*?" Ramon asked.

"That woman, Shari!"

"I've met Shari before," Carlos said grimly. "And her employer, Nate Shea. We are in worse trouble than we were before, Ramie."

"But doesn't she look just a little . . . weird . . . to you? I mean, you saw it, right? Her face? Her eyes? Her *ears*?"

"Stop talking nonsense, girl," Carlos said. "Her ears are just like the rest of her. We have serious business to talk about now."

They didn't see it, neither of them saw that she isn't human. Kayla stopped for a moment on the stairs, staring at Carlos and Ramon. *How could they miss it? She's got bigger ears than Mister Spock! Maybe she got those eyes from a fancy pair of contact lenses, but those ears were real! Come on, guys, I know you're not blind!*

Maybe there's something else going on here. She recognized me the minute she saw me, she knew what I can do. Maybe this is some kind of thing that most people can't see, something to do with magic. I can see her for what she is, but no one else can.

This is too weird for words!

Kayla followed them back into the apartment.

Roberta was all over Carlos a half-second later, crying and hugging him. He said something gentle to her in Spanish, and she went back to the couch, picking up little Juanita, who had started to roll toward the edge of the sofa.

Carlos sat down heavily next to Roberta. For a moment, he played with baby Juanita, letting her tug on his fingers, before he spoke again. "I don't know what to do, Ramie. This is an impossible situation."

"What's so impossible about it?" Kayla spoke up. "Seems like it's the perfect solution, everything works out great for everyone."

"It isn't that easy, *bruja*."

"Why not?"

Ramon explained quietly, as Carlos stood and paced the room. "Nate Shea, that is why. He is a major drug supplier to most of Los Angeles, a very dangerous man. Our fight with the T-Men is bad, but not as bad as angering Nate would be. At least in the war with the T-Men, there's a chance we could win, or force them to quit."

"But what she talked about was terrific! It could work!"

Carlos whirled to face her. "But what if it doesn't? Then we are in a war with not only the T-Men but also Shea, who owns his own private army! We can't win!"

"But you don't have to fight!"

Carlos sat down on a chair across from her. "*Bruja*, you know that the T-Men are trying to kill all of us. I think they might kill you, or worse, if you go with them. We can't trust them. Perhaps we can trust Nate Shea, but I don't know. The T-Men are a lot of business to Nate, millions of dollars a year, and he may decide to go along with what they want rather than lose their business. We're nothing beside that. And next to that, what are you?" He shook his head. "No. I won't risk it."

"But don't you see, it could stop this war! I'm willing to take the risk," Kayla said, trying to keep from getting angry.

"And why are you so willing to take this risk for us?" Carlos asked. "You're not one of us, you've said that yourself. Call 911, you said. Why have you changed your mind?"

Kayla flushed, and glanced at Ramon across the room. "I don't want anyone else to die. That's all. If I can make a difference, then I want to give it a try."

"She has a point," Ramon began. "I agree that it's dangerous, but it could be worth a try."

"But how do we know?" Carlos paced to the window, looking out. "How do we know?"

"It's a leap of faith," Kayla said. "There isn't any way to know. Ramon . . . Ramon could go with me, make sure that they don't do anything bad to me. They ought to agree to that."

"Eh, I like that idea," Ramon said, smiling at her.

"Be quiet!" Carlos snapped at him. "Can't you see that all of this could be a trick? They'll take the *bruja* away from us, and then there'll be nothing to stop them from killing all of us! Can't you think for once with something other than your *pene*?"

Ramon's face flushed suddenly. "At least I'm not afraid to admit that I care about someone," he said, looking down at his shoes.

"No," Carlos said. "And that's final. I'm going to call this Shari woman and tell her that there is no deal. And you, girl, go pack up your clothes. We're taking you to another house, a

safer place. Roberta, you too. I want you to call
Luisa and your cousins at work, tell them not to
come home for a few days. The T-Men know
that you live here, and I think they'll be back."

I don't know if we'll be safe, even here, Carlos
thought, walking with the *bruja* into Luis' home,
an old house several miles away from Roberta's
apartment. It was plainly furnished, but clean
and neat. Luis and his wife showed Kayla to a
small spare bedroom, as Carlos and half a dozen
of his homeboys set up chairs in the living room,
carrying in pizza boxes and six-packs of beer.

He tried not to think about it as they ate
pizza for dinner, watching the football game on
the television. Luis tried to make a joke about a
bad football play, but no one laughed. Everyone
was tense, even Ramon.

*They know that the T-Men are going to come
after us, and maybe Shea's people, too. Did I
do the right thing?* he asked himself, glancing
at the *bruja* seated across the room from him,
watching the game.

The girl excused herself after the game ended,
disappearing into the spare bedroom down the
hall. Carlos caught Ramon watching her as she
walked away, and smiled to himself. Now *that*
was a good way to keep the *bruja* with them
and happy, if only he could be certain that it
wouldn't affect her magic. He needed to talk
with his grandmother again, to find out more
about whether letting Ramon sleep with the girl
would hurt her magic.

He yawned and stretched. It was too early to
be sleepy, not even 10 P.M. yet. He drank from
his beer and yawned again.

Luis was already asleep, sitting on the couch with

his arm around his wife. Ramon, too, looked like he was about to nod off. It had been a long day, true, but he knew he needed to tell one of the boys to stay awake, keep a watch for the T-Men. . . . The empty beer can slid from his fingers onto the floor as he yawned again. . . .

Kayla tried to concentrate on reading the book about the magical white horses, but it was impossible. *I can't believe Carlos is doing this. It'll never end now, not until everyone's dead . . . oh God, I don't want that to happen, I don't want to see Ramon dead. . . .*

She stared at the open page of the book until the words blurred. Angrily, she brushed the tears away from her eyes.

It's not fair, it's not right. Maybe Carlos will change his mind, though I think there's a snowball's chance of that. But it's not too late. Hell, maybe I can convince Ramon to go over his head, call that Shari lady himself. Ramon understands, he knows we should do this. But he lets Carlos make the decisions.

She didn't know when her mind had changed so much, from wanting to get away from Ramon and the homeboys to wanting to make sure that nothing bad happened to them. *I should get out of here while I still can, before it gets worse. Wait for the right opportunity, maybe later tonight, and slip out of here when everyone's asleep. . . .*

Through the wall, she could hear Carlos and the other homeboys talking about something. *Don't think they're going to call it a night anytime soon.*

She yawned, covering her mouth with her hand. She didn't know why she was so tired,

she'd slept late enough in the morning . . . it
didn't make any sense, didn't . . .

Kayla rubbed her eyes and picked up the
book again. Maybe she was still exhausted from
everything that had happened, maybe this was
her body's way of telling her to chill out and get
some rest. Maybe . . . maybe . . .

The book slipped from her fingertips as she
drifted off to sleep.

Sharanya stepped quietly into the house, past
the sleeping figures in the living room. She
paused in front of Carlos, deftly reaching into
his shirt pocket to remove her business card.
The card glowed slightly at her touch. No need
to leave this behind, with its odd set of runes
and glyphs disguised as a business logo. True,
she might need to track down Carlos again, but
better not to leave any clues behind. There was
always the risk that someone else among the
Tyrone Street Boys would have some magical talent and figure out how she had tracked them to
this place.

She walked down the short hallway, following
her magic sense to a closed door. She opened it
silently. Inside, the young mage was asleep on
the bed, a book fallen by her open hand.

Kayla dreamed of dancing. It was a warm
moonlit night, and she was standing in an open
meadow that was ringed with tiny mushrooms,
watching the dancers. All those strange people
with the pointed ears and delicate, inhuman
faces, dressed in elegant flowing clothing,
whirled and turned to the music. The women
wore long gowns of bright colors, silver and
blue and green and gold, and the men were in

short jackets and odd-looking pants, laughing and speaking among themselves as they moved through the dance. Kayla could hear the melody but she couldn't see the musicians, the slow strings and soft flutes, the delicate sound of a harp, playing from somewhere unseen. So she watched the dancers, entranced, as the beautiful people moved in graceful patterns on the silver-edged grass.

Someone was calling to her, asking her to join them. She shook her head, terrified that she would ruin the beauty of the dance. She wasn't dressed for it, she didn't know how to dance . . . a silver-haired man smiled at her, and she saw that she was now dressed as they were, in a heavy gown of black velvet and pearls, swirling skirts that brushed against her bare feet.

Their hands reached to her, drawing her in. The silver-haired man bowed to her as he took her hand, leading her in the steps of the dance.

Everything blurred around her as she danced: the world seeming to fade away to nothing but this meadow and the dancers, their laughter and words blending in with the music. The lights of the city beyond the car window blended in as well, melting into the moonlight and the dancing figures.

Kayla came back to herself with a start. The dancers faded away, to be replaced with the smooth leather seats and dark interior of a BMW convertible. The dark-haired woman with the pointed ears—Shari?—was in the driver's seat next to her, watching Kayla with a small smile.

"Almost there," Shari said. "Are you awake now?"

"Where?" Kayla tried to say, but her voice

wasn't working right. She felt like she was still dancing, whirling and spinning in the patterns of the dance, with everything moving around her.

"I thought so," the woman said. "That's good . . . you'll need to be awake. Nataniel wants to talk with you."

Nataniel? Kayla wanted to ask, but decided against it. None of this made any sense. One minute she'd been asleep at the house, now she was halfway across the city in a car with the weirdest lady she'd ever seen, with no memory of how she'd gotten there.

I have to get out of here!

She casually moved her hand to the door handle, ready to shove the door open and jump. The car wasn't going too fast; she could roll out and probably be okay, nothing worse than bruises. Kayla tensed to shove the door, then felt her hand lift from the handle, drifting back to her lap of its own accord. She looked over at the odd woman in shock.

Shari smiled.

Kayla clenched her hands into fists, trying to keep from shaking. It was all too weird, too much for her to understand. She thought about hitting the woman or grabbing for the hand brake to stop the car . . . her hands froze in place, she couldn't feel them anymore, couldn't even wiggle her fingers. "Just another few minutes, girl," Shari said without looking at her. "Sit there quietly, we'll be there soon."

How can I sit here quietly when you're screwing with my brain? Kayla wanted to scream at her, but her voice wasn't working any better than her hands. She sat quietly in the passenger seat of the car, because she didn't have any choice in the matter.

She could still turn her head, though, so she looked out the window. They were driving down a residential street near the ocean; she could see the wide expanse of white beach beyond the houses.

Shari brought the car to a stop in front of a two-story house. "It's just a few stairs up to the door. You can walk, can't you?"

For an answer, Kayla felt her legs straighten and her hand push open the car door. She followed Shari up the steps and through the front door of the house, into the darkened hallway and back to an open patio door. Someone was outside, standing in the shadows on the deck, looking out at the bright moon on the blackness of the ocean.

"I've brought her, my lord," Shari said, and Kayla was surprised to hear the respectful tone in her voice.

The man turned. He was tall, with pointed ears and short pale blond hair, wearing a long robe that looked Japanese . . . *and he has blue eyes, those same catlike blue eyes that she has. And those slitted eyes are looking at me like a piece of dead meat*, Kayla thought. *Even Shari looks friendlier than this guy*. Kayla wished she could run, just get anywhere away from these two, run away as fast as she could. . . .

With a start, she felt her legs unlock, and fell backwards into a deck chair with a thump.

"Sit down, girl," Shari said unnecessarily.

"So, this is the new human mage," the man said quietly, walking closer. "She doesn't look like much, Shari."

"There's no way to know what she can do," Shari said.

Kayla felt like a bug under a microscope, with

the two strange people staring down at her.
"Who are you, and what are you?" she asked, as
calmly as she could. "And why can't other people
see what you are?"

The man nodded. "Good questions. I suppose
I'll answer them." He pulled another deck chair
closer and relaxed into it. "I am Nate Shea. Sharanya, you've met. To answer your second
question: we are elven, the faerie folk." He
smiled as Kayla sat up straighter, staring at him.
"Yes, all the old legends are true. The elf-folk
who live under the hill, dancing in the faerie
ring in the moonlight . . . all quite true. When
times became difficult, many centuries ago, we
left the Old Country and came to America."

His voice tightened. "I was a lord of our
Court, a Prince. But many years ago, I was
banished from our court because of my . . .
ambitions. I came to the human world to begin
again, with my faithful Sharanya and other
followers at my side." Kayla saw Shari's mouth
twist at those last words, looking down at her
hands. *Not so faithful as all of that*, Kayla
thought. *This guy's not so smart. Can't he see
that Shari hates him?*

"And to answer your last question," Nataniel
continued. "The humans don't see us as what we
are because we don't want them to. Surely you
can understand that, being what you are."

And what does he think I am? Kayla wondered.

He smiled, as if knowing her thoughts. "A
very frightened human child, who also knows the
ways of magic." He took her hands in his, looking into her eyes. She couldn't look away,
couldn't pull away . . . the room tilted around
her, strange colors and scents moving past her.
She saw a blur of images: herself, standing next

to the racks of potato chips with the fire burning over her hands; Billy's blood on her fingers, the wound slowly sealing itself as she watched; the crazy man in the jail, shouting at her.

Devil's daughter! You're the Devil's daughter!

The images faded as her hands burst into flame, cold blue fire flickering over her fingers. It illuminated the patio, the light reflected in Nataniel's and Shari's catlike eyes.

"As I thought," Nataniel said, a note of satisfaction in his voice. He leaned back in his chair, watching her. "So, what shall we do with you, little girl?"

He makes my skin crawl, Kayla thought. *I don't know who this guy is, or what he wants with me, but I don't like the way he looks at me.*

"Do you think she's strong enough to go against Queen Lilith, my lord?" Shari asked quietly.

Nataniel's eyes never left Kayla's face. "Possibly. Quite possibly." He steepled his fingers together. "I have a business proposition for you, girl. As I said, I am a banished prince, unjustly exiled from my homeland. If you're powerful enough, you could help me regain my position in the Unseelie Court. And I'd reward you greatly. What do you wish for?" He spread his hands wide. "Cars, jewelry, money, property . . . anything could be yours. Is there a man that you want? We can make sure that he'll always want you, that he'll never even think of anyone else."

Kayla thought about one particular man and his laughing dark eyes. She thought about how she'd feel if she knew that he'd never leave her, he'd always love her . . .

No. That's not right. They shouldn't do this to

anyone. Playing with people's minds, treating them like they're toys—that's not right.

"What—what if I don't want to?" she asked hesitantly. "What if I just want to go home?"

Nataniel shrugged. "Then you can leave, of course. We won't stop you."

"You mean it?" Kayla stared at him in surprise.

"Of course." He smiled. "I'm asking for your help, not demanding it. If you don't want to help me, you can leave, just walk out the door."

Shari and Nataniel exchanged silent looks. Kayla thought she could hear a whisper of sound in the silence, something quieter than the waves against the sand, but it was too faint to make out all of the words. . . .

: . . . *through the Door, my lord?:*

:*If she survives, then she's of value to me. If not, then it makes no difference* . . . :

Kayla decided she didn't like the look in their eyes at all. There was something in the way they were watching her, as if they were trying not to smile about a joke that she didn't know about.

"I'd like to go home and think about it," Kayla said at last. "If that's okay by you?"

"Just walk out the door, girl. We won't stop you," Nataniel said.

It sounded like the best idea yet. Maybe she could get some more information from Shari on the way home. . . .

Kayla started through the patio door to walk through the house, and stopped in mid-step.

Something was wrong. It was too quiet. It took her a half-second to realize that the sound of the ocean waves had suddenly stopped.

And it was too dark, as though the streetlights had suddenly gone out, too. She squinted, trying to see anything in the pitch darkness, and then realized what else was wrong as well.

She was standing on uneven ground, not on the carpeted floor.

Kayla concentrated hard, imagining the blue fire coiling over her outstretched hand, the lines of light rippling over her fingers. . . .

Her hand brightened with fire, enough to illuminate what was around her. She looked around quickly, and blinked.

She wasn't standing in the house. It was too dark to see, but she knew that she was Somewhere Else. Somewhere that smelled of trees and dead leaves and another smell that she couldn't identify, a strangely foul but sweet smell, like something dead and rotting. And there was something squishy underfoot that she couldn't identify, either. She stood very still, too startled and scared to move.

The area brightened suddenly with another light, as the full moon emerged from behind the thick dark clouds overhead, illuminating the trees around with a silvery light.

Trees!

It was a forest, she could instantly see that much. Not a house in Los Angeles, but a forest. A dark, apparently endless, forest, surrounding her with trees for as far as she could see in the dim light.

Toto, I don't think we're in Kansas anymore, Kayla thought in shock, staring at the forest around her.

Chapter Ten

Kayla stood in a clearing, the damp dark leaves squishing beneath the soles of her sneakers, with a faint whispering wind through the trees the only sound around her. All she could see was the faint outline of dead, barren trees in all directions, dripping with slimy-looking ivy and covered with ugly molds. And nothing else. This forest, whatever and wherever it was, was more desolate than anywhere she'd ever seen before.

She leaned against a tree trunk, not wanting to look at the gnarled, wiry shapes of the trees, with long, sinuous tendrils coiling around the lifeless branches.

Maybe I should just sit down and cry, she thought. *No, that won't help anything. I don't know where in the hell I am, but this sure isn't Los Angeles anymore.*

I've read a lot of books, but none of them had any advice for what to do when some pointy-eared slimeball dumps you out in the middle of nowhere in the dark! This is probably his idea of a great joke.

Something was watching her. She turned

quickly, only to hear the rustle of branches and the cry of some forlorn bird, flying away. For a moment it was silhouetted against the moonlight, then she was alone again.

Well, I can't stand here all night. Might as well pick a direction and start walking.

After a few minutes, she was convinced that she'd picked the wrong direction. But nothing here looked at all familiar, or even like any other forest she'd heard of, for that matter. Most forests had trees that looked like they were alive, at least! This forest looked like it had been dead for a long, long time. *Dead and left to rot,* she decided.

And there was something else about it, something she couldn't quite put her finger on—a feeling that more was wrong here than just rotting wood, a feeling of malevolence, as though the trees were dead but the forest was alive. As though there was something else here, hidden beneath the surface, watching her and laughing to itself.

And it doesn't like me very much.

She continued walking, just because there wasn't anything else she could do. She sure didn't want to sit down in the muck and wet leaves and stay here in this awful place.

The moon slid away again behind the dark clouds, and then she had to stop, just because there was no way to see where she was going in the pitch darkness.

As she waited for the moon to reappear, she heard a whisper of sound, something so faint she wasn't certain what it could be.

I wish I could've spent some time in Girl Scouts instead of in detention at school, she thought. *They could've taught me to make fire*

out of nothing but sticks and my shoelaces, prob-
ably. As it is, I don't know what I can do.
There's nothing here.

This has to be a dream. I'll wake up and find
myself somewhere else, anywhere else. Even
Roberta's apartment would be better than this!

I just don't understand. Why did Shari and
Nataniel do this to me? What kind of game are
they playing?

She heard the sound again, closer and more
distinct, and with a chill touch of fear, knew
what it was: the howling of wolves. She didn't
know whether they could hear or smell her, all
she knew was that she didn't want to be there
when they arrived.

She picked a direction and started to run.

"The Hounds have scented prey," the Master
of the Hunt said to Lady Catt, as he cantered
easily on his horse. His eyes narrowed as he
looked around the moonlit forest.

"Have they now?" she replied in an uninter-
ested tone. She turned away from him, ignoring
the way his eyes flashed angrily within his
horned helmet. His face was hidden by the helmet's dark mask, the way his leather and
armor-garbed body was hidden by his cloak, but
she could sense his anger. And she didn't care.

There was nothing for them here. They had
long since exhausted any interesting prey for the
Wild Hunt, and even the Master of the Hunt
admitted it. And there would not be any more
prey, ever again. Unseelie sorcery had stripped
this forest of its native magic, killing the trees
and every other living thing that needed some
touch of magic to survive, and Unseelie hunters
had destroyed the last of the animals. They had

drained this land so much that their own sorceries were limited by it; only the Queen, of the entire Unseelie Court, could still work her wreakings with the Greater Magic. As for Catt, she could not even work enough magic to conjure up the lovely clothes that she had once worn to these Hunts or change magically between those silken gowns into the heavy silver armor that she now wore.

But one of the ravens had said it had sighted something, perhaps a Seelie elf. A Seelie lord would be good sport. More than one would be a true battle, something none of them had seen in a long time. The mere thought of it had been enough to rouse the lethargic Unseelie from their Court, make them put on armor and swords dusty from disuse, and send them out on Hunt.

Lady Catt thought the bird was insane, personally.

There was nothing in this wilderness, not a Seelie or anything else.

So much for the grand entertainments of the Unseelie Court, she thought wryly. *Is this what we've come to, we who once hunted Seelie High Court elves like deer in this forest? Chasing the illusions of Seelie prey? Is this what we are now? Brave hunters of squirrels?*

"They've picked up a scent!" the Master said, pointing to where the Hounds eagerly sniffed the dark ground. One of the Hounds bayed, then another, a fierce sound, and the others took up the call. The Hounds surged forward, away from the Unseelie lords and ladies astride their horses.

"It's a human!" the Master shouted, bending low over the neck of his horse and spurring it into a gallop.

A human? But there are none left alive here, only the slaves and servants . . . it's not possible!

Catt raced after him, her own magic reaching out to find the source of the Hounds' eagerness. The other Unseelie lords followed them, no longer the disinterested, bored band of courtiers that had left the Queen's castle a few hours before.

"A human mage," Catt called, sensing the lure of power like a beacon in front of her. She could feel the incandescent glow of magic, bright against the deadness of the surrounding land and trees. It moved quickly through the trees before them. She sensed the sudden taste of fear rippling through the human's magic.

"We'll take it alive," she shouted, loud enough to be heard over the pummeling hooves of the horses on the damp ground. "A gift to our Queen!"

She was close enough to him that she could hear the snarl that transformed the Master's face beneath his horned helmet. "Do as I say," she hissed, "or risk *Her* wrath!"

He nodded once, then spurred his horse to even greater speed. The elven horses strained beneath their riders to follow him, moving quickly through the shadowed forest.

Kayla slid down a slimy embankment, landing on her knees in the icy water of the stream. She lurched to her feet again, scrambling for a handhold on the opposite bank.

Come on, run, they're closer, they're getting closer, they're—

She grabbed for the low, glistening roots that extended out from the muddy bank above her head and screamed in sudden surprise as those roots came to life, wrapping themselves tightly around her hands and wrists. Kayla struggled to pull free, unable to stop screaming.

She could feel the roots doing more than holding her fast; they were pulling at something inside her, feeding off the magic inside her. She tried even harder to pull free, then felt a surge of magic coursing through her hands from within, culminating in a bright flash of light. The roots fell away, shriveling and dying instantly, and Kayla fell backwards into the water with a splash.

For a moment, she couldn't do anything but hold her hands to her face and cry.

This place is so horrible, it's awful, please, somebody get me out of here!

Stop it! Got to keep running, keep running . . .

The wolves were getting closer every second. Regaining her feet, Kayla staggered down the streambed, sloshing through the cold water and trying not to slip on the wet stones. She clambered up a sandy bank, carefully not touching any of the tree roots that dangled near her, and stopped for a moment at the top to catch her breath. She could hear the wolves howling frantically and eagerly.

Then, with an inhuman scream that echoed through the trees, a wolf burst from the cover of the trees on the opposite bank of the stream. In the split-second that it paused there, she saw it wasn't a wolf at all, but a black hound with yellow eyes, nearly as tall as she was. It howled once, triumphantly, and then leaped across the wide stream directly at her.

Kayla didn't even have enough time to scream as the gigantic hound knocked her to the ground. She tried to roll out from under it, but its jaws clamped down on her arm, painful but not breaking the skin, holding her fast. Her struggles sent them rolling off the bank and into the icy water, but the dog's teeth wouldn't let go.

Desperate, Kayla grabbed for the dog's nose, twisting it sharply. The huge dog yelped in surprise and let go of her. She staggered to her feet and then ran as fast as she could, splashing down the stream.

As she ran, she could hear the whimpers and whining of the hound behind her, joined by the barks and howling of the rest of the pack.

The stream widened suddenly into a still lake, quiet and dark beneath the moonlight, surrounded by a meadow of tall grasses. Kayla fell onto the sandy shore, too exhausted to go any further. She crawled into the thick grass and lay there for a moment, trying to catch her breath.

Please, just let me wake up now, make them go away, please please . . .

The howls of the hounds were all around her now, and a new sound: the stomping of horses' hooves and the jangle of metal. She tried to get up, and something kicked her back down again, something heavy and hard as stone.

She rolled away and managed to get up onto her knees, and saw the milling crowd of riders on horseback and dogs surrounding her. Another pair of hooves kicked close to her, and she ducked back, falling against the legs of another horse.

Someone laughed, a cruel sound, as Kayla made a wild dash to get past one of the horses. Something tripped her and she fell again, landing hard.

"Enough." The woman's voice was quiet, but

loud enough to be heard above the sounds of the horses and the snarling dogs.

Kayla got up slowly as a single rider moved to face her. She couldn't see much of the woman, just a glint of bright eyes, some kind of metal visible beneath her swirling long cloak. Her horse stamped angrily as it moved toward Kayla at its rider's urging, one slow step at a time.

The woman spoke again. "Well, well, what do we have here?" Now that she was closer, Kayla could see that she wore metal armor under the cloak, the bright steel reflecting the moonlight. The woman's face was as emotionless and as finely chiseled as glass. She stared at Kayla, who could now see the tips of pointed ears beneath the hood of the woman's cloak.

They're elves, they're all elves. . . .

This can't be real, it can't be happening to me!

The other riders moved in, surrounding Kayla with stomping horses, the huge hounds circling her. The riders all wore silver and leather armor, which jangled with their laughter as they closed in around her. And in their faces, she saw hatred and cruel pleasure, malevolent smiles on their fine features, moonlight reflected in a dozen pairs of eyes, ice blue and green, pale violet and silver. None of those eyes looked even remotely friendly.

"Is it human?" a man's voice asked.

"It has magic!" another voice crowed exultantly.

"Can we kill it now?" a third voice asked, dry and dusty as death.

"I want to wake up now," Kayla said to no one in particular. "This is an awful nightmare, and I really want to wake up now."

She waited to see if anything would happen. The riders watched her in silence, the horses shifting and making odd snuffling sounds.

"It's only a human child," the woman said at last. "A little human girlchild with some magic. Nothing more than that."

Maybe they'll be nice to me because I'm a kid? Kayla thought hopefully.

"Tie it up and bring it along," the woman said.

Kayla was more exhausted than she'd thought was possible. It felt as though she'd been running behind the horses for hours, with the sweat dripping down her forehead and into her eyes. With her hands tied and the rope fastened to the saddle of the woman in the silver metal armor, there was no way she could even wipe her face.

I'm sure I'm going to wake up any second now, she thought, feeling the burning pain in her legs getting worse by the minute. *Any second now, I'll wake up and be somewhere else . . . any second now . . .*

The moon was higher now, illuminating the entire forest with silvery light, and it was by that moonlight that Kayla first saw the castle, rising from the hill like something out of legend. Tall spires of gray stone arched upward, covered with ivy and hung with tattered cloth banners. Maybe once it had been beautiful, but now it looked as dead as the surrounding forest, dead and decaying.

There was no sign of life as they rode slowly over a creaking wooden bridge through the castle gates. She had to walk carefully to keep from falling over the pieces of wood and stone lying on the ground. The group of riders stopped in the open courtyard.

"I must change into court clothes before I go

before Queen Lilith," the woman in armor said, dismounting from her horse and taking the rope that held Kayla's hands. "Come with me, girl," she said, tugging at the rope.

"Hey, I'm not a dog on a leash, lady!" Kayla snapped.

She saw the smile that drifted across the woman's face beneath her cloak hood. "No, you are not," she agreed, and with a deft movement, drew the knife at her belt. Kayla flinched back, but the woman only cut the rope. Kayla rubbed at her sore wrists, which were red and raw from the chafing of the rope. Without even thinking about it, she let the magic simmering within her rise to the surface, sparks of pale blue flickering over her skin. The abrasions and pain disappeared a moment later.

"A healer!" someone murmured close to her, and the words were repeated by the others, gathering close around her. One of them reached for Kayla's hand with grasping long fingers, a broad-shouldered man wearing dark leathers and, oddly enough, a bright red cap on his head. She stepped back, not liking the look in his eyes.

"Don't touch her," the woman said. "She's mine, not any of yours. Unless you wish to fight me for her?"

The elf wearing the red cap backed away a step.

"I thought not." The woman pulled the hood of her cloak away from her face, staring at Kayla with an odd look in her green eyes. Without the hood, she looked much younger than Kayla had thought, short sandy-colored hair tousled around the fine features of her face and those long, pointed ears.

"Come with me, girl," she said, abruptly turning and walking away. Kayla wondered whether she should follow, then saw the guy in the red cap watching her with eyes that burned. She headed quickly down the hallway to catch up with the woman.

Silently, they walked up a crumbling stone staircase, down shadowed hallways. *What a dump*, Kayla thought. *This isn't how I imagined a faerie castle would look. I wonder why they've let it turn into this mess?*

"Once this was a lovely hall," the woman said, as if answering Kayla's unspoken question. "Once this was one of the finest castles of the Unseelie, gold and silver and glittering with magic. Once I was Lady Catt of the Unseelie Court, the Queen's right-hand confidante, wearing fine silks and jewels in our moonlight dances, leading our Host to war against the Seelie. Now that is no more."

I'm surprised she's talking to me like I'm a real person! Kayla thought. "What happened?" she asked.

Catt didn't answer. She shoved at a closed wooden door, which creaked open slowly. Inside was a small room, not much different from a prison cell. There was only a cot with blankets laid over it, what looked like a large rack for armor, and a standing closet. Ignoring Kayla, Catt undressed quickly, dropping her cloak and pieces of armor on the floor.

Kayla bent to look at it curiously, then blinked. *It's not steel . . . it's solid silver!* She turned, to see Catt lifting a lovely blue and silver gown from the closet, slipping it over her thin shoulders. Her very thin shoulders. *I'd think the lady was sick, she's so thin, but all these people look like that. . . .* "Hey, this is silver, isn't it? That's worth a lot."

"Is it worth much in the human realms?" the elf-woman asked, lacing the front of the gown. "Silver is not very rare here in the Unseelie lands." She fastened on the gown's long sleeves with ribbon ties, and Kayla saw that the gown wasn't as beautiful as she'd thought—it was faded, marked with old stains, obviously old and worn. "I've thought of visiting the human worlds," Catt continued as she smoothed the heavy skirts of the dress. "To see the realm of folk who live without true sorcery, building their tall towers and mechanical magics."

"Why don't you go there?" Kayla asked.

"Only those who are banished can go to the human lands. That is by the Queen's command. But I am curious about them." She shook her head. "Come. It is time to bring you before the Queen. I wish I could delay that longer, because I have many questions to ask about the human lands, but the Queen will already be impatient."

"Hey, you can ask me those questions after I talk with her, right?"

Catt didn't answer.

This doesn't sound very good, Kayla thought, following Catt down the stairs and through the rabbit warren of twisty hallways. *I guess I could try to run away from her, get out of here, but where would I go? I don't know this place, don't know anything about how to get home from here. . . .*

As they walked down a last curved flight of narrow stairs, hands suddenly grabbed Kayla and pulled her away from Catt. Laughing, the Unseelie courtiers, garbed in faded velvets and silks, dragged Kayla out into the huge hall. They

spun and pushed her around, until all she could
see was a blur of colors, red and blue and gold
and green, and their laughing, cruel faces. As
they shoved her forward, she had one glimpse of
a huge room with vaulted stone ceilings and
giant fire pits along the sides of the room, filled
with glowing coals. Stained and torn tapestries
hung from the walls, which were black with soot
and filth. Half-seen shadows flitted through the
darkness of the hall behind the waiting crowd of
brilliantly clothed elves.

The mass of people parted to admit her and
her captors, revealing a silver-haired old woman
with eyes the color of ice, seated upon a carved
stone chair. A long velvet gown the color of
blood draped her thin figure, and two silent
guards stood on either side of her, so motionless
that they could've been carved from stone.

"So what have you brought me, my dear
Catt?" the old Queen asked in a thin voice, her
eyes not wavering from Kayla.

Catt stepped forward and knelt gracefully. "A
human child of magic, a gift to your Majesty,"

"Indeed," the Unseelie Queen said thoughtfully. "And do you have nothing to say for
yourself, human child?" she asked, gazing at
Kayla with her colorless eyes. "Or are you so
awed by the glory of the Unseelie Court that
you have been struck dumb?"

The courtiers tittered at the remark, and Kayla
agreed with them. This place was shabby, not
anything like what she'd imagined a queen's
court would be.

"I'm not dumb," Kayla said, "And besides, this
is only a dream. I don't believe in you!"

The elves laughed.

"I'll wake up in another few minutes, I'll be

back in bed, and I probably won't even remember that I dreamed about you!" Kayla said hotly.

"I want this one's blood," a chill voice said from behind her. She turned quickly, to see the broad-shouldered elven man dressed in leather, with the red cap perched on his head. "I want this one's blood to dye my cap!" he repeated, staring at Kayla with hungry eyes.

She felt a chill run down her back. "Okay, I admit it," she said. "This isn't a dream, this is a nightmare. It's an awful nightmare, a real, genuine, honest-to-God nightmare, but I'm going to wake up from it, any minute now."

There was another titter of laughter from the crowd, and the Unseelie Queen smiled. "What you believe and what will happen are two different things, child," she said. "But, for the moment, you amuse me. So I will let you live, I think, at least for now."

"Look, lady," Kayla said, starting forward. The sound of a dozen swords being drawn stopped her in her tracks. She glanced around nervously and then stepped back from the Queen's throne.

"You amuse me, child, but don't push your luck," the Queen said dryly.

Kayla nodded, her mouth dry.

"Now, tell me, how did you come here?" the Queen asked. "Did you conjure a doorway with your own magics between the human lands and our own? You look too young and unskilled to accomplish such a feat."

How do I explain what happened? And why in the hell should I explain anything to someone who's only part of a dream?

"You may think this is only a dream," the Queen said, idly viewing the jeweled rings on her long, tapered fingers. "But I assure you that it is quite real, and if you defy me, you'll discover the reality of it in a most painful and immediate way. So, answer my question: how did you come here?"

"I don't know what you're talking about with doors and all of that," Kayla began. "All I know is one minute I was in Los Angeles—well, Santa Monica, I think, but I'm not certain about that—and then all of the sudden I'm out here. I bet Shari and Nataniel think this is some kind of a great joke. . . ."

As she said Nataniel's name, she felt a sudden chill run through the crowd, a tension as the smiles froze on the faces of those graceful figures.

"Let me kill it now!" the man with the red cap hissed.

"In a moment," the Queen murmured. "First, I would hear all of this one's story. So, you admit that you are in league with Nataniel, who was banished many centuries ago to the human lands? I would have killed him for attempting to murder me," she added in an undertone, "but he had too many loyal followers, and a war would have destroyed the Unseelie Court. Instead, I sent him and his followers to the human lands, where now, apparently, he is recruiting young humans to do his work for him."

"I'm not working with him at all!" Kayla protested. "Look, he kidnaped me, asked me if I wanted to work with him, I said no, and so he sent me here!"

"I see." The Queen was silent for a long moment, then spoke. "Despite your words of innocence, I cannot believe that Nataniel would have brought you here if you were not allied with him and somehow part of a plot to

overthrow my rule. Therefore, my Lord
Skullcleaver . . ." She gestured at an Unseelie
in dark armor, who stepped forward with a
sword raised, firelight glinting off the blade.

Kayla swallowed. *Even if this is a dream, this
is getting way too real for me.* She glanced at
the Queen, who was sipping dark red wine
from a crystal goblet, and felt a shock run
through her. Something was wrong about the
Queen, she could feel something was very
wrong, and as the Queen brought the glass
again to her lips, she knew what it was.

"You've been poisoned," Kayla said.

The swordsman stopped in mid-step.

The Queen stared at her. "What did you say?"

"You've been poisoned," Kayla repeated. "And
there's more of the poison in that glass. At least,
I think it's poison. I don't know what it is, but I
can see what it's doing to you, eating away at
your mind and body. . . ."

The glass slipped from the Queen's hand and
shattered on the stone floor.

"And how did you know this?" the Queen
asked, all traces of amusement gone from her
voice. A sudden silence had fallen over the
crowd.

"She's a healer," Catt whispered from behind
her. "We saw her heal herself only a short while
ago."

"Is that true?" the Queen asked Kayla.

She nodded. "It's what I do. I guess it's what
you'd call my magic. There's something wrong
with that goblet, I can't tell exactly what, but
when you drank from it, I could see the poison
affecting you."

The Queen rose unsteadily from her throne,
and the crowd parted instantly before her. She

strode across the hall, toward an arched doorway
on the far wall. "Bring the girl, Lady Catt," she
said without looking back.

Catt pushed Kayla ahead of her, walking
quickly. "Say nothing unless she speaks to you, if
you value your life," the woman said tersely to
Kayla.

*Not a problem, I don't want to get in that
lady's way, not when she's got that "To hell with
patience, I'm going to kill someone" look in her
eyes!*

A moment later they were in the kitchen,
walking past the greasy wooden tables and cowering servants dressed in rags who were kneeling
on the straw-covered stone floor.

"Who poured my glass of wine?" the Queen
demanded, glancing around furiously at the terrified servants.

No one moved or spoke.

The Queen walked forward, her eyes moving
over the servants' faces, and stopped in front of
a kneeling woman. *She's human like me*, Kayla
realized, seeing the woman's normal ears showing
beneath her tangled mop of dark hair.

"I know what you did," the Queen said dangerously. "What did you put in my wine?"

"It wasn't me, milady," the woman wheezed,
her face pale white beneath the grime. Impatiently, the Queen shoved her out of the way,
searching through the items piled on the wooden
table next to her, bowls and platters clattering
haphazardly onto the floor. A moment later she
straightened, something small and white clenched
within her hand.

"What is this?" she said, turning quickly to
Kayla. "This is not of my realm. Do you know what
this is?"

No-Doz? What is a bottle of No-Doz doing here?

"Uh, it's pills, Your Majesty," Kayla said, looking at the white plastic bottle. "No-Doz. They're caffeine pills."

The Queen's fingers whitened on the plastic bottle, and Catt made an odd choking sound. "Caffeine!" the Queen said in a voice like ice. "Heads will roll over this," she whispered. "Heads will roll!" She turned quickly to Kayla. "Can you counter the poison, healer?"

"I think so," Kayla said uncertainly. "I mean, you didn't drink very much of it, so there's only a little in your system. . . ."

"Even small amounts of pure caffeine is deadly to our kind," the Queen said. "Work your magic, child. Heal me of this poison."

Hesitantly, Kayla touched the Queen's pale white hands. In that instant, fire welled up from within her, blossoming around her. Suddenly she could see beneath that pale skin, the swirling patterns of power and lifeblood, and the darkening stain of shadow that was moving through her body. She could see the deadly effect of the caffeine upon the Queen, and before she could blink, the magic caught her up and plunged her into the healing.

She coaxed the poison out of the Queen's blood, changing it to something harmless that drifted away. It was more difficult than anything she'd ever done before, tracing those tiny molecules of death through the Queen's body and changing each one. When she finished, she realized that Catt was holding her up, keeping her from falling onto the stone floor. The Queen was standing silently, sparks of blue fire still flickering over her skin.

"Thank you," the Queen said stiffly. Kayla thought that maybe she'd never said those two words before. "Thank you, child." The Queen glided away without another word, walking back through the kitchen. After a moment, Kayla felt strong enough to follow her. In the throne room, the Queen, calm and expressionless, seated herself without a word. The gathered courtiers watched her nervously.

"It is true, what the human child said," the Queen said at last. "I was poisoned."

The Queen's eyes traveled through the crowd, glancing at one elven lord and then another, until they fixed upon an elderly, gray-haired elven man garbed in black velvet, who was watching her with a composed face but terror in his eyes. His lips twitched once, and before he could smooth his features into another mask of impassiveness, the Queen pointed at him.

"He is responsible!" the Queen said, gesturing with a pale finger at the elderly elf. "Take him outside and make him pay for his treachery!"

How . . . how did she know?

The silent swordsman and the Redcap moved to the old elf. They had taken him by the arms and dragged him halfway across the hall before he reacted, shouting protestations of innocence and begging for mercy. The heavy twin doors of the hall shut upon his wild pleadings.

They're going to—they're going to kill that old man!

"Wait . . ." Kayla began, then saw the look in the Queen's eyes, intense hatred mixed with a cruel satisfaction, and knew that she couldn't say anything that would save the old man's life.

"Well, that's that," the Queen said, rubbing her hands together. She glanced at Kayla, who

realized she was standing with her mouth open.
"You have a question in your eyes, human child,"
she observed. "What is it?"

*I don't want to say anything to this lady, I
don't want to be here, I don't want to know
what they're doing to that old man . . . how can
she sit there, smiling, having just ordered those
people to kill him?*

Kayla felt sick to her stomach, thinking of the
look on the old man's face. *How can she be so
cruel?*

*She's looking at me. I'd better say something,
anything, before she gets angry at me. . . .*

*Oh God, I hope this is a dream . . . this can't
be real, it can't . . .*

"How . . . how did you know that he was the one
who tried to murder you?" Kayla asked, hoping her
voice wasn't trembling as much as she was.

The Queen shrugged. "I didn't. But I had to
punish one of them. That particular lord had no
loyalty among the others, none who would fight
for him. And it certainly impressed the rest of
these useless traitors." She gestured at the elven
courtiers, who were casually but obviously making their exits from the hall. Only Kayla and the
wordless guards remained close to the Queen,
and Catt, who stood near the Queen, watching
Kayla silently. "So, human child, the question
remains of what I shall do with you," the elf
queen continued.

Kayla thought about the elf lord who had just
been dragged off to his execution and decided that
maybe, just this one time, she wouldn't make any
wise-ass remarks. "Well, uh . . ." she started
awkwardly.

"Set your fears at rest, human child," the elf
queen said, smiling indulgently. "I owe you a

debt, and I would repay it. What do you wish for? Gold, jewels, fine clothes?"

These elves tend to think alike, Kayla thought, remembering a similar list that Nataniel had offered her. *I wonder if she's going to offer me a Mercedes next?*

"Actually, Your . . . Your Majesty, I'd really just like to go home. I didn't want to come here in the first place—I mean, not that this is a bad place or anything, I kinda like the dead trees and the moldy castle and all, and it's sure been . . . been interesting, but I'd really like to go home. You don't need to give me anything else, that'd be more than enough."

The Queen nodded. "A wish that is easily granted," she said. "Though I am surprised that you do not wish for anything more than that. I will draw a Doorway that will take you home." The Queen closed her eyes, her fingers moving in an odd pattern. Pure white light began to appear around her fingers, lines and angles growing brighter and brighter.

"Thanks. Thanks a lot." *Except, what's home for me now? Not Suite 230—no, that really had never been home, and it sure wasn't now, not after everything that had happened. . . .*

Maybe Elizabet's would be home someday, but I never spent much time there, not enough to make me feel like I belonged.

Another thought came to mind; she thought about someone else, the young man with laughing dark eyes and unruly hair, the way he smiled at her, the way he made her feel so happy and safe. . . .

She yawned, feeling very sleepy. Not surprising after everything that'd happened, all she wanted now was a comfortable bed, someplace warm to curl up and go to sleep. . . .

The room was very bright as the Queen wove her magic spell, so bright that she had to close her eyes against the light. She stood in the light, feeling the warmth against her skin and seeing it through her closed eyes.

"Fare thee well, human child," the Unseelie Queen said in a quiet voice, her words very faint, as though falling away. Kayla smiled and yawned again, pulling the blankets tighter around her. The bed was definitely warm enough, soft and comfortable. She snuggled up against the source of warmth, hearing an indistinct murmur in response. She smiled as she drifted off to sleep.

Something awakened her suddenly, someone shoving her away. Kayla yelled as she felt herself sliding out of the bed, unceremoniously dumped onto the floor. The light switched on suddenly, and she saw Ramon, a blanket clutched desperately around his naked body, staring down at her in surprise.

"*Madre de Dios!*"

Chapter Eleven

"Ramon, what's wrong?" someone called from outside the bedroom, then the door was flung open. Roberta stood in the doorway, looking down at Kayla on the floor, and Ramon, wrapped in a blanket, on the bed. She began to laugh.

"It's not funny, Berta," Ramon began indignantly. Carlos appeared in the doorway, looking over Roberta's shoulder, his hair still dripping from the shower and a towel wrapped around his midriff.

His eyes darkened when he saw Kayla, and she felt a shiver run down her back. *This is going to be bad. He's furious, I can tell by his eyes.*

"Where did you find her?" Carlos demanded of Ramon.

"I don't know, she just appeared, I woke up and she was here."

Carlos crossed the room, reaching down to grab Kayla by the shoulders and hauling her to her feet. "Where have you been, all this week? How did you get out of Luis' house?"

Kayla shook her head. Carlos' eyes narrowed, and he raised one hand. "You will talk to me, girl! You'll—"

"Carlos, stop it!" Roberta caught Carlos' raised hand, held it tightly in her own. He glared at her; to Kayla's surprise, Roberta glared right back at him. "She came back, right? That's all that matters. She is here now."

"But she's—"

"Carlos, you've dropped your towel," Roberta observed tartly, and Kayla quickly averted her eyes. "Go put on some clothes."

With a last fierce look at Kayla, Carlos stalked away, slamming the bedroom door shut behind him.

"And you, Ramie!" Roberta turned on him. "What were you doing with this girl in your room?"

"Roberta, I didn't do anything!" Ramon protested.

Yeah, that's the pity, Kayla thought. *If he hadn't yelled so loudly . . .*

"You didn't do anything because you didn't have enough time to do anything!" Roberta countered.

"'Berta, that's not—" Everything blurred around Kayla, dizziness suddenly overwhelming her. She leaned against the wall, shaking her head.

Roberta said something terse in Spanish to Ramon, then to Kayla, "Girl, you're pale as a ghost. Come, I'll make you some hot chocolate, you'll feel better."

"Just a second . . . I'm not feeling so great . . ." Everything was spinning too fast. She closed her eyes and swallowed, wishing it would all just go away. She heard the sound of the bedroom door opening; Carlos and Ramon's voices, speaking in quiet Spanish.

"Where has she been for the last week?" Ramon asked in English.

"I want to know how she got into your room," Roberta said, "when I know she didn't come through the front door. How did she get up to the third floor and get inside without opening a window? The window's still locked, Ramie, from the inside."

The dizziness cleared, slowly. Kayla straightened to meet Carlos' level gaze.

"She's a *bruja*, she can do many things," Carlos said, looking at her with expressionless dark eyes. "And now we have her back."

Kayla sat next to the living room window, sipping from a steaming mug of spicy hot chocolate, listening to Ramon and Carlos arguing in Spanish across the room. Roberta sat near to her, watching her intently.

"Why did you come back?" the Hispanic girl asked suddenly.

Kayla looked down at her mug, not answering.

"I don't understand it. I know you don't like Carlos . . ."

That's the understatement of the century, Kayla thought.

" . . . and you never wanted to be here at all. So why did you come back?"

I wish I knew. I must've wanted to come back here, or the Unseelie Queen would've sent me somewhere else. And what happens now?

"It's settled," Carlos said, standing up. "Ramie will take you to the apartment. You'll be safe there, safer than here. We'll need to keep some homeboys there to protect you all the time."

"Listen . . ." Kayla began, then faltered, seeing the look in Carlos' eyes. She marshaled all the courage she had—*which isn't much,* she thought. "Carlos, can we . . . can we talk about this? I don't . . . I don't want to be a prisoner, locked up somewhere. I want to go home. Please. That's all I want."

Carlos stood silently, looking at her with unreadable dark eyes.

Ramon broke the awkward silence. "You don't know what's happened in the last week, *querida.* The *bastardos* have been coming around here all the time. None of us can go out alone. It's very dangerous. I think Carlos is right, you should go to the safest place we know. There are many lives depending on you."

But I don't want these people depending on me! she thought. *I just want to be what I was before, just plain, ordinary Kayla, no one special, no one that anyone cares about.*

"You're going to live in the apartment," Carlos said in a tone that allowed no argument. "And Ramon will stay with you. He can watch over you. And Fernando will be there too," Carlos added, as Ramon grinned at Kayla. "Just to watch over Ramon!"

"But first we'll stop at the hospital, where you will heal our people. It's too dangerous to leave them there; the *policía* won't let us guard them. There's no one to make sure that the bastards don't come after them. And there's no way we can leave them guns to defend themselves with. We'll go there and you'll heal Luis so he can leave the hospital, then take you to a safe place."

"But—"

"No more arguing," Carlos said, cutting off Kayla's words. "That is what we're going to do."

*   *   *

In the bedroom, Kayla stuffed her other pair of jeans into the plastic shopping bag, throwing in some socks after it.

God, why did I come back here? I'm never going to get free of Carlos, ever. . . .

"*Querida?*"

Kayla turned to glare at Ramon. "What do you want?"

"I wanted to see if you needed any help getting your things together. You sound like you're a little angry?"

"A little angry? Look, I don't want to talk to you about it! You're as bad as Carlos—you just think of me as a walking medical kit, not a person!"

He moved closer, taking the shopping bag from her hands. "You know I don't think of you as that. I'll take this to the car. By the way," he said as he walked to the door, "your leather jacket is in the closet."

Kayla opened the closet door. She yanked the jacket from the hanger and pulled it on. The warm smell of leather touched with a hint of Ramon's aftershave surrounded her. *This is what I'm going to be,* she thought. *As tough as leather, as hard as the studs on this jacket. It's what I have to be.*

There were several safety pins on the dresser. She took out the silver hoops and dropped them into her jeans pocket. She fastened a safety pin in each of her ears, then followed Ramon downstairs to the car, where Carlos and Roberta were already waiting.

They were halfway up the steps to the hospital entrance when Kayla stopped, unable to walk any further.

"Come on, it's too dangerous to stand out here," Carlos said impatiently, glaring at her.

The sensation of pain and fear emanating from the hospital crawled over her skin, tightening around her throat. She couldn't speak, almost couldn't breathe. "Ramie," she whispered, "I don't want to go in there. It hurts too much."

Ramon took her hand, his fingers tight around hers. "I don't like hospitals, either," he said. "You can do it, *querida*. I know you can."

"Come on," Carlos urged, looking around nervously.

Holding onto Ramon's hand, Kayla walked through the hospital doors. The emotional noise hit her like a fist, and she nearly fell. Ramon's arm was around her shoulders, holding her upright.

She moved blindly, holding onto him with all her strength, unable to see or hear anything with the cacophony raging around her. Her vision cleared, and she saw that they were in a deserted corridor. There was a policeman seated on a folding chair outside the closest room, watching them with narrowed eyes.

"We're here to see Luis," Carlos said to the policeman, not bothering to disguise the hatred in his voice.

The policeman glared back at Carlos. "No visitors, homeboy. Visiting hours won't start for another couple hours."

"Please, he's our friend, can't we see him?" Roberta pleaded.

The cop's expression softened a little, looking at Roberta. "Okay, okay, but only for a few minutes. And only you two, the girls. The boys will have to wait outside."

"But—" Ramon began. Carlos put his hand on Ramon's arm.

"That's fine," he said quietly. "Kayla is the one who needs to see Luis, not us." They sat down to wait outside, as Roberta and Kayla went into the room.

Inside the hospital room, Luis was asleep in his bed. A bandage covered him from his shoulder down to his waist, and a drip line was connected to his wrist, the IV bag hanging from a rack next to the bed.

Kayla touched him lightly, trying not to awaken him. She could feel the wound beneath the bandage, the track of the bullet that had shattered his collarbone. They'd fitted the pieces back together, but the bone would take months to heal.

But I can change that. I can heal him.

She closed her eyes and let the magic move through her.

She didn't know how long she stood there, lost in the magic. The world vanished around her, and all she could feel was the sensation of the magic coursing through her. She carefully knit the shattered pieces of bone back together, drawing the pain away from him as she worked. When she was done, she sat down abruptly, feeling all the power draining away from her and leaving her an exhausted, empty shell.

Luis opened his eyes and smiled at her and Roberta. "'Berta, it doesn't hurt," he murmured sleepily.

"Sleep for a few hours, Luis," Roberta said gently. "When you have the chance, just walk out. Leave your door open so you can hear when the policeman goes to have a doughnut break, and just walk away.

"I will, 'Berta," Luis said. He smiled at Kayla again, closing his eyes to drift off to sleep.

"You did well, Kayla," Roberta said, smiling. Kayla stood up unsteadily; Roberta held out her arm, and Kayla leaned on her gratefully.

They walked slowly from the room. In the hallway, Carlos looked at Roberta with an unspoken question in his eyes. She nodded.

"Now we'll take you to the apartment," Carlos said, glancing at Kayla.

The street looked like a war zone, much worse than any neighborhood she'd ever seen before, with abandoned cars left like corpses on the pavement. Children played between the rusting hulks. The kids ran for the sidewalk as Ramon drove Carlos' car down the street. He parked the car in front of an ancient-looking apartment building.

Fernando stepped out of the car first, scanning the street quickly, then gestured to Ramon and Kayla. Kayla picked up the shopping bag of her clothes and followed Ramon up the creaking flight of stairs, through a hallway littered with stinking trash and abandoned children's toys, to an unmarked door on the second floor.

"You'll like staying here," he said, and Kayla thought he sounded like he was trying to be cheerful and failing completely. "You'll have a room to yourself, you won't have to share with anyone. It's not as crowded as Roberta's."

"Yeah, but at least Roberta's place was clean," Kayla observed, stepping over some garbage on the landing.

Ramon shrugged. "No one really lives here. We keep this place only for selling . . . what we sell."

"Drugs, you mean?" Kayla asked.

He unlocked the door and they walked in, Fernando following them. She looked around curiously. The living room was a little cleaner than the rest of the building, but completely without any furniture, except an old couch.

Ramon walked down the short hallway, glancing quickly in each of the rooms. He said something in Spanish to Fernando, who nodded. "No one has been here since we left," he added. "You will be safe here. If any other of the homeboys come here, stay out of the first bedroom—that's where they work. We don't sell drugs here, they do that downstairs. When someone wishes to buy, we lower baggies through the hole in the floor of the bathroom. That way, if the *policía* or someone else breaks through the downstairs door, there isn't anything around."

Ramon said something else in Spanish to Fernando; the other man smiled and left, closing the door behind him.

"Fernando's going to make sure everything's okay downstairs," Ramon said. "Later, he'll go get some groceries for you. I don't think there's anything but Coronas in the fridge."

"Great. I'm starving." She looked at the sofa, some of the springs poking through the fabric, and decided against trying to sit on it. *Doesn't matter, I'm not going to be here very long. Ramon won't be that hard to get away from—a lot easier than Carlos. It's only about fifteen feet to the ground; I can jump out the window, that won't be tough at all. I'm not sticking around here, that's for sure. These guys can carry on their war without me.*

The silence was becoming awkward. "So, do

you make a lot of money selling drugs?" Kayla
asked.

Ramon turned away, moving to the fridge
without answering. She watched as he popped
the cap off a bottle of beer. "What, the money's
not good? I don't believe that."

He turned to face her. In spite of herself,
Kayla took a step backwards. "You don't understand!" he said angrily, then shook his head and
repeated quietly, "You don't understand.

"No, I don't," Kayla said.

He gestured for her to sit on the couch; carefully, trying to avoid the deadly-looking metal
springs, she sat down next to him. He took her
hand in his, looking down at her grubby fingers.
He glanced up at her and smiled. "You need a
bath, *querida.*"

"Thanks for reminding me," she said wryly.

"Fernando will bring back some towels when
he goes to get groceries; you can bathe later.
Just put a towel over the hole in the floor, otherwise the homies downstairs may play jokes on
you. Kayla . . . what do you dream of?"

"I—I don't understand," Kayla said, a little
confused.

"What do you want to be when you grow up?"

"I don't know." Kayla looked down at her
hands. "Before everything . . . went wrong,
before my parents disappeared, I wanted to be a
doctor, I think. I don't remember."

Ramon nodded. "I've always dreamed of being
someone who could make a difference. I wanted
to be a lawyer, to change the way the law treats
Hispanics. I studied hard in school, thinking that
even though my family couldn't afford to send
me to college, I'd get a scholarship and go.

"But what I didn't know as a kid is that the

system, it doesn't let you do that. You go to school, but they can't teach you, not here in the *barrio*. They don't have enough teachers, or books, or anything. If you're lucky, you can stay in school through most of high school, like I did. Carlos wasn't so lucky, he had to quit school and work after Papa left.

"All they can teach you is that nobody cares. Nobody really cares. What they teach is that you can't win, that if your name ends in Z, all you can hope for is a job at McDonald's. The teachers don't expect you to get through high school, let alone go on to college. Most of my friends can't speak English, they can barely read, even in Spanish, they can't hope for anything better than a job as a night watchman or a cook.

"And then there are the gangs. You have to stick with your own kind, otherwise you're dead. They'll find you alone somewhere and cut you up. I was ten years old when they started carrying knives and talking tough. Junior high is worse. By the time I got to high school, it was a war.

"I quit high school after the first time I was stabbed, walking to classes one morning. I wanted to go back, but Carlos made me quit then. He said that they knew I was his brother, and he couldn't protect me at the school. Next time, he said, they'd kill me.

"But one of my teachers visited me in the hospital." Ramon's eyes were distant as he smiled, remembering. "Mrs. Webster. Mrs. Jennifer Webster. She was beautiful, with long dark hair and blue eyes. Such pretty blue eyes, like I'd never seen before.

"She knew I wanted to go to college, and she

said to me: 'Ramie, you're bright enough, but you need to learn so much. You need to learn how to learn.' She convinced me to go back to high school. She'd spend an hour with me every day after her other classes, working with me, teaching me, helping me prepare for the SATs. She said that if I scored high enough, it wouldn't matter that I couldn't afford even the community college fees, that there would be scholarships to pay for my education.

"She was young and beautiful, and she cared about me. I think I was a little in love with her." His voice fell to a whisper. "But then one of the Bloods attacked her in the hallway early one morning. He cut her face . . . here." Ramon's finger traced a line down Kayla's cheek. "She had the most beautiful face, with those pretty blue eyes.

"I wanted to visit her in the hospital, but they wouldn't let me into her room because they thought I was a homeboy. Mrs. Webster never came back to the high school after that, not even to say goodbye."

He shrugged. "Carlos needed my help, especially when the T-Men started coming after us. So I quit high school again, to work with my brother and hang with the homeboys. What else is there for me?"

He stood up suddenly and walked to the window, looking out at the street. "I need to go take care of other business," he said. "Fernando will stay here and watch over you. Don't leave the apartment, it's not safe. You look very tired, *querida*," he added. "Do you want to rest?"

"Yeah." She nodded. "I think that's a good idea."

She picked up her plastic bag of belongings and

carried it into the bedroom. The bedroom was almost as plain as the living room, with just a mattress and some blankets on the floor. She stretched out on the mattress and pulled the book about the magical white horses from the bag.

Through the open bedroom door, she could hear the clatter of a metal chain from the other room and Ramon's voice quietly calling to someone in the apartment below. *I'll just rest for a few minutes,* she thought. *Just a few minutes . . .*

They were walking on the wet sand, the waves surging only a few feet away. Little tongues of water trying to reach their feet. Kayla held tightly to Ramon's hand, hearing Elizabet talking about something as she walked near them, but the words didn't register. Just the way that Ramon was looking at her, that's all that mattered right now, his dark eyes glinting with hidden laughter, some kind of promise . . . The sound of gunfire awakened her abruptly.

She half-rolled to the floor, sliding off the mattress and onto the cold linoleum. The sound erupted again, echoing from the street below. Kayla crawled to the open window, peering carefully over the sill, just enough to see.

There were several cars parked in front of the apartment building, including the white Mercedes convertible with the trashed fender. She ducked back out of sight, not certain what to do next. There was nothing here she could use as a weapon, and no way out except down the stairs, past whatever was going on down on the street.

The apartment door opened and slammed quickly shut, and she heard muffled voices from the living room, speaking in fast Spanish.

"*Querida?*" Ramon called softly, and she ran out into the living room. Fernando was standing at the side of the door, a pistol in his hand. Ramon was reloading a small handgun, his eyes wild. "Go hide in the bedroom closet," he said to Kayla. "Stay low, don't get up for any reason."

"What's—" she began.

"They're trying to kill us all," Ramon said, his voice tight. With a start, Kayla realized that he'd been crying, that there were smeared stains of tear-tracks on his face. "Roberta is dead. They shot her and Luisa half an hour ago. They were trying for Carlos, but he got away. Someone must have told them about the drugs here—I don't think they know we're up here. Quickly, now, go to the bedroom."

Kayla nodded, too stunned to speak. She started for the bedroom, then all of them froze, hearing the sound of footsteps on the creaking stairs outside. Then the sound of a door being kicked in down the hall and a woman's shrill scream, combined with a baby's crying. "Shut the bitch up," she heard someone say from the hallway, muffled by the closed door.

Her own breathing sounded very loud in the silence, loud enough for someone to hear from miles away.

They could hear whispered words from beyond the closed door. Ramon pushed Kayla down behind the couch with one hand, his other hand bringing up the pistol to aim at the door.

The world exploded around her.

She screamed and huddled against the floor, as the room was filled with the noise of automatic gunfire. She couldn't hear anything but the endless sound of bullets ripping through the air around her.

It was over as quickly as it had begun, a sudden shocking silence. There was no other sound, only her own breathing. She crouched against the floor, unable to do anything but breathe.

Someone grabbed her by the shoulder and yanked her up. Two young black men, one cradling a stubby machine pistol in his arms, were staring at her.

She looked down, and saw Ramon.

He lay several feet away, his hand still clutching the pistol. All around him was blood, staining his shirt and the floor. His eyes were open, staring blankly.

Oh God . . . oh my God . . .

Fernando was lying a few feet beyond him, a long smear of blood staining the wall where he'd been thrown by the impact of bullets, before sliding down to the floor.

She tried to pull away from the T-Men holding her. He was saying something, but she couldn't understand the words, nothing made any sense.

He brought up his hand and slapped her across the face.

The sudden pain snapped something in her. Her shock and terror giving way to something else: hot, deadly anger.

All right, you bastards . . .

Chapter Twelve

She grabbed his hand.

For a moment, nothing happened. Then the magic coursed down through her with a force that she'd never felt before, leaping between them. She touched his own magic, the light that was his life . . . took hold of it, and pulled.

He screamed and jumped back, staring at his hands, which were engulfed in blue fire. The skin of his hands shriveled, as though rotting in front of her. It crawled up his arms, moving up to his face. What staggered and fell to the floor wasn't a young man, but something wrinkled and bloodless, with bone showing through the tatters of skin of his hands. He twitched on the floor, making small whimpering sounds through what was left of his lips.

The other T-Man dropped his gun and ran.

Kayla didn't notice that for a few seconds, until the apartment door slammed shut; she was too busy throwing up. She couldn't stop shaking, her stomach heaving even though there was nothing left.

Out of control, she thought, trembling. *Like Elizabet said, out of control.*

Got to get up. They'll come back and kill me.

The T-Man was moving feebly on the floor, trying to crawl away from her. She could feel a little life left in him, barely enough for her to touch.

I did that. I did that to him.

And it felt . . .

She didn't want to think about how she felt, because right now she felt wonderful, as though every nerve ending in her body was singing. She'd never felt this good before, and it was a dizzying high, overwhelming her with giddiness.

It's wrong . . . I shouldn't feel like this . . . I shouldn't . . .

She turned away from the T-Man, looking to where Ramon lay on the floor. She felt tears burning her eyes. *He's dead. I didn't even see it happen. I didn't even have my eyes open to see it.*

She felt the magic stir within her, trying to reach out to him. She was next to him a split second later, kneeling; her hands touching the bloody wound.

He's not dead, but . . .

Her healing sense widened, brightened; blurring the rest of the room to invisibility until all she could see was the track of the bullet and how it had passed through skin and muscle to nick the major artery that was pumping out his lifeblood with every second. She felt herself falling into the healing and stopped with a sudden thought.

They're going to be back in a minute. I won't have time to do this and get away. I have to get out of here, I have to . . .

No. I won't let him die.

She let the magic sweep through her, everything else fading away. She felt the electricity surge down through her hands, knitting the pieces of muscle back together, sealing up the rip in the artery, closing the flesh around it.

The magic let her go suddenly and she fell forward. Her cheek lay against Ramon's chest and she could feel his breathing growing stronger, his heartbeat strengthening.

She came back to herself with a start, hearing voices through the open window. Fighting off the waves of exhaustion, she lifted Ramon and dragged him into the bedroom, setting him down in the closet and closing the door. She laid her hand briefly on his face, feeling the glowing light of his life becoming stronger and brighter with every passing second.

He'll be okay, she thought. *I don't think they'll find him in here. Now I'd better get my ass out of here.* . . .

She paused in the bedroom long enough to grab her jacket and sneakers, yanking on the shoes and quickly knotting the laces. She ran back into the living room, heading for the shattered door.

"Please . . ."

Kayla stopped, looking down at the source of the whisper. The T-Man boy, sprawled on the dirty floor, staring up at her with terrified eyes. "Please, don't . . ." he whispered again, his voice failing.

"You would've killed me," she whispered. "I'm sorry, I didn't want to hurt you that way, but . . . I need to get away from here, I can't . . . I can't . . ."

His dark eyes stared at her, filled with pain.

I can't leave him like this. I can't.

She knelt beside him and rested her hand on his forehead, closing her eyes. Her other vision kicked in a moment later, and she was horrified to see what she'd done to him—*pulling out the energy that his body needs, the energy of the cells themselves.*

She reached into herself, for the heat of magic within her, and poured it back into him. She could feel his body changing beneath her hand, grasping desperately for life, and willing itself to live. When she opened her eyes, he was unconscious, but alive.

Now I'd definitely better get my ass out of here. . . .

"There she is!"

"Oh, shit!" Kayla looked up at the three T-Men in the broken doorway and saw the leader raise a pistol to fire. . . .

She closed her eyes and called the magic.

Blinding light filled the room, light and a warmth that felt like sunlight on Kayla's face. It was too bright to see, so bright that the light imprinted itself on her closed eyes. Kayla blindly leaped for the doorway, crashing into someone who fell out of her way and half-falling, half-rolling down the stairs. On the landing, she managed to open her eyes, though the world was still filled with glowing afterimages. She scrambled down the remaining stairs and paused at the bottom, listening closely, and then reaching out with that other sight.

She could feel the light of human lives around her: two just beyond the apartment wall that she was leaning against, close to a third life that was fading to nothingness even as she touched it. There were two others outside, beyond the building walls.

She took a deep breath and leaped out the door. The two T-Men standing at the car reacted a half second too late as she dashed past them and into the alley. She heard a gunshot ricochet off the wall just behind her, and a window just ahead of her shattered, splinters of glass flying past her.

"Stop her!" she heard someone yell from behind her. She ran without looking back, her legs pounding against the uneven pavement, her heart thudding in her chest.

She didn't bother to stop for traffic at the next street, just ran across the intersection and dodged the cars, which screeched to a halt around her. She heard another squeal of tires off to one side and glanced up to see the Mercedes tear around the corner, barely missing a collision with a truck. Kayla dashed into the next alley, too crowded with boxes and trash cans for a car to pass through, then around a corner and into a wide empty parking lot, next to a desolate-looking area of warehouse buildings and parked trucks.

Keep running . . . keep running . . .

I don't know what I'll do if they catch me. I can't do whatever it was that I did to that guy, not again. If they find me, I don't know what I'll do.

She paused long enough to catch her breath, gasping as she leaned against a graffiti-covered wall. She thought for a moment that maybe she'd lost them, and then she saw the Mercedes turn into the parking lot ahead of her, moving silently like a gliding shark.

She ducked into the shadow of the closest building, but heard the roar of the Mercedes' engine accelerating and knew that they'd seen her. Kayla ran further into the shadows between the tall warehouses, plain flat walls without any place to hide, nowhere else to go.

Suddenly, ahead of her in the shadows, she

saw a light glittering from a warehouse window.
She ran for it, half-blinded with the sweat dripping in her eyes, her lungs aching.

Beside the lit window was a closed door.
Kayla shoved at it; to her surprise, it opened,
apparently unlocked.

She slipped inside and shut it quietly behind
her. She looked around quickly to find a light
switch, planning to hide herself in the darkness,
and found herself face-to-face with a short, wrinkled old woman dressed in tattered, filthy rags,
looking at her with an odd smile on her face.

"My, my," the old woman murmured, in a
voice thick with a foreign accent, "what have we
here?"

"Two guys, chasing me," Kayla gasped.
"They're . . ."

"I know," the old woman said. Kayla could
recognize the accent now as Irish, but a heavy,
slow Irish accent, not like what she'd always
heard on television. "But they won't dare to
enter here," the old woman added.

"B-but, they're . . . they're . . ."

The old woman smiled, showing several
pointed, yellow teeth. "You're not very observant,
for one who bubbles with magic like Bridget's
Well," the woman said. "Can't you see it? Can't
you feel it?"

Kayla shook her head, wanting to explain to this
nice old woman that they were in terrible danger,
that they had to do something, call the cops, get
the Feds, call in the U.S. Marines. . . .

There was something else here, something
that Kayla realized with a start. *She's not . . .
there's something very different about this bag
lady. That odd face . . . the heavy cords of muscle beneath the rags, this lady could be a pro*

*weightlifter without any training . . . the teeth,
too long and pointed to belong to a human . . .
the long fingernails, crusted with dirt . . . no,
they're claws, sharp claws. She's not human, not
anymore than the elves, she's something else,
something completely different. . . .*

She felt more than saw the burst of magic,
flowing from the old woman like dark water, racing
toward Kayla . . . a shadow reaching out past her,
moving through the door. She nearly fell, stepping
away from it. She pressed against the wall,
flinching where the dark light brushed against her,
feeling a sharp pain as though she'd been cut and
was bleeding . . . and sensed that it was delighting
in that, enjoying her fear and pain.

There was a strangled sound from outside the
closed door, and then the boneless thump of
something heavy falling, and then again, a similar
noise. Kayla listened, but she couldn't hear anything else, not a single sound.

"Well, that takes care of that," the old woman
said, a small satisfied look on her face. She
turned to Kayla, who was still crouched against
the wall. "They won't trouble us," the woman
said, "or interfere in any way. Now, come with
me. I was about to set the table for dinner." The
old woman tottered away toward a lit doorway
down the hall.

Kayla glanced at the closed door, sensing that
hungry darkness still lingering outside, and
decided that maybe, just this once, she didn't
want to look.

She didn't really want to follow the old
woman anywhere, either. *Just what did she do?
It felt like magic, but it wasn't any magic I'd
ever seen before, nothing I'd want to know . . .
I'd better be polite, at least until I figure out*

*who—or what—she is, and what's going on
here. . . .*

"Coming, dearie?" the old woman asked, peering back at her.

"Uh . . . yeah," Kayla said uneasily. "I'm coming along right now."

The next room was dimly lit by several huge candles, their flickering light half-concealing the furniture draped with dark cloth and the odd object in the corner, a huge metal cauldron hanging over a pit of bright coals. The cauldron was blackened and old, and the old woman was now standing in front of it, adding seasonings from a small clay pot.

"Make yourself comfortable, dearie," the old woman said, sniffing suspiciously at the open clay pot in her hand. Something leaped out of it and skittered across the floor. The old woman yelped, dropping the pot.

Kayla gingerly sat down on the couch. "Can I help?" she asked hesitantly. *As long as I don't have to eat whatever she's cooking for dinner. I'm not into cockroaches, thanks.*

"Oh, possibly in a minute," the old woman said, reaching for another clay pot on the shelf above her. "For now, just make yourself comfortable."

"Uh, thanks," Kayla said. There was a low table, also draped in a dark sheet, directly in front of the couch. Several dozen pieces of paper were spread out upon it. Curious, Kayla picked up one of them.

It was covered with beautiful, twisty designs drawn in many colors: bright blues and reds and golds, all coiling together to form patterns. In the center, there was what looked like the image of a cow drawn out of a knotwork of twisty lines.

The paper was odd, too: a heavy, tanned paper with darker lines running through it. "What is this?" she asked the old woman.

The old woman sighed. "That is a drawing I made from the *Book of Kells*," she said, reaching for a wooden spoon with a long handle, maybe three feet long, and stirring the contents of the black cauldron furiously. "I've been drawing my own version for the last two hundred years or so."

"Two hundred years!" Kayla repeated in shock.

The woman laughed, an odd creaking sound. "I suppose I should be explaining to you who I am. An Caillach Beara, that was what they called me in the Old Country."

"An Caill . . . ?"

"Call me Beara, dearie, if you can't pronounce the Gaelic."

"Beara. Okay, I can handle that. What's the Old Country?"

"My, you're full of questions! I was born in Eire many years ago, what they now call Ireland. I came to America when foul times and famine befell the land. Not that I ever cared to eat potatoes, mind you, but if the people were starving, so was I.

"And, to make it worse, they wouldn't believe in me anymore. Once they feared me and my magic, but now no one believes in me. Nobody believes in magic anymore, not even you; and you're so strong with it, it's skittering out around your edges even when you're not using it."

"I believe in magic," Kayla said, a little uncertainly.

"Do you now? Seems to me that all you've done is try to pretend that it isn't real, ever since the magic first touched you."

"How do you know that?" Kayla asked, bewildered.

"I wasn't born yesterday, dearie. I can read it in you, read you like a book. I understand power, and humans, and what you have simmering inside you. Some of us appreciate magic, believe me. It was quite a surprise, though, to have someone as talented as yourself come wandering across my doorstep. Hmmm, I think this stock will need more salt, don't you?"

Kayla got up from the couch and walked over to her as Beara lifted the wooden spoon, dripping with broth, from the cauldron.

This smells awful! Kayla thought, as soon as she was within a couple feet. *I'm not going to try any of that, no way!* "Er, uh . . . I'm really not a good judge of cooking," she said quickly. "But it smells like it needs some salt, yeah."

"Why don't you stir it, while I get everything else ready?" the old woman asked, and immediately plunked the huge wooden spoon into Kayla's hand without waiting for an answer.

Oh no, this means I have to stand next *to this stuff and stir it!* "Ah, listen, it's nice to meet you and all that, but I really need to be getting out of here. It's getting dark outside, and I really want to get out of this neighborhood, y'know, and . . ."

"You can't leave before dinner, I won't hear of it," Beara said. She hobbled away to another table, picking up a large gleaming knife from a huge knife rack on the wall. She hummed an odd melody as she ran a honing stone over the long blade.

"Okay, sure," Kayla said, looking apprehensively at the knife. *I don't think I want to tick this lady off. She has some kind of weird, dangerous magic, and she keeps really long knives around—lots of them.*

Absently, Kayla stirred the soup and wrinkled her nose as another blast of foul odors wafted up at her. *What's in this stuff? It smells worse than anything* . . .

She looked down at the thick, grayish soup and stared.

There was a human finger floating in the soup.

"YAAAAAAHH!"

Kayla leaped backwards, the spoon flying, soup spattering everywhere.

"Is something wrong, dearie?" the old woman asked, turning to look at her with the knife raised in her hand.

Oh . . . *oh, this is bad, this is really bad* . . . *Kayla, you've really done it to yourself this time.*

"Uh, no, not at all," Kayla said nervously, glancing from Beara's face to the sharp knife in her hand. *Probably the same knife that sliced the finger off of* . . . *whoever it is that's in the soup. Don't panic, don't panic, just get out of here.* . . . "There's just something . . . about the soup . . . it's . . . it's not . . . not what I was expecting."

"Ah, of course," the old woman said, nodding. She set down the knife and picked up another wooden spoon, hobbling back to the cauldron to stir it. "That's the problem nowadays: it's hard to find good meat. How can you make good stock from something like this?" She fished the floating finger out of the soup and tossed it into a trash can several feet away. Kayla flinched as she saw the large pile of white bones in the bin.

"I thought that young man looked so tasty,"

the old woman continued. "After all, he was very muscular. He broke into my house without even working up a sweat. You just can't tell with these things, though. It's terribly difficult to cook a decent meal when you have to work with raw ingredients like that."

"Yeah, I can guess," Kayla said weakly, glad she didn't have anything left in her stomach that could come up. She glanced at the knife lying on the table. She could grab it, maybe threaten this lady long enough to get out of here. Then she remembered that flash of dark magic, the sound of two bodies hitting the floor in the alley.

Come on, Kayla, think fast . . . think of something, anything . . .

There was a sudden knock at the front door; the old woman looked up at the sound, startled.

"Would you like me to answer that?" Kayla asked hopefully, already imagining how quickly she could be out that door and running down the street.

"Oh, that's all right, dearie. I'll get it myself," the old woman said. "I'm just a little surprised. I wasn't expecting any other guests." She walked slowly to the door; Kayla took the opportunity to pick up the long-bladed knife from the table. She held it with one hand behind her back, hoping the old woman wouldn't see it.

"My, this is a surprise!" Beara said from the hallway. "Two guests for dinner! Come with me, come with me." She returned a moment later, followed by . . . *Elizabet?*

Kayla blinked. It was Elizabet Winters, looking very calm, but with a simmering anger half-hidden in her eyes. "Elizabet," Kayla gasped, so overwhelmed with relief she thought she was about to fall over. "You . . . you can't guess how good it is to see you right now!"

Elizabet walked to her, resting her hands on Kayla's shoulders. Her dark eyes searched Kayla's. "Are you all right, child?"

"Yeah, yeah, I'm fine, but listen, there's—"

"Later, child," Elizabet said, turning that glare on Beara. "All right, old woman, I want some answers from you. To start with, why are there two dead black boys lying on your doorstep?"

"Trespassers." The old woman shrugged. "Hoodlums. Thugs. Cheap stew meat."

"Elizabet," Kayla began, her voice squeaking a little. "She's a, uh . . . she's a . . ."

"Ogress," Elizabet said firmly. "And a cannibal, from the looks of her kitchen," she said, glancing around and wrinkling her nose. "And what else are you?"

"I am An Caillach Beara, The Hag of Beara," the old woman said, straightening slightly from her bent-over position. "I came here from Ireland hundreds of years ago, like many of the Wee Folk and the Tuatha De Danaan. And who are you who comes so boldly into my parlor?"

"I'm Elizabet Winters," the black woman said quietly. "I'm a witch and a healer and guardian of this young girl. I've spent weeks chasing down any trace of magic in the city, trying to find her."

"But I've spent time and magic on her as well," the old woman said, smiling. "It was my magic that called her here, reaching out to her across the city. Who, then, has the greater right?"

"Uh, can I . . . I mean, I didn't . . ." Kayla could feel the currents of power rising between the two women, like the smell of rain before a storm. "Listen, Elizabet . . ."

"Be silent, child," Elizabet said, not unkindly. Her eyes never wavered from Beara. "So, old woman? What will it be? You may be a powerful Irish ogress, but there are two of us, and we can't be discounted that easily."

The old woman stared back at her. "For five hundred years, no one has dared threaten me."

"Get used to it, lady." Elizabet's voice was tight.

"I'm really not that much of a villainess," Beara said, looking away. "Yes, I feast upon the mortals, but only the worst of them—the thieves and muggers and punks who would prey upon a helpless old woman. The predators, the ones who laugh at me and my magic. They chased me out of Ireland, those ones, and so I came to this New World. The land of the free, the home of the brave. Even here, they hound me." She sighed. "It's just as well, I suppose . . . one still has to eat. Still, if I let you go, then I'll have to deal with the police. . . ."

"I'll make you a deal," Elizabet said quietly. "Let us leave now, unharmed, and we won't interfere with what you do."

"What?" Kayla said, and stopped as Elizabet put her hand on her shoulder, holding her back. *What's she saying? This lady is a murderer, a cannibal, an ogre, God knows what else! We can't just walk out of here and let her keep doing this!*

"So, old woman, what do you say?"

"We are alike in many ways, you know," the ogress said. "You've learned what it took me many years to understand: any woman with power is to be feared and hunted. At least we should not hunt each other, eh?"

"They don't burn witches these days, but they

sure don't invite them to join the P.T.A., either,"
Elizabet said with a faint smile.

*I don't understand this. She's acting friendly
with this—this thing!* "Elizabet—" Kayla began.

"Shush, child," Elizabet said without glancing
at her. Kayla realized that Elizabet's gaze had
never wavered from the ogress for a moment,
not even when she was smiling.

"I would enjoy speaking with you again, Elizabet," the hag said. "You are a woman after my
own heart, reminding me of my long-lost sisters."

"As long as you're not after my heart," Elizabet said. "I don't think I'd like to come over for
dinner, thank you very much."

"Oh no, we'll have high tea with scones and
crumpets," the hag said with a chuckle. The old
woman's smile faded. "I have a small truth to
confess. I knew I couldn't harm this girl from the
moment I saw her. Even though I was very tempted,
when she picked up one of my knives. . . ."

Kayla suddenly remembered the knife in her
hand. A little self-consciously, aware of the
raised-eyebrow look that Elizabet was giving her,
Kayla put it back on the counter.

"But there is a danger for all of us on the
horizon: a black cloud on our future, a danger
to the magic in this place and all who need
that magic to live," the hag said. "In six moons'
time," she continued. "Whatever is going to
happen, it will happen in six moons' time. You
have that long to prepare this young one to
help counter it." She pointed at Kayla. "Her
skills will be needed. You have six months to
teach her what she needs to know."

"I don't want to think about six months from
now," Elizabet said wryly. "I'm just worried about
getting Kayla through the next two weeks."

"Gee, thanks a lot," Kayla muttered.

"Nothing happens by accident, young healer," the hag said, gazing directly at Kayla. She looked down, not wanting to see the dangerous power that burned behind the old woman's eyes. "Not magic, not this meeting, not you wandering across my doorstep." Beara turned away, hobbling back toward the other room. "You should go now. I still need to put supper on the table, and there are more of those young thugs on their way here."

"We'll leave," Elizabet said.

"No problem," Kayla said under her breath. "I've been ready to get out of this place since the minute I walked in."

"Quietly, child," Elizabet said in a low whisper. "We'll talk more when we're safely out of here." Elizabet waited until the hag had left the hallway, then quickly pushed Kayla out the door. Kayla flinched back on the doorstep, seeing the lifeless face of a young man, his eyes dimly lit by the light from the window, his body lying on the pavement a few feet away from her. Another boy lay facedown several feet further away.

"Walk, Kayla," Elizabet murmured behind her. "Start walking. We have to get out of here."

Kayla didn't need any encouragement. Walking quickly, they left the shadowed alley, stepping out into the bright, welcoming light of the streetlights.

Chapter Thirteen

It feels like it's been years instead of days since I was here, Kayla thought, sprawling out onto the comfortable couch in Elizabet's living room. "Elizabet, I didn't say it before, but . . . thanks for getting me out of there. I thought I was a goner."

"You probably were, despite what the ogress said about the magic being endangered in this area," Elizabet said, wearily pulling off her boots.

"I still can't believe you said we wouldn't do anything about her," Kayla said. "I mean, we should call the cops to go stop her. Or maybe the Feds . . ."

"I'm surprised you don't understand."

" . . . or the National Guard? Maybe we should call in the Marines?" Kayla shivered, thinking about what was brewing in that cauldron. "That's one nasty lady." She glanced at Elizabet. "What do you mean, you're surprised that I don't understand?"

Elizabet leaned back against the couch with a sigh of pure exhaustion. "Well, what do you think would have happened if we'd had to fight

217

our way out of there?" she asked. "Who do you
think would have won?"

*Good question. That old lady looked pretty mean.
Then again, Elizabet's a tough cookie, too. . . .* "I
don't know," Kayla said.

"That's why," Elizabet said. "Don't ever take
on a fight unless you think there's a good chance
you can win, child. Not unless the stakes are
very high." She yawned. "Well, I'm for some hot
chocolate, and then it's probably time for bed.
Would you like some?"

Kayla consulted her stomach, which was still a
little queasy but seemed to be settling down at
last. "Yeah, some hot chocolate would be great."

She followed Elizabet into the kitchen, sitting
down at the table as the older woman began
hunting for the ingredients. *In a way, it feels
like none of that really happened,* she thought.
*Maybe it's all been a dream, and it's the same
night when Billy got hurt. Elizabet's making me
another cup of chocolate, and then . . .* Elizabet
reached for a small box of Mexican chocolate
and broke off several pieces, setting them in the
pot to melt.

That yellow and red box . . . Roberta . . .

Kayla felt something tighten inside her, and
tears blurred her vision. She rubbed at her eyes,
which only made it worse, as she thought about
Roberta and Luisa, and Fernando, and Jose . . .

Elizabet turned. "Kayla? What's wrong?"

"It's, it's just . . . that's the same chocolate that
Roberta made for me. Roberta, she's dead now. . . . I
thought she was such a bitch, but she was nice to me,
and they killed her, she's dead now. . . ." It was
hitting her all at once, all the shock and anger and
terrors of the last few days, falling down on her like a
wave. She couldn't keep from sobbing. "And Ramon,

they tried to kill him, they shot Fernando right in front of me, I couldn't do anything to help him . . ."

Elizabet knelt next to Kayla, putting her arms around her. Kayla felt her tears soaking into Elizabet's blouse. Elizabet didn't say anything, only held her.

"I'm . . . I'm okay," Kayla said, after a few minutes. "Really, I'm okay."

"Do you want to talk about it?"

Kayla thought about everything that had happened and nodded. She told Elizabet what had happened from the moment that Carlos and his friends had broken into Elizabet's house to get her, and what had happened to her with the homeboys. And the strangeness of the Unseelie's world, and how she'd saved the life of their Queen—though, thinking about it, she wasn't certain that anybody except the Queen herself was going to benefit from that. And how the T-Men had come after them at the apartment, and . . .

I should tell her. I should just tell her what happened.

"What is it, child?" Elizabet asked, as though reading her thoughts—*which she probably was,* Kayla reflected wryly.

"Something happened tonight," Kayla began hesitantly. "Something really awful."

Elizabet listened as Kayla told her what had happened earlier that night at the apartment. She felt her stomach turn over and took several deep breaths as she described what she had done to the young man, the T-Man who had nearly died.

Elizabet was silent for a long time after Kayla finished the story. "I should be saying I told you so," she said, "but you know that already, don't you? The magic within you doesn't have a conscience of its own. You can hurt people or help them. You're the one who has to decide which."

Yes, but . . . "But I couldn't stop it," Kayla said. "I couldn't do anything about it."

"You'll have to learn to control it," Elizabet said. "The magic isn't going to go away. It's a part of you now, a part of what makes you yourself. Right now, your magic is as dangerous as a loaded shotgun in the hands of a three-year-old. But we can change that." She glanced up quickly. "Oh Lord, the chocolate is burning!" Elizabet moved quickly to the stove, turning off the burner as the room filled with the smell of burnt chocolate.

"So much for the hot cocoa," she said, returning to the table.

"What do you mean, we can change that?" Kayla asked, wrinkling her nose at the burnt smell. She yawned and rubbed at her eyes.

Elizabet smiled. "My grandmother, she was the one who taught me. Of course, my talent isn't anything compared to yours, but I should be able to teach you a few things that she taught me. Gram was an amazing lady. I wish you could have met her." She looked up at the clock as Kayla yawned again. "It's definitely past your bedtime, though," she said. "We'll talk more about this in the morning."

Kayla hesitated for a moment at the open door to the spare bedroom. She stood there, toweling her hair dry and wiping the last of the water from her face. Looking into the bedroom, it really did feel as though the last few days hadn't happened at all. There was the bed, still slightly rumpled from when she'd been reading a book the night that Carlos and Ramon had come to the house. *In a way, it feels like a dream,* she thought. *Like I'm waking up from an awful nightmare. But now it's okay, I'm home.* She stopped short at that thought.

Home? I guess that's what this is now. It feels like home. And Elizabet? I don't think she'll ever be like my mother. I don't think I'll ever feel she's my parent, but my friend, definitely my teacher. Someone who can help me figure all of this out and make sense from my life.

She put on a pair of pajamas and, on an impulse, moved to the bookshelf that lined one wall of the small bedroom. Just as she'd hoped, there it was: the book about the dragons. Smiling, she took it back to bed with her, opening up to the page where she'd stopped reading before.

She awakened with a start at some noise she couldn't identify. The room was still dark, with only a hint of light filtering in through the closed curtains. She reached out, and her hand brushed against the novel on the pillow next to her, lying where she'd left it before she fell asleep. She heard another sound, a rustling of the bedsheets. Someone was in the room with her—no, someone was sitting on the edge of the bed. . . .

She picked up the book and threw it hard in the direction of the noise.

She could see the person now, a dim outline in the faint light. The book flew through the air and then *through* the person, bouncing off the far wall.

Oh no . . . it's something magical again, I know it, it's something magical . . . can't I even get a night's sleep without something weird happening around me?

"That ain't very polite, girl," the person said
with a laugh, in a woman's low, rich voice, heavy
with a Southern accent. "I would think that
Elizabet might've taught you better manners.
Then again, you ain't been Elizabet's ward for
very long now, eh? Just a couple days?" She
stood and moved closer. Kayla blinked.

The old woman, her wrinkled black face
creased with a broad smile, was only an outline
of pale blue light, nothing more than that. *I'm
going crazy . . . that's it, it's all finally hit me
and I'm going crazy . . . now I'm seeing ghosts.*

"You're . . . you're . . ." Kayla's voice wasn't
working quite right.

"Elizabet's gram, that's right."

"But you're . . . you're dead!"

Gram chuckled. "I think that's obvious, girl.
Most normal folks don't go around floatin'
through walls, y'know."

"But you're dead!"

"Been that way for a few years, now."

"But . . . you're . . ."

"Yes, I'm dead. Now shut up, girl, and let me
talk." Gram seated herself next to Kayla. "That's
why I'm here, girl," she said cheerfully in her
slow Southern drawl. "Since Elizabet thought it
was important that we meet, I figured I'd go
ahead and meet you. You ain't never seen no
ghosts before?"

"Uh, no!" Kayla blurted.

"Ah, no wonder you're surprised. Some people
just can't handle the concept too well. Elizabet
now, I tried appearin' to her once, not too long
after I left this world. She just couldn't handle it
at all. Thought she was losin' her mind. You, on
the other hand, look like you're doin' just fine,
honey." She stood up, stretching wearily. Her

outlines thinned even more as she stretched; Kayla could see the walls through her. "Now, girl, we have to talk with Elizabet. . . ."

Elizabet set down the sociology textbook she'd been reading and reached for the light switch next to the bed. Kayla's voice, muffled through the closed bedroom door, stopped her in mid-motion.

"Elizabet, can we come in?" Kayla asked.

"Of course," Elizabet said, then suddenly realized Kayla had said the word "we" instead of "I." "Kayla, is someone . . . ?"

The door opened and Kayla stepped in, followed by someone that Elizabet had thought she would never see again, at least not in this lifetime. Her grandmother glided into the room, smiling wickedly, with her feet not quite touching the ground. She sat down at the foot of the bed. "Evenin', honeychild," Gram said.

Elizabet just stared at her.

In the long silence Kayla finally piped up. "Uh, Elizabet, she's your grandmother, you know? Your grandmother, the dead one."

"I know who she is," Elizabet said. "What I'm wondering is what is she doing here? And why I'm dreaming about her."

"Ain't no dream, Elizabet," Gram said. "You're in trouble, an' that's why I'm here. You are in one heap of serious trouble. I can't see exactly what, my sight isn't too good looking very far into the future, but something evil has set its sights upon you, and on this girl here, too."

This must be a dream, Elizabet thought. *Or maybe I'm insane. That would explain this.*

"Shoot, girl, you're not crazy, any more than I am! Lordy, you believe in magic, right? Why so much trouble believing in ghosts?" Gram spoke in an aside to Kayla. "That's why I never showed up before now. I knew she wouldn't believe it."

"All right, then, I'll take this at face value," Elizabet said. "What I don't understand is how you can be here."

"You don't have time to understand," her grandmother replied. "What you have to do is teach this child what she needs to know, and quickly. You don't have much time, granddaughter. Only six months."

As she spoke, Gram's translucent body was becoming even more faint. She faded away to a mere brightness, a hint of light in the air. "Teach her what she needs to know before it's too late."

The words lingered in the empty air where Gram had sat a moment before.

"Kayla, do you know what's going on?" Elizabet asked.

Kayla shook her head. "It's not my fault," she said quickly.

"I know it's not your fault, child," Elizabet said with a sigh. "Six months. I wonder what's going to happen in six months?"

"I wish I knew," Kayla said.

"Well, we'll find out when it gets here. Alternatively, we go ask Beara, since she obviously knows something about it as well. I'd just as soon not do that, though. It might be significantly harder to get out of her home a second time."

"Yeah, that's for sure." *I don't want to go back there without the Marines, or maybe the National Guard.*

"Now, go to bed, child," Elizabet said. "We'll start your lessons in earnest in the morning."

"Okay," Kayla said. "I'll let you know if any

more of your dead relatives show up to visit," she said, grinning.

"You do that," Elizabet said with a smile, and turned off the bedlight.

Back in her bedroom, Kayla picked up the fantasy novel from where she'd thrown it and set it down on the nightstand. "All of this is really just a little too weird for me," she said aloud, thinking about the events of the last week.

"Well, it's only going to get weirder, honey-child," Gram said from behind her.

Kayla turned so quickly she nearly fell. "I thought you were gone," she blurted.

"Naw, I was jus' doin' that for dramatic effect," Gram said, an impish grin across her wrinkled dark face. "I've always wanted to do that to Elizabet. She's always been so unflappable, even as a child; I just couldn't resist it."

"So why are you still here?" Kayla asked.

"Because, honeychild, you an' me have to talk. Let's go for a walk, okay?"

Silently, Kayla followed the ghost of Elizabet's grandmother through the darkened house to the front door. The ghost drifted effortlessly through the door, vanishing from view. Kayla followed, and barely stopped herself in time to avoid bashing her nose against the door. She opened the door very quietly, so Elizabet wouldn't hear, and stepped outside.

Outside the house, the street was very quiet, with the faint echo of the late-night traffic on Laurel Canyon as a distant noise, sounding almost like waves on a shore. Kayla followed Gram around the side of the house, along a winding trail that led to the top of the hill—or, rather, Kayla walked and Gram floated.

"Can you tell me a little bit about this ghost stuff?" Kayla asked, trying to catch her breath as they paused at the top of the hill. She looked out at the lights of the city, spread out like a glittering carpet of jewels around her. From this viewpoint, she could see the lights of Los Angeles to the south and the San Fernando Valley to the north.

"Oh, you'll understand that eventually," Gram said, also admiring the view. "There's not much to it. The basics are simple. There are two kinds of ghosts: people with unfinished business, and ones like myself who are too stubborn and meddlesome to leave. You want to watch out for those folks that don't have all their business taken care of, girl—they can be nasty. But we have more important things to talk about." Gram sat down in midair as though on a chair, folding her legs under her. "I was born in 1860," she said. "In Georgia, on a farm. You know anything about American history, girl?"

"A little." Kayla nodded. "Wasn't that right around the time of the Civil War?"

"You're right. I was born into slavery, just like my folks, my grandma and grandpa, and my great-grandparents had been. When I was a little girl, they outlawed slavery, and suddenly we were free. Even as a child, I understood what that meant.

"But I'll never forget that for the first few years of my life, someone owned me. That's the choice you'll have to make, girl. There are people out there who want to own you. And the question you have to ask yourself is: will you let them? Right now you're surviving more by luck than anything else; luck and my granddaughter Elizabet watching over you. But this choice, this

has to be yours. Elizabet can teach you the ways
of magic, what you need to know to control your
talent and not hurt the people around you. But
me, born a slave in Georgia, I can teach you
about freedom."

"I don't want anybody to control my life,"
Kayla began. "But how can I stop them? It's not
like—"

Gram cut her off with a sharp gesture. "It's
not a question of wanting, it's a question of
whether you're willing to fight right down to
your last breath to be a free woman. Are you?
They may gild the cage for you, make it seem
like a lovely place to be, but slavery is slavery.
And not just for yourself, but others."

"What do you mean?" Kayla asked.

Gram glanced at her quickly. "You're a part of
more than you know, girl. Things, they're gonna
be happening around here. You'll need to be
ready for 'em."

Kayla didn't know what to say to that. Gram
pointed off to her right, away from the glittering
carpet of lights of Los Angeles, across the dark
hills between L.A. and the San Fernando Valley.
"Can you feel it, girl?" she asked.

Kayla shook her head. "I don't understand.
Feel what?"

"Look there, in the hills. Can't you feel it?"

Kayla squinted, trying to see what the old
woman was talking about.

"No, no! Not with your eyes! With your
heart," Gram said in an annoyed voice.

Kayla closed her eyes and reached out her
hand, trying to sense what the old woman was
talking about. There was nothing there. . . .
No, there was something. A faint glimmer of
magic, very far away, a dim point that glittered

in the night. As she looked more closely at it, she could feel a sense of power, drawing her toward it.

"That's the source," Gram said. "That's the source of magic for all of Los Angeles. There are a lot of folks that need that to survive. Keep that in mind, girl, that folks' lives are depending on that little place."

"What folks? I don't understand."

"You'll see," Gram said, "you'll see." She glanced up at the sky, where the moon was setting behind the distant hills. "My, it's time you were in bed. Go home, girl; go home and learn, and think about what we've talked about."

Without another word, the old woman faded away.

Kayla stood on the hillside, looking down at the lights of the city. *I don't know that I'm strong enough,* she thought. *Gram can talk about freedom till she turns blue . . . well, she is blue, already! But I don't know that I can do it. Carlos terrifies me. I don't know how to stand up to him. And Nataniel and those other nasty elves . . .*

No way. How am I supposed to do it? She's nuts; the old lady is just crazy.

But if I don't learn how to stand up to them . . . what then? I'll be hiding from them all my life. I don't want that, either.

She turned away and started back down the hill, lost in her thoughts.

"Concentrate!" Elizabet said from somewhere behind her.

"But you just told me *not* to concentrate!" Kayla protested from where she was sitting on the living room floor. Her eyes were tightly closed, but she wanted to open them and scream. *These "mental exercises" are making me crazy!*

"Well, you're not getting it that way," Elizabet said, "so we'll try the other way. Since you're having trouble relaxing enough to use your Sight, we'll try this instead. We have to train to you to where you can rely on your talent, not just have it happen accidentally, uncontrolled. So concentrate on something, anything. Think about it as hard as you can."

Kayla nodded. *There is,* she decided, *a hell of a lot going on in my life that I can think about. Magical powers, healers, killer elves, gateways into other worlds, an ancient ogress who likes to have muggers for dinner . . . literally. Yeah, there is quite a lot going on in my life lately,* she concluded.

"Think about something specific," Elizabet said.

"Okay, okay, give me a break!"

"That is the one thing I won't do," Elizabet said, her voice tinged with humor.

I'm getting tired of this bullshit! Kayla thought. *There's Elizabet, standing right behind me and smiling. Oh yeah, I'm sure this is a lot of fun for you, too! She's—*

Kayla sat up straight, opening her eyes in shock. "I saw you! I really saw you! With my eyes closed!"

"See, you're learning, child. It's not *entirely* hopeless." Elizabet smiled. "It only *looks* that way. Now, think of something, really concentrate on it."

Kayla tried to think of something to concentrate on. It was a beautiful day outside, really great, not too smoggy, a perfect day to go to a park. . . .

That would be nice, she thought, smiling. *To go to the park next to the house. . . .*

She thought about the park down the street from her house, the house where she'd lived with her parents before . . . before the Awful Day. She loved that park. Mom and Dad used to walk with her there in the evening, as the sun was setting through the tall trees. It was different from all the other parks she'd ever seen: a wild, untamed place where the gardeners and keepers seemed more interested in the little community gardening project at the back of the park rather than the park itself. The trees were left alone to grow into unruly shapes tangled with ivy and surrounded by shrubs. The paths through the park were hard to find and harder to follow, but that was something she loved. There was one tree that she loved best, a huge old oak tree with broad spreading branches which filled the sky. Dad said that the tree was at least two hundred years old. Sometimes Kayla had thought she could hear laughter from the tree, the flickering movement of someone climbing in the branches, but Dad always said that it was only the wind, there wasn't anyone there.

She'd run to that tree on the Awful Day, the day she'd come home from school and found the police cars in front of her house. Old Mrs. Liddy had called the cops after hearing gunshots from next door and seeing some cars leave fast. They wouldn't let her into the house, into her own house; she heard some of the cops talking about how they'd found blood, but no bodies.

She remembered running to the park, falling onto the thick moss under the tree and crying. That's where the cops had found her, hours later.

She could feel the tears starting down her face, remembering.

"Are you all right, Kayla?" Elizabet asked, concern in her voice.

"Yeah, I'm fine," she said. "I'm fine."

"Kayla," Elizabet said. "Keep your eyes closed. Can you see me?"

She could. There was a faint brightness against the inside of her eyes, a glow that moved as Elizabet walked around her, matching time with her quiet footsteps. "You're doing it, child," Elizabet murmured. "You're doing it. Now, look at yourself."

She felt herself moving away; no, she was sitting still, but somehow she was moving in that quiet darkness. She turned and looked back at herself. What she saw was fire, blue-white centered around a core of brilliance, with flowing tendrils of light flickering and dancing over the surface. Kayla opened her eyes suddenly, startled, and blinked. "What was that?" she asked.

Elizabet was sitting close to her; she laughed, little lines crinkling at the edges of her eyes. "Yes, that's you. That's why everyone can find you, because you look like a neon sign when you're using your magic. But we're going to see if we can do something about that now. Close your eyes again. Now look at yourself and try to make the glow a little less bright. Dim it down. Not completely, but see if you can slowly fade it."

Kayla concentrated, imagining that brightness fading away to nothingness.

Make it go away . . . dim it down, like turning down a light. . . .

A wave of dizziness hit her like a fist. She

opened her eyes and grabbed for anything to hold onto, afraid she was going to faint. Elizabet caught her, keeping her from falling over.

"Not too much," Elizabet repeated, "just a little bit. Carefully. Slowly."

Kayla nodded, taking a few deep breaths. She closed her eyes and tried again. This time she could do it. She could bring that simmering pool of fire down to embers, glowing with restrained power. She concentrated, letting the fire slowly die down, dimming the light to a faint glow. "Did it work?" she asked.

"You did it just right," Elizabet said. "Now, you're going to have to learn to keep it like this all the time. Otherwise, anyone that's looking for you will be able to find you easily, just by tracking your magic. Good work, child."

"Are we done now?" Kayla asked.

"Not by a long shot. Lesson number two. This one will be a little tougher. We'll do this and then take a break. It's almost visiting time at the hospital where your friend Billy is staying. We can go over there and see him. I called the hospital while you were still asleep, and he'll be expecting us."

"Great!" Kayla said, grinning. *It'll be terrific to see Billy. I've got so much to tell him. . . .*

Except I can't, can I? He won't believe any of this. He'll think I'm crazy. My old friends . . . are they still going to be my friends? I don't know about that. "Where's Liane? Do you know?" she asked.

Elizabet shook her head. "No, she's still missing. Though I'm hoping once you have a little bit of control over what you're doing, you might be able to find her yourself. The police haven't turned up any leads at all." She reached into the

pocket of her jeans, pulled out a small Swiss
army knife, and sat down on the floor next to
Kayla. "Now for the next lesson." She opened
out one of the blades and glanced up at Kayla.
"What you're going to do now," she said, "is *not*
heal me."

"I don't get it," Kayla said. "What are you . . . ?"

Elizabet brought the razor-sharp knife down
on the palm of her hand.

Pain! It echoed through Kayla like a shock-
wave. She felt the magic inside her answer that
pain, welling up through her. Kayla reached out
to where the blood was slowly pooling in Elizabet's palm.

"Stop it!" Elizabet said sharply, and Kayla
drew back, startled. "You have to learn to control
it, not let it control you."

"Elizabet, I—"

"Just sit there, child," Elizabet said. "Just sit
there and control it."

That's easy for you to say, Kayla thought
resentfully, feeling the magic pulling at her like a
riptide, trying to surge through her, reaching out to
Elizabet.

Her hands were shaking. She clenched them
into fists and closed her eyes. *I will control it,*
she thought desperately. *I will!*

Slowly, like an ebbing tide, she felt the pressure
easing. The electric touch of the magic fell away
from her with each breath she took, slowly
receding.

She opened her eyes to see Elizabet smiling
at her. "Not bad," Elizabet said, "not bad at all."

Kayla smiled in relief. *Thank God this craziness is over,* she thought. *Now I'll just heal
Elizabet, and then we'll be done with this.*

"Very good," Elizabet continued. "We'll sit like

this for the next forty-five minutes or so, until you think you've really got it down."

Kayla stared at her. *She's got to be joking!*

"No, I'm not," Elizabet said, in a voice that didn't allow any argument.

Kayla sighed. It was going to be a very long forty-five minutes. . . .

Chapter Fourteen

"I think that was a rotten trick, Elizabet," Kayla said, helping Elizabet carry the dishes from the breakfast table to the kitchen sink.

"Learning isn't supposed to be easy, child," Elizabet said as she set the dishes down into the soapy water.

"Yeah, but I didn't think it would be this hard," Kayla said. "I mean, you never—"

Across the room, the phone rang. Elizabet grabbed a dishtowel to dry her hands and then hurried over to answer it. Kayla rolled up her sleeves and began scrubbing the dishes. She listened to one half of the conversation. "Good morning, Nichelle . . . I didn't think there would be any news . . . Well, thanks for calling. I'll see you later tonight at the office."

Elizabet's forehead was slightly furrowed with a frown as she walked back to Kayla.

"What was that all about?" Kayla asked.

Elizabet began drying the dishes Kayla had washed. "That was Detective Cable. She wanted to tell me there had been no update on your case. You're still officially kidnaped as far as the LAPD is concerned."

"You didn't tell her that I'm here?"

Elizabet shook her head. "I haven't told anyone anything. I'm still not entirely certain what to do in this situation. I really should take you downtown and have you tell everything to the police. You're a witness to multiple crimes, including homicide."

"No!" Kayla shook her head. "Don't you understand if I do that, it'll never be over? They'll always be after me."

"Not if they're in prison, they won't be," Elizabet said grimly.

"You can't guarantee that! I just . . . I just want to live. I want them to leave me alone." Kayla thought about it for a moment, wondering whether she should ask the question that had been bothering her all morning. *What the hell*, she thought, and plunged forward. "Elizabet, if you were serious about maybe, like, adopting me, which I think would be really great, I thought maybe we would want to leave Los Angeles. I mean, I've got this whole crowd of people that may be looking for me, and Carlos knows where you live. Sooner or later, they may come looking. So, I thought, hey, maybe we should just go somewhere else. Like New York, maybe?" *Or Alaska. South America. Burma?*

"Is that what you want to do?" Elizabet gave her a long look. "Run away? Again?"

New Zealand? Ireland? Antarctica?

"Well . . . yes! I mean, I don't want to be here when the trouble arrives. What if those killer elves start looking for me again? Or Carlos?" *Or Ramon . . .*

Kayla thought about Ramon, his laughing dark

eyes. *Guess I'll never see that guy again,* she thought. *If I do, his big brother will be right behind him. I know he's okay; I healed the guy, I shouldn't worry about him. But I do. . . .*

"No," Elizabet said firmly. "We're not going to run away. These are problems, child, that you'll have to learn how to face, because if you don't, they'll just find you again and again. You'll have to go to the police and tell them everything . . . well, almost everything," she amended. "We'll deal with this trouble together. I want you to do this because you know it's right, not because I'm compelling you to do it. But you must know that you have to do it, you have to go to the police and help them put these people behind bars. You have to be willing to confront them."

Kind of a scary prospect, that, Kayla thought, remembering about Carlos, the T-Men, and the Unseelie Court. *It's a whole lot of trouble. More than I want to deal with, that's for sure. How did I get myself into this kind of trouble?*

"I'll have to go into work in a few hours," Elizabet said, stacking the clean dishes in the cupboard. "I'll stop by the county office and file papers to see about formally making this your foster home. You, on the other hand . . ." And she gave Kayla a stern look. "You will stay here, try to keep out of trouble, and do some schoolwork. I have a number of textbooks in my library that you can start with. I imagine you've missed quite a bit of school over the past few months."

"Oh, just a few classes," Kayla admitted. *Like most of this school year. . . .*

"And I'll call downtown," Elizabet continued. "We'll get a regular patrol to stop through here on their circuit, plus whatever else they think is appropriate to a key witness. You'll have to testify, Kayla. It'll probably take a couple of days for them to get the paperwork started on this, but you will have to testify against the gang. I don't know whether the L.A.P.D. can do anything against elves and that ogress . . ."

They'd better take in a platoon of Marines with them, if they try!

" . . . but we can certainly do something about the gangbangers," Elizabet continued. "If we see any sign of the gang or . . . anything else, the police will probably want to take you into protective custody. So don't be alarmed if a policeman stops by to see how you're doing during the day, while you're studying. And you'd better start cracking the books. You'll have some serious catching up to do if you want to graduate high school with a high enough grade point average to go to college."

"College?" Kayla glanced at her. "I can't go to college!"

"Of course you can," Elizabet said, smiling. "I'll help you with the tuition. But you'll need to get your grades into shape or you won't be admitted. It'll take a lot of hard work, but I think you can do it."

"College?" Kayla repeated, her eyes wide. *College . . . I never thought I'd be able to do that. I wonder what I'd study? I'd like to learn more about how this magic thing works, but somehow I don't think they'll have classes in Magic 101 at UCLA.*

Elizabet laughed, reaching out to ruffle Kayla's hair. "Of course, imp. College. Who did this to your hair? It looks like it was hacked off with a knife."

"I like it this way," Kayla said. "Wow . . . college. I never thought I'd really be able to do it."

"We'll get you there," Elizabet said. "Just you wait and see. Well, we do have a few hours before I need to head into the city. Shall we go visit Billy?"

"You bet," Kayla said immediately. "And I'd like to go looking for Liane, too. I know that no one's seen her around, but I'd like to try to find her. I don't know where she'd be exactly, but we could go back to Suite 230. Maybe she went back there."

"The police have been checking there once a day or so," Elizabet said. "There hasn't been any sign of your friend, but we can go look if you like."

"Yeah, I'd like that."

Walking into the hospital was easier this time. It was the same, the overwhelming pressure of pain and emotions pouring down on her, but she was able to push it back, to hold it away from her almost without thinking about it. She moved it away from her, closing it off to where it was only a quiet, distant clamor rather than an overwhelming wave. She caught a glimpse of Elizabet's smile as they walked through the hospital lobby.

Maybe I am learning. Maybe I'm getting better at this.

"They've moved him to the third floor," Elizabet said as they walked to the elevators. "He's doing fine, last I saw him."

"You've been here?" Kayla asked, surprised.

Elizabet nodded. "I asked that they assign him as one of my cases. I also asked that they keep him here for a little while longer even though he could have been discharged from the hospital a couple days ago. Downtown, they're still trying to figure out what to do with this young man, but Billy has his own ideas. I'm sure he'll tell you."

Kayla only followed Elizabet from the elevator down the hall to room 341. Through the closed door, she could hear an exuberant yell: "Yeah, go Niners!" She grinned, recognizing Billy's voice.

"Come on, Billy!" someone else shouted. "They're history, they're toast, they're outta here!"

Elizabet opened the door, leaning inside. "Is there room for two more Niners fans in here?" she asked.

"Elizabet! Come on in!"

Kayla walked in after Elizabet, a little nervously. Billy, wearing a San Francisco Forty-Niners shirt over his hospital gown, was sitting up in bed. Another boy, very thin and pale and wearing a baseball cap, was in the next bed. Both of them were watching the game on the television set high on the wall across from them.

Billy winced as one of the Niners fumbled a catch and glanced at Kayla and Elizabet. His eyes widened, and he let out a yell that filled the room. "KAYLA!"

"Hiya, Billy," she said. "How's tricks?"

"You're looking all right," he said, grinning. "The 'do is awesome. Did you do your hair with a knife? Can I get your leather jacket if you get hit by a truck?"

"In your dreams, dude," she said, grinning back at him.

"Shhh, come on, guys, put a cork in it, the Niners are trying for a touchdown," the other boy said, lying back so that he was only half-visible behind the row of IVs and medical equipment.

"Chill out, Rick!" Billy shook his head. "He's stressed out 'cause tonight's dessert is riding on this." He added more quietly, "An' the chemo's got him down today." Billy glanced over at Elizabet, a little hesitantly, Kayla thought. "So, Elizabet . . . any news?" Using both hands, he shifted his leg, encased in a heavy white cast, so he could sit up straighter. "You got any news for me?"

Elizabet sat down on the edge of his bed. "Oh, nothing much. Just a new home for you. It's up in San Francisco and your foster parent is an engineer, just like you asked for."

"Really?" Billy's eyes were wide. "You did it, Elizabet! I knew you could do it!"

Kayla glanced between Billy and Elizabet, not understanding. "An engineer?" she asked.

Elizabet nodded. "We've been trying to do that, match kids with parents who are in the profession the kid would like to pursue. Billy told me that he wants to study civil engineering; if he can get into college, that is," she added, giving him a stern look. "After talking with your teachers at your last high school, that may be tougher than you told me. But I think you'll like this lady, Billy. I talked with her on the phone. She's been working on old buildings, making them more earthquake-proof."

"Cool!" Billy said. "That's great. We'll have something to talk about over dinner."

"I didn't know you wanted to be an engineer," Kayla said. *When did he decide he wanted this? It couldn't have been when we were at the foster home; he never talked about it, never said anything about it. . . .*

"Well, it didn't look too likely when all I was doing was ditching class and trying to run away from lousy foster homes. But talking with Elizabet made me think about what I'd like to do with my life. So I'll give it a try. If it doesn't work out, maybe I can go work for the CIA or something. I've got all that experience in breaking and entering, I bet they'd hire me in a minute!"

"Don't you even think it, scamp!" Elizabet said sternly and Billy laughed.

I never would've guessed this about Billy, Kayla thought. *I never thought that maybe he had dreams, dreams of more than just getting through a few days without getting arrested, or how to break into an apartment quicker and faster the next time. I never thought he might want to be an engineer. He's so different. I mean, it's only been a week, and he's changed so much. Or maybe he's not so different, maybe he's been this way all the time, and I just didn't know it.*

"Have you guys heard anything about Liane?" Billy asked, his face suddenly very serious.

Elizabet shook her head. "Nothing new."

"We're going to go look for her," Kayla said. "Right after we leave here, we're going into Hollywood."

"Well, then get your asses out of here," Billy said with a smile. "And I'll go back to watching the football game. Come back and visit me after you've found her." He looked down, away from them. "I've been worried 'bout her. Kayla, I figured that you'd be able to take care of yourself, even if you never did before. . . ."

"Hey, thanks a lot, dude!" Kayla said, glaring at him and then grinning in pretend anger.

"No, I'm serious! I always took care of stuff for all of us, after we left the foster home, but it wasn't because I was the only one who could do it. You could; you always could. You just didn't . . . just didn't believe enough in yourself. But Liane's different. I hope she's okay."

"We'll find out," Elizabet said reassuringly. "My guess is that she's still somewhere in the Hollywood area, that she wouldn't have gone far, which means . . ."

Elizabet's voice faded, and Kayla glanced over at Billy's roommate, now asleep. His face was very pale and drawn, white even against his pillow, only a few stringy wisps of hair visible beneath the baseball cap. *Something's very wrong there,* she thought, *something's very . . .*

Without warning, the room disappeared around her. It was as if she was falling into a whirlwind of pain and chaos, sliding between the layers of skin and muscle, until she could see the cells of his body. The cells that were fighting a hopeless battle against each other, killing him piece by piece. It was too overwhelming and confusing; she didn't know how she'd start to heal this. *It's not just a single cut or a wound,* she thought, *it's all the way through his entire body, it's everywhere. . . .*

She felt Elizabet's hand on her shoulder, pulling her back into herself. "Control, Kayla," Elizabet murmured. "Disengage from it. Control it."

Kayla blinked and shook her head, trying to clear the image of the millions of cells fighting against each other from her vision. Then she was standing in the hospital room again, Elizabet's hand on her shoulder keeping her from falling.

She glanced at Billy; he was staring at her.

"Your eyes!" he whispered. "Your eyes were filled with blue fire. It's true. I thought I

dreamed it, but it really happened. That scar
that the doctors found, the one they said must've
happened a few months back. Except it didn't;
I'd never had it before. It was you. What is it,
Kayla?"

"We'd better go," Elizabet said quietly, urging
Kayla toward the door.

"Kayla?" Billy called. "Please, I need to know!"

Still dizzy from the magic, Kayla looked back
at him. "I don't know, Billy," she said. "I don't
know what it is. But I'm going to try to figure it
out."

"And I'm going to help her," Elizabet said.

"Yeah, you do that, Elizabet," Billy said, settling back against his pillows. "Elizabet can help
you figure things out, Kayla. She's good at that."

Kayla glanced back at her friend. *It's not the
same,* she thought. *It's never going to be the
same. We're different people now.* "Take care of
yourself, Billy," she said.

"You, too, Kayla," he said, and smiled. "Try to
stay out of trouble, hey?"

No bets on that, she thought, walking out into
the corridor.

In the hallway outside his room Kayla turned
to Elizabet. "Do you know what's wrong with
Rick?" she asked. "All that craziness, everything
fighting itself?"

"Leukemia," Elizabet said. "That's what Rick
has." She was silent for a moment as they
walked past the nurses' station. "Everyone has
limits, child," she said at last. "You'll have to
learn what yours are."

"Can you do it?" Kayla asked. "Can you cure
cancer?"

Elizabet shook her head. "No. You forget,
child, my talents are much more limited than

yours. I can't cure a cold, not the way that you can. Some small things, yes, but I'm not in your league. Maybe you can learn how to cure cancer eventually."

Kayla thought about it as they walked out to the car. *That would be great, if I could. I mean, what am I supposed to do with this magic thing, anyhow? It's like . . . there has to be a meaning to it, some reason for it. Elizabet's the only other person I know who has this magic talent that I have, not counting the killer elves, or whatever they are.*

If I go to college, and med school after that, then maybe I'll learn just what I can do with this. If I'm a doctor, then I can help people and they won't know that it's magic; they'll think it's medicine. Maybe I can learn how to cure cancer.

She was quiet for most of the drive into Hollywood, thinking about that.

"Want to talk about it?" Elizabet asked, as they drove through the slow-moving traffic onto Hollywood Boulevard.

"It's just . . ." Kayla began, then faltered. "Well, I keep thinking there has to be a reason for this, this magic stuff. I mean, why else would I have it?"

Elizabet smiled. "Thinking that you were put on God's Earth for a reason, child, that's ego. What you have is a gift, and you have to figure out how best to use it." She braked as the street light changed to red and glanced at Kayla. "Where did you want to start looking for your friend?" she asked.

Kayla looked at the street, the cars moving slowly through the intersection ahead of them. It was only late afternoon, but already the night people were starting to appear: men in dirty clothes slouching against the storefronts, women walking by in high heels and tight skirts. Two motorcycle cops were parked near the intersection, watching the traffic go by.

"Oh, I don't know," Kayla said. "I guess we should stop back—" She stopped, realizing that she was about to use the word "home" for Suite 230. And that that word didn't fit it anymore. "I guess we should look at the office building first," she finished awkwardly.

"All right," Elizabet said. She waited for the signal to change and parked in the lot at the corner of Hollywood and Cherokee.

Kayla was very quiet as they walked down the street. She led Elizabet down the narrow alley between two tall buildings and up to the broken window at the back of the office building. "Watch out, there's some glass on the floor," she said, climbing through.

Elizabet nodded, clambering in after her. Kayla stepped around the pile of dirty blankets and old newspapers, where someone else had obviously set up their digs, and to the stairway down the hall. A few minutes later, they were on the second floor, and Kayla pushed the door of Suite 230 open with her foot, glancing around inside.

Suite 230 looked just like it had the night when all of this started. The blankets were still piled in the corner, and the three half-eaten cans of spaghetti, the contents looking very green and moldy, were still on the sink. "I don't think Liane has been back here," Kayla said, looking around. She looked into the other room and saw her old backpack on the floor, open and obviously searched, then abandoned. "I don't think she's been in here."

Elizabet shook her head. "The police were here, but I know they were careful to leave everything the way it was."

Kayla pulled her jacket a little more tightly around her, not from physical cold but something else. This place looked so empty, depressing. It was hard to believe that she'd lived here. When Billy and Liane had been with her, somehow the place hadn't looked so bad. It'd been more of an adventure than a dump. "I'm glad I don't have to live here anymore," she said.

"Me too, child," Elizabet said, smiling.

Kayla bent to pick up her backpack. She unzipped the main pocket, looking inside. There wasn't much there: half a candy bar, some change, and a bent photograph. She zipped it up again quickly, not wanting to look at the photo of her and her mom and dad in the backyard of their house, at her last birthday party. *I shouldn't have kept that; I should have left that at the house,* she thought. *I should have—*

"Is something wrong, Kayla?" Elizabet asked.

Kayla shook her head quickly, rubbing at her eyes. "No, I'm fine," she lied. She slung the backpack over her shoulder. "I guess we should ask around out on the street, see if anyone has seen Liane. Folks would remember that I'm a friend of hers, maybe they'd tell me." Kayla took one last look around Suite 230, then walked to the door.

Out on the street, she saw a few people she recognized, but not many. There was the old bearded man who sat on the sidewalk not far from the McDonald's, panhandling for change. The shopkeepers were still the same after only a couple weeks, but she'd never talked to any of them before, figuring that they'd only call the cops on her, so they probably wouldn't be much help.

She stood on the street corner, looking around, not certain where to go next. There was the elderly man who sold hot dogs from a wheeled cart. He'd smiled at her before and given them a couple extra hot dogs for free when they'd bought from him. Maybe he'd know something about Liane.

"Elizabet, I'm going to talk to that guy," she said.

"Sounds like a good idea to me," Elizabet said. "I'll go get us some Cokes from the McDonald's."

"Great," Kayla said. She waited for the light to change, then walked across the street to where the old man was slathering onions on a hot dog for one of his customers.

"Excuse me, sir," she began, then she saw Liane walk out from a bar entrance three doors down the street.

Liane!

She looked totally different. The old sweatshirt and jeans were gone—she was wearing a tight white blouse and a black leather miniskirt, with four-inch spike heels. Kayla stared at her, too surprised to say anything. She walked to the edge of the curb, obviously waiting for someone. She looked around the busy street, then glanced in Kayla's direction.

Her eyes met Kayla's; she blinked, staring. "Kayla?" she called, her voice mirroring her surprise. She took a few quick steps in Kayla's direction, then stopped.

"Liane?" Kayla walked hesitantly toward her. Liane hugged her, smiling. *She's okay, thank God she's okay. . . .*

Kayla sniffled and rubbed at her eyes as she stepped back, looking at her friend. "Oh, hell, I smeared your makeup! I'm sorry, I didn't—"

"Who cares? I'll fix it! But what did you do your hair?" Liane asked. "It's wild!"

"What did you do to the rest of you?" Kayla asked. "The way you're dressed, you look like—"

A car pulled up on the curb with a squeal of tires—a blue Chevy. Kayla glanced at it and froze. In the driver's seat was Nick, looking just like he had the night all of this started, wearing a white sportscoat with his hair all slicked back.

For a half second Kayla wanted to run away, but she stopped herself. She didn't have to run from Nick, not now.

"Who's that you're talkin' with, Liane?" Nick got out of the car, walking over to them. "Liane, what are you doing with this punkette?"

Before, just that look would have sent Kayla running, especially without Billy around to keep her from being scared. *But now, things are different.* Kayla glared back at him. "I'm talking to my friend, bozo. What's it to you?"

"Nick." Liane put her hand on his arm. "Listen, I'll just be a few minutes. Can I talk to her?"

She's asking permission from him. This isn't right, this really isn't right. "Liane—"

"Two minutes. You got an appointment now, remember? Can't keep people waiting."

Kayla pulled Liane a few feet away, closer to a wall. "Liane, what in the hell are you doing? Nick? You're hanging out with Nick? With that total sleazeball?"

"It's not like that," Liane said, glancing at where Nick was waiting, leaning against the door of the Chevy. "Really. Nick is a cool guy once you get to know him, and he gives me lots of clothes to wear, takes me out to restaurants, buys me jewelry, and we get high all the time. It's really a lot of fun."

"Jesus, Liane, you can't mean that!"

"Kayla, you know I hated living up in Suite 230. It was dirty all the time and there was never all that much food to eat. This is so much better. I'm happy now. I'm really happy now."

"Come on, Liane, time to go," Nick said, straightening up and walking toward them.

"Liane, don't you want to . . . I mean, things are working out okay by me. You don't have to be here—"

Nick reached out suddenly and grabbed Kayla by her jacket, shoving her against the wall. "Shut your mouth, chickie. Liane knows what she's doing. She knows what's good for her."

Kayla twisted, trying to get free. Behind Nick, she could see that Liane's face was pale, her eyes wide.

I could toast you, slimeball, she thought. *I could call up the magic and fry your ass.*

In her mind's eye, she saw the black boy lying on the bloody apartment floor, twisting in pain.

No. Not that.

"Nick, please don't—" Liane pleaded.

Nick glanced at her, then let go of Kayla abruptly. "Sure, baby, anything you say," he said. "Take a hike, chickie, don't bother us an more."

"Kayla, is there a problem?" It was Elizabet, standing a few feet away from them, holding two cups of soda. She surveyed the scene before her calmly, glaring at Nick.

"It's really okay," Liane said. "Kayla, this is what I want. I don't need your help."

"Let's go, Liane," Nick said, taking her by the arm and walking with her to his car. He opened the car door for her and gave Kayla a last furious glance. The Chevy screamed away into traffic a few seconds later.

Elizabet stood quietly next to Kayla. "I'll call Nichelle downtown," she said. "I'm sure they can find Nick again, and Liane."

"She didn't want me to help her," Kayla said. "She didn't want any help."

"Come on, child, let's go home," Elizabet said gently.

Nataniel leaned back in his chair, gazing out at the lights of Las Vegas. It never ceased to amaze him the way the humans squandered so much electricity on this useless display of lights. It certainly was eye-catching, though, and garish, but still beautiful in its own way.

Such an incredible waste of energy, he thought, *like so much about the humans, especially those with the gift of magic. They live their short, useless little lives, never dreaming what they could truly accomplish. Now that would be an accomplishment worthy of an Unseelie prince . . . to gather the power of all of those untapped resources, guiding it where he will.*

A knock at the door interrupted his thoughts. "Come in," he said sharply.

Shari entered the room. She bowed, fractionally less than the last time she had approached him, he noted with a hidden smile. Shari, in her own way, was becoming dangerous, he had decided, more questioning, edging toward disobedience. She spoke more often now of when they would return to the Unseelie Court, and he knew that she hated life among

the humans, even more than most of his
followers.

Still, she been the first one to follow him of
her own free will when he had been cast out of
the Unseelie Court. That was worth something,
and he would tolerate a small amount of inso-
lence in the remembrance of it.

"What is it?" he asked.

"The human girl," Shari said, unable to keep
the excitement out of her voice. "The young
mage. She's back in Los Angeles and growing in
power even as we speak."

"Oh, really?" Nataniel asked, smiling. He wondered briefly how the human child had survived
the Unseelie Court, then shrugged. She was
alive, and that was all that mattered, that she
was powerful enough to return to the human
lands of her own will.

"Razz and his boys, they found her in Los
Angeles. She nearly killed one of them with her
magic, but apparently healed him afterwards.
Several others of their gang disappeared, so
they're still searching the area.

"I find it a little hard to believe," Shari continued, a touch of surprise tinged with something
else—admiration?—in her voice. "She nearly
killed someone and then healed him. Healing an
enemy. Can you imagine that?"

"She's human, and a healer." Nataniel
shrugged. "She probably can't bear the pain of
others. We'll change that once we have her here
again." His voice tightened. "Tell the others to
prepare for war. Razz has been useful to us, but
we can't let him win this prize. We go to Los
Angeles."

Chapter Fifteen

"Wake up, sleepyhead!" Kayla said, leaning around the edge of the open door. "Come on, Elizabet, time to get up!"

Elizabet groaned, burying her face in her pillow.

"Elizabet, it's almost seven-thirty. You have to get up and drive me to school, remember?" *She looks a little tired,* Kayla thought. *But it's time to go; I need to get to school!*

"To think that I asked for this," Elizabet said, her face muffled by the pillow. "I asked them to sign the papers, setting you up as my foster child. I must have been on drugs to do that. . . ."

"Elizabet, it's gonna be great. It's my first day at the new school!" Kayla sat down on the edge of the bed, watching her expectantly. "Come on, let's go!"

"Child," Elizabet said, slowly getting out of bed and reaching for her bathrobe, "there is one major difference between us that you had better understand. I am a night person. I work the night shift at the station and sleep during the morning. You, on the other hand, are a day

person. You go to school in the daytime and
sleep at night. As long as you're not too cheerful
in the mornings, we should be able to get along
just fine."

"Well, there's one solution that would be really
easy. You could buy me a car, since I'll be able
to get my driving permit in a couple months,
and then you wouldn't have to get up early in
the morning anymore, right?" Kayla asked hopefully.

"I'll think about it," Elizabet said, but Kayla
caught the quick flash of her smile, like a hint
of sunlight from behind clouds. "First we'll have
to see how you do in high school," Elizabet continued, walking to the bathroom. Through the
open door, Kayla could hear the sound of water
running from the tap and Elizabet splashing
water on her face. "Then we can maybe talk
about a car."

Elizabet emerged from the bathroom drying
her face with a towel. "So are you ready for
your first day at the new high school?" she
asked.

"You bet!" Kayla said, though suddenly she
was much less certain. *I think I can deal with
it*, she thought. She'd thought quite a bit about
it over the last three days, what it would be
like to be back in school, meeting new kids and
teachers. She hadn't felt nervous at all yesterday
when Elizabet had taken her downtown to
complete the foster parent paperwork. And then
they had driven to the school so Kayla could
register for classes. The school secretary had
kept them waiting outside her office for ten
minutes, but Elizabet only had to deliver a few
seconds of what Kayla privately was starting to
think of as The Eyebrow, a stern look that

allowed no opposition, before the secretary quickly filed the forms, muttering something about needing Kayla's transcripts later. So now Kayla was a registered student at Laurel High School. And now, as of this morning, she was totally terrified.

It won't be so bad, she tried to tell herself. *They're just kids like me.* That thought stopped her. *No, not like me. Not anymore. I don't think any of them can call magic with their hands or heal somebody or hear someone else's thoughts. I'm different now, totally different.*

As if hearing her thoughts, Elizabet said, "Don't worry so much, child. It'll be fine. You'll see."

"Yeah, but what . . . what if I run into one of Carlos' guys or something? You don't seem to be worried about that, but there are a couple of street gangs out there who don't like me very much, remember?"

Elizabet walked to her closet, reaching inside for a blouse and skirt. "They did come by," Elizabet said. "Twice. But they haven't been back in several days."

"What?" Kayla asked, surprised.

"They came by when you were gone. From what you told me, my guess it that it was when you were in the elven lands. I think time moves a little differently there; you were there for only a few hours, but a week went by for the rest of us. Several boys pulled up in their cars at the foot of the driveway and sat there for a while. They came back, looked around, and always left without causing any trouble."

"I wish you'd told me that," Kayla muttered.

"I didn't think it mattered too much," Elizabet answered. "After all, they haven't been back in several days. And we have the LAPD keeping an eye on the house, while they get their warrants amd subpoenas together."

"But what if they come back?" Kayla asked. "What will we do then?"

"We'll deal with it then," Elizabet said, taking some pantyhose from her dresser drawer. "Go get some breakfast, child," she continued. "We'll have to get out of here in the next few minutes if we're to get you to the school on time."

Kayla was lost in her own thoughts as Elizabet drove. *I wonder what kind of people I'm going to meet at the school? I wonder if there's going to be any good teachers? Like that teacher Ramon was telling me about. I wonder if . . .*

"Stop that, child," Elizabet said from the driver's seat, not taking her eyes off the road.

"Stop what?" Kayla asked, surprised.

"I can sense the magic around you," Elizabet said. "When you worry, when you're not paying attention, you let your magic show. That's the real danger, child. You can't lose control of that, not for a minute. At home, you don't have to worry about it because I've taken steps to prevent any magic traces from leaking out. But if anybody is going to find you, it'll be because of your magic, not because of a street address."

"Yeah, right," Kayla said. She pushed all her worried thoughts away from her, concentrating on calmness, trying to find the burning fire inside her and quiet it down. *Chill out in there,* she thought, talking to the flickering blue flames as if the magic was a misbehaving child. *Just chill out for a while. We'll probably do magic lessons again tonight. You'll get to do stuff then.*

In the magic lessons, where Kayla was now learning to "hear" better, that was something that

Elizabet had taught her, to think of the magic as a little child, somebody who wouldn't always do what she wanted but could be convinced if you talked fast enough. Her ability to hear people's thoughts and talk directly to Elizabet with her mind was getting better, as well. *Maybe I'm finally starting to get the hang of this magic thing,* she thought, and smiled.

"Well, here we are," Elizabet said, pulling into the high school parking lot. "Try not to raise too much hell on your first morning, will you, child?" She smiled at Kayla, who grinned back her. "I'll be waiting here at the end of your last class," Elizabet continued, "but now I'm going home and definitely going back to sleep."

"See you later," Kayla said, climbing out of the VW.

This is a great-looking school, she decided. *Twenty million kids all running into their classes. And a few of them even have hair that's more punked out than mine. Not too many with this kind of cool leather jacket, though.*

Ramon's jacket. I wonder how he's doing?

She felt smugly proud at having achieved black leather superiority over the other students.

Kayla walked to the school secretary's office. The gray-haired woman assigned a student worker to escort her to her first class, who also introduced her to the instructor of the English Literature course. The dark-haired man with the handlebar mustache gestured for Kayla to take one of the empty chairs, then continued his detailed explanation of the relationships in Shakespeare's *Romeo and Juliet*.

Kayla listened in spite of herself, fascinated by the teacher's command of language and the way he stopped every few minutes to recite a few lines from the play, becoming that character for several seconds, bringing the play to life. "And tomorrow we'll watch a film version of *Romeo and Juliet,* and then compare that to *West Side Story,*" he concluded, just as the bell rang. Kayla blinked, realizing that the hour had gone by without her even noticing it.

Now all I have to do is figure out how to get to Building 12, Room 3, Kayla thought, gathering up her notebooks. She waited until the rush of students leaving the room had died down a bit before walking out into the hallway.

"You looked like you were really into that Shakespeare stuff," someone said from directly behind her.

Kayla glanced back and saw a young man with an unruly mop of wild red hair. He was grinning at her.

"Yeah, I thought it was pretty cool," she said. "Listen, maybe you can help me out. I need to figure out how to get to my next class."

"Hey, no problem," the redhead said. "My name's Mike, what's yours?"

"Kayla," she said. "Kayla Smith."

"Oh, you've got Tokugawa next for biology, too," Mike said, leaning over to look at her class schedule on top of her notebook. "She's a killer, probably the toughest teacher in the whole school. And you've got Wilson for English Grammar after that. Looks like we've got pretty much the same schedule, which makes sense if you're in the Honors program, too."

"Honors program?" Kayla said. "I didn't know Elizabet signed me up for that."

"Who's Elizabet? Your stepmom?"

"No, my . . . uh . . . my guardian. It's a long story," she added at his confused look.

"Yeah, well, tell it to me over lunch. We'd better get ourselves to class." They walked quickly across the quad to another building, where Mike introduced her to two of his friends, Stephanie and Bert, just before the bell rang to begin biology class. Miss Tokugawa, a tiny Oriental woman, began her lecture on genetics. Kayla realized that Mike was absolutely right: this class was going to be a killer. But an hour later, she knew a lot more about genetics than she had before.

English Grammar was almost a relief after that, and Kayla was rather pleased when Mrs. Wilson turned out to be a cheerful, exuberant young woman who obviously loved what she was teaching.

After the class ended, Kayla caught up with Mike and his friends in the hallway. He saw her and smiled. "Hey, Kayla, we're thinking of going and getting burgers for lunch. Do you want to go?"

"I thought you needed a lunch pass to leave the school," Kayla said. "At least, I thought that's what the secretary told me."

"Well, yeah." Mike shrugged. "Or you could just climb the fence, which is what we usually do. It's no big deal; they don't really care all that much. We should all take journalism next semester. That way you get an automatic gate pass. Let's go, guys."

Kayla followed them out the building and around the school auto shop to a deserted area of fence. *I hope Mike's right about this. I'd really hate to get busted on my first day at a new school.*

Mike scaled the wire fence with the ease of someone who's been practicing it for a long time, and Steph and Bert started up as well. Kayla sighed and began pulling herself up the chain links. She jumped down lightly to join the others on the other side. *This isn't too bad,* she thought. *First day here, already making some friends, some cool guys who aren't afraid of a little adventure. Though I bet they wouldn't believe the kind of adventures I've had lately.*

"We usually go to the Burger Shack just over there across the street," Mike said, starting across the wide boulevard.

"Mike, watch out!" Steph yelled. Mike looked up, too late.

The oncoming driver slammed on his brakes, but not fast enough.

He's going to hit him! He's going to—

Mike yelled once, a hoarse sound, and then the blue car hit him, knocking him up the hood of the car. He landed hard against the windshield. The blue car squealed to a stop a few feet further down the road. Mike slid off the hood onto the asphalt, lying very still on the street.

"Oh, shit . . ." Kayla was kneeling next to him a minute later. He was still conscious, staring at her, his mouth moving but not making any sound.

She put her hands on his shoulders and her other vision peeked in a moment later. *He's hurt on the inside, bleeding. No broken bones, but I'd better stop that bleeding.* Relief swept through her as she realized that he'd be okay. And then she called the magic out from that tiny safe place where she'd hidden it away from sight, freeing it to run through her. She could feel it skittering down her arms beneath the leather jacket, tickling her hands. She knelt closer over Mike so her body would shield the light, closed her eyes, and let the magic flow through her.

From a distance, she could hear Stephanie's voice. "Oh my God, Mike!" And Bert: "Kayla, is he okay?"

Kayla didn't answer; all of her concentration was on the magic, caught up in the healing.

"Hey, girl, is he okay?" an older voice asked, rough with concern. Someone grabbed her shoulder, pulling her back. Magic flared, bright enough that Kayla could see it through her closed eyes. She damped it immediately, knowing that she'd done what she needed to.

He's okay, he'll be all right.

She opened her eyes and saw Steph staring at her, a last hint of blue fire reflected in the other girl's eyes. "Kayla, what . . . ?" she began, and then stopped.

"It's okay, he's okay," Kayla said quickly. "Mike's gonna be fine."

The driver of the car shook his head. "I must be seeing things . . . hey, kid, you all right?" he said to Mike, who was sitting up slowly with Bert's help.

"Yeah, I'm fine," Mike said, then glared at the driver. "Jesus, man, can't you watch where you're driving? You could've killed me."

"Yeah, well, you should look before you run into the street! Goddamn kids," the driver said, then sighed. "Listen, kid, here's my business card. If you decide later in the day that you're not all right, get yourself to a hospital. Don't worry about it, I'll pay for it. Just don't tell my insurance company, okay?"

Mike stood up slowly, a little wobbly on his feet, and Kayla and Bert both reached out to steady him. "Yeah, sure."

"You sure you're all right, Mike?" Steph asked.

He nodded. "Yeah, yeah, I feel fine. Just a couple bruises maybe, that's all." He glanced in the direction of the school. "Hey, look at that!"

Kayla turned and saw the row of students staring and pointing at them through the chain link fence. *Great,* she thought. *That's all I need now. I know Steph saw the magic, and the driver, though I don't think the driver believed in it. Mike was too out of it to notice anything, but who knows how many of those kids saw what I did.*

"We'd better get out of here before the principal shows up," Mike said. "How 'bout we skip on the burgers for lunch? Somehow I'm not all that hungry anymore."

"Good plan," Kayla said, and they headed back onto the sidewalk, climbing the fence to get back into the school. She saw Steph watching her as she jumped down from the fence, and looked away, not wanting to answer the questions in Steph's eyes.

No one commented on it, though, and by the end of the day Kayla had almost forgotten the incident. Each of her classes was more fascinating than the last, and she'd met a dozen interesting people ranging from the quiet Sandra to Mike's best friend Steve, who described himself as a computer hacker and offered to take Kayla on a guided tour of the AT&T network. Mike had to one-up that offer by saying that he'd teach Kayla how to pick locks and get herself out of a pair of handcuffs, to which Steve said that he figured he'd break Bank of America's security codes by next week and wouldn't that be a fun place to check out?

Kayla was laughing so hard at their attempts to impress her that it took her a few moments to notice the two businessmen that were loitering just outside the school's wire fence. Loitering and watching them. A moment later, Kayla noticed their ears.

Their long, curved, pointed ears.

"Uh, excuse me, guys," Kayla said. She walked quickly into the closest building and stood there for a moment, leaning against the row of metal lockers. *It's the elves. They know I'm here. What am I supposed to do now?*

As if for an answer, Kayla saw one of the business-suited elves walk into the building, scanning the hallway. He saw her, and for a brief moment, they stared at each other. Then Kayla turned and ran.

She didn't hear footsteps running behind her, but a split second later there was the startling crackle of displaced air and then the elf was standing ten feet ahead of her, right in the middle of the only doorway out of the building. He smiled at her. Kayla didn't lose a step, but slammed into him at full speed like a high school football player. The elf had time for one startled expression on his finely-chiseled features before he was knocked flying. Kayla heard him crash into a locker as she fell, then she rolled to her feet and kept going.

Can't believe it. Elves invading my new high school, and it's only my first day here! She dodged into the next building, running past the startled faces of other students, then through the open double doors and past the library.

The main entrance to the school was just ahead, and the parking lot behind it. Kayla went through those gates as though all the demons in hell were hot on her tail. *Well, at least one of them is!* She stumbled to a stop in the parking lot, looking around quickly.

Ten feet away, she saw Elizabet's VW, parked with the convertible top down. She ran for it. Elizabet smiled as Kayla flung open the door and dived into the passenger seat.

"So, how was your first day at the new high school?" Elizabet asked cheerfully.

Chapter Sixteen

"Drive, drive, let's get out of here!" Kayla said, glancing back to see whether the elf was following her. She couldn't see him, but . . .

"It wasn't that bad, was it?" Elizabet asked, turning the key in the ignition and slowly backing the VW out of the parking spot.

"Yes, it was! It was awful!" She stopped, realizing that they were talking about different things. "I mean, school was fine, great, but . . . but . . . what were you doing around lunchtime, like a few minutes after noon?"

"Sleeping," Elizabet said, the VW slowing to a stop at the next streetlight. "I work night shift, remember?"

"Oh yeah, that's right," Kayla said. "Well, it's kinda like this. . . . "

"You got yourself into trouble," Elizabet said. It wasn't a question, it was a statement. "On your first day at your new high school, you got yourself into trouble."

"Well, not exactly school trouble," Kayla said, wondering exactly how she was going to explain this. "Not like getting sent to detention or

anything like that. I got into, well . . . another
kind of trouble."

"What do you mean by that?" Elizabet asked,
glancing at her and raising one eyebrow.

Kayla glanced out the car window, wanting to
look at anything but Elizabet's face. She didn't
want to see Elizabet's annoyance with her, or the
disappointment that she knew was there, that
her ward couldn't even get through one day at
school without getting into trouble. . . .

The light changed to green, and the VW started
forward. Kayla saw a green BMW that looked like
it was going to run the intersection. . . .

A green BMW, with the pointy-eared businessmen in the front seat.

"Oh no, it's them!" Kayla shouted, pointing
through the windshield. "The killer elves!"

"Kayla, that's a remarkably childish way to try
and change the subject," Elizabet said. "You're
really—" Her words were cut off by a squeal of
tires as the green BMW skidded through the
intersection just behind them, missing the little
VW by a few inches. Elizabet swerved their car
sharply, barely missing an old Volvo that was trying to make a lane change.

Kayla glanced back to see the BMW scream
through a tight U-turn, accelerating after them.
"Elizabet, get us out of here," Kayla yelled,
hanging on to the dashboard.

For an answer, Elizabet gunned the engine,
the VW seeming to leap forward past the other
cars on the road. Kayla looked back again to see
the BMW deftly dodging two cars in a near collision to stay close behind them.

"Hold on, child," Elizabet said calmly.
Without warning, Elizabet yanked the steering
wheel hard, bringing the VW to a sharp stop

and spinning the tail end of the car around in a perfect circle to face in the other direction. She floored the gas again. Kayla saw, through the BMW's windshield, the wide-eyed faces of two elves in business suits as the BMW went past them in the other direction. She turned to see what they did, but the BMW was lost in traffic within a few seconds, apparently unable to make an emergency turn to follow them.

Elizabet drove in silence, making several more turns through small residential streets, before taking them back to the 101 Freeway.

Kayla was still trying to catch her breath. "Elizabet, that was . . . that was *scary*," she said at last.

"My younger brother used to race stock cars in the seventies," the older woman said. "I learned a few things from him. And now," she said in a voice with a lot more edge to it, "I would like you to tell me exactly what happened to you at school today. *Everything.*"

"Okay," Kayla said, a little meekly. *At least we're away from the killer elves—now all I have to deal with is* Elizabet.

Enrique Ramirez glanced around the empty hallway outside the high school gym, before fishing in his jeans pockets for some coins. He dialed the pay phone quickly.

"Hey, Carlos, *mi amigo* . . . yeah, yeah, I'm fine . . . listen, got some news for you . . . that little white girl, the *bruja*. Well, she was here at the high school today. A kid was hit by a car, everyone's still talking about it, and listen, you'll never guess what I saw her do. . . . "

*   *   *.

"Those idiots," Shari said, slamming down the phone receiver into its cradle. "They're useless, totally useless."

"Then you shouldn't use them, my dear," Perenor said from across the room, his feet propped up on the end of the couch. He looked the picture of an indolent elflord, sipping from a glass of wine, his suit tie undone and lying on the couch next to him.

"What are you suggesting, my lord?" Shari asked tartly. *He's ceasing to be amusing,* she thought. *He's as cold in bed as he is outside of it. And it's because he's toying with me; I know he is. He wants something more from me, and he's only playing games until he gets it. . . .*

"Just that this could be done much more easily by you and me than by some of those rejects of the Unseelie Court."

Shari stiffened at that remark, and Perenor smiled.

"Does that bother you, my dear?" he asked silkily. "I would have thought not. That you would care as little about your exile from the Unseelie Court as I do about mine from the Seelie Court."

He gestured at the view of the ocean through the pane glass windows. "Isn't this much better than living in the Unseelie Court, in that dark, desolate place? I've been to the Unseelie lands, so lifeless and lacking in magic. Do you really want to go back there?"

"I will return home," Shari said, a touch of steel in her voice. "My lord Nataniel will see to that."

"Ah, Nataniel," Perenor said. "An interesting fellow . . . ambitious, intelligent. I just wonder what he'll be able to accomplish with it."

"I am loyal to—" Shari began, but Perenor cut off her words with a gesture.

"I know you are, Sharanya. That is one of the things I admire the most about you. I just wonder whether that loyalty might be misplaced." He rose from the couch, walking to the wet bar to pour himself another glass of dark red wine.

"What do you mean, my lord?" Shari asked.

Perenor turned, the glass of wine in his hand. "Just this. Imagine for a moment you, Nataniel, my daughter Ria, and I are to meet and discuss various business ventures tonight. We have dinner reservations for five o'clock, as I recall."

"Yes. What of it?"

"Let's say that you and I were to leave now, to go to that high school where your inept associates completely failed to capture the young human mage. There will be records of where this little mage lives somewhere in their files. We search through the records, or use the administrators to find the information. . . . "

"Easily done," she said. "They are only humans, after all."

"Agreed. Some simple magic to force them to tell us what we need to know. Then, at dinner tonight, we convince Nataniel that we should go pick up this mage immediately. After all, that's a pet project of his, isn't it? And then, somehow, during the course of capturing it . . . something unfortunate happens to Nataniel." He raised his glass to her in a toast. "And then you, my dear, would be free to return to the Unseelie lands with your elven host, with the human mage at your side to defeat the Unseelie Queen for you."

"But I wouldn't . . . "

"Think about it," Perenor said, smiling. "Nataniel cares too much about this human world. That's why he's built an empire here. Do you really believe him when he says that he wants to go home?"

"I don't know," Shari admitted. "Sometimes I believe him, but . . . " She glanced up at him, eyes narrowed. "And what do you get out of this, my lord Perenor?"

He shrugged. "I could say I do it simply out of my regard for you, that I care about you and I want to see you happy. But you would assume that was a lie, of course. Let's say this, instead: I help you gain the Unseelie throne, and then you'll grant me your aid to use against the Seelie Court. I have no great desire to return there, but I do owe them something for exiling me."

"Now *that* is a motivation I understand," Shari said. She moved past him, pouring wine into another glass. "You could lie to me, though," she said, "Just a little. Pretend that you're doing this because you care for me. That you'd love me infinitely, the way the humans do."

"Should I?" Perenor said, an amused tilt to his lips. "Do you want me to lie to you, Shari? Should I tell you about the beauty of your eyes, the way that your hair falls in such lovely flowing waves to your waist?" He moved closer to her, smiling that wicked smile, stray rays of sunlight from the window glinting off his silvery hair. "What other lies would you have me tell you?"

"All of those and more," she said, taking a sip from her wineglass, close enough that she could have leaned forward to touch him.

"Let's drink to the one thing we both know is true," Perenor said, raising his glass. "To partnership."

"To partnership," she echoed, and drank slowly, her eyes never leaving him for an instant.

To partnership, she thought, *and all the pleasures of it . . . until the moment when I don't need you anymore, my lord Perenor.*

Razz sat back in the back seat of the white Mercedes, his fingers drumming an idle pattern on the leather upholstery. Something was wrong and he knew it, but he couldn't put a finger on it. Maybe everything looked like it was fine, but he knew something was wrong. Here he was, in the back seat of his favorite car, good blow drawn out on the mirror in thin little lines on the seat next to him, and his best girl promising to meet him later tonight. But something was wrong.

His mother had said it when he was just a little kid, that he had something special. The eyes, she'd called it, talking about how her mother had had it. A way to know when something bad was going down. And that was what he felt right now, with the hair prickling on the back of his neck and the tight feeling in his belly.

The car phone rang. Flyboy, Razz's driver, picked it up, listened for a moment, and then handed it back to Razz. "It's Hotshot, bro," he said. Razz took the phone from his outstretched hand.

Hotshot's voice was thin and faint across the crackling phone line. "We've been following Shari's people like you asked," Hotshot said. "Just like you thought, they led us straight to that white chick, the one that did the number on Marcus. I saw the kid take off like a bat out of hell in a VW with some black mama, heading toward L.A."

"You got license plates on her, bro?" Razz asked.

Hotshot laughed a little. "More than that, Razz, I know the sister. It's the lady that works with the cops downtown. Winters, her name is. I met her last time they booked me. She's a good sister, Razz," he added. "She helped one of my cousins get a job, sent a friend of mine's little brother to the gangbanger camp in Malibu, kept him out of county jail."

"Yeah, well, we won't do shit to her, but I want that little white bitch," Razz said. "I don't know what she did to Marcus, but it was some serious shit, you hear me? You find out where this mama lives; we'll go drop by and pay our respects later tonight."

"You got it, bro," Hotshot said. Razz heard the click of him disconnecting.

He held the cellular phone in his hand for a moment longer, thinking about things. That feeling of something being wrong still wouldn't go away.

He leaned forward to speak to his driver. "Stop by the house," he ordered, "I want to pick up some heavy shit, some of the Uzis and automatics. I have a feeling about tonight. I think we'll need it."

The sun was setting at the far end of the San Fernando Valley, a disc of dark orange light disappearing behind the hills, turning the sky to shades of pink and pale blue. It was an effect that Perenor knew was caused by the smog, but it was beautiful in spite of that. He heard Shari's breath catch as she looked at the gorgeous sunset.

"Such beauty from such filth," she commented, handing her car keys to the valet as she stepped out of the car. Perenor took her arm and walked with her to the entrance of the restaurant where the doorman stood, holding the door open for them. This was his favorite Japanese restaurant in the Valley, an elegant restaurant nestled against the hills. It was, fortunately enough, also close to where the young mage lived. *Five minutes away, just off Laurel Canyon,* he thought with a satisfied smile.

Inside the restaurant, Perenor glanced past the tables where humans sat talking and eating, looking for his daughter and Nataniel. They were seated in a far corner, talking animatedly. As he and Shari walked toward them, Perenor could hear the edges of their business discussion.

"But you're going to have to amortize, which means that your return on investment will drop over the five-year period down to forty percent!"

"But what if I recapitalize at the end of the fifth year?" Nataniel asked. He glanced up and saw Perenor and Shari as they walked up to the table. "Ah, my friend Perenor! It's good to see you again," he said, standing and clasping Perenor's hand. "Your daughter has amazing insights into this new venture of mine. I'm delighted that you were able to introduce us."

"I guessed that it might be profitable for both of you," Perenor said, holding out a chair for Shari, then seating himself at the end of the table. "Ria is an extraordinarily talented young woman, as we've seen from the success of her Llewellyn Corporation."

He saw that Ria smiled at that, but her eyes were cool and assessing. *She's learning,* he thought with a touch of regret. *She no longer blindly worships me. Which is a pity, really. If she ever becomes a danger to me . . .*

"But we should talk of other things," Perenor continued. "Shari has some interesting news for you, Nataniel."

"Oh, indeed," Nataniel said, turning to his liegewoman.

Shari crumpled her napkin into her lap . . . a little nervously, Perenor thought. "It's that young human mage that you were so interested in, my lord. Morendil and Keryn found her this afternoon. And Lord Perenor was kind enough to suggest a visit to the girl's school, where we found the school administrators to be . . . quite helpful in giving us the information we needed to find the girl."

"How interesting," Nataniel said, smiling. "I knew you wouldn't fail me in this, Sharanya."

Shari colored slightly, a faint touch of pink creeping across her face. *She does poorly at these games of deception,* Perenor thought. *Nataniel has some skill at it, but Shari is a child beside him—or me.*

"I took the liberty of calling together the Host, my lord," Shari said. "They can meet us at the girl's address after we finish our supper here."

"That sounds like an excellent plan," Nataniel said. "We can have a delightful dinner here in the company of good friends," he smiled at Ria, who glanced away from him, "and then go pick up this useful little human girl."

Nataniel's gaze drifted back to Shari, and his eyes narrowed slightly. *He knows,* Perenor thought. *He knows that something is amiss. Like a wolf near a trap, he can sense it. But will he figure it out before the trap closes in on him?*

Nataniel turned back to Ria. "So, Ria, what else can you suggest for increasing return on investment in this venture?"

Kayla tried to concentrate on her geometry homework, but she couldn't stop herself from listening to Elizabet's voice from the other room. "Yes, Nichelle . . . no, I agree unfortunately . . . well, then, it's settled." There was the click of the phone being hung up, and Elizabet walked into the living room a moment later, frowning.

"So, what did you tell her," Kayla asked, "And what did she say?"

"That police patrols around the house weren't good enough. She'll arrange a safe place for you to be while they get the warrants together. They're sending over a patrol right now to take us in."

Elizabet sighed. "We'll probably spend tonight downtown, and tomorrow they'll send us over to a witness shelter. I just hope you can give them enough information that they can find these people."

"I'm sorry, Elizabet," Kayla said in a small voice. "I never meant to be this much trouble for you."

Elizabet smiled and reached over to ruffle Kayla's short pelt of hair. "You certainly know how to make an old woman's life interesting, child," she said.

There was a knock at the front door, a polite rapping.

"Could that be the police already?" Kayla asked, glancing at Elizabet.

"They might have had a patrol car in the area," Elizabet said.

"I'll let them in," Kayla said, bounding up from the couch.

"Then again, I don't think they'd be here so quickly—wait a moment, don't—" Elizabet said, just as Kayla unlocked the front door.

The first thing she saw was the gun. It was a shiny silver revolver, pointed right at her, the large barrel of the gun right in front of her eyes. Then she saw the face of the young black man holding the pistol, his smile half hidden beneath the hood of his bright blue sweatshirt.

Behind him, Kayla could see two more young men wearing blue caps and sweatshirts, and two cars parked in Elizabet's driveway. One was the white Mercedes convertible with the bashed front fender, a car that she'd hoped she'd never see again.

"Elizabet!" Kayla said in a voice that came out as a squeak.

Kayla felt Elizabet's hand upon her shoulder. Elizabet's voice was calm, almost too calm, as she surveyed the three gang members standing in her doorway. "Maybe you boys should come inside?" Elizabet said quietly.

"Thank you, sister," the young man with the revolver said. "Don't mind if we do."

She's inviting them in?

As if hearing her thoughts Elizabet murmured to Kayla, "Don't worry, child. Everything will work out fine."

I don't think so, Kayla thought. *I really don't think so. . . .*

Chapter Seventeen

"Are you gonna stay chill about this, mama?" the leader of the three young men asked as they walked into the living room. "You're not going to try to fuck around with us, are you?"

"No, I certainly don't intend to do that," Elizabet said evenly.

The young man nodded as if satisfied and glanced at his associates. "Holster 'em, homies," he said. "Show some respect for the sister."

Kayla breathed a very small sigh of relief as the young men put the guns away, sliding them under their shirts or behind their waistbands.

"So, mama," the leader said, sitting down on the edge of the couch, one knee propped up under his chin. "We're here with a businesslike proposition." He glanced at Kayla, still standing by the door. "My name is Razz. These two are my lieutenants."

"I can't exactly say it's a pleasure to meet you, Razz," Elizabet said as she sat down in the chair across from him.

She's so calm, Kayla thought. *She's got to be as scared as I am, but she's sure not showing it.*

"The white chick should sit down, too," Razz said, "'Cause she's part of the business deal."

Somehow I don't think I like the sound of that. . . .

He gestured at her, and Kayla sat down gingerly at the far end of the couch, as far from the young men as she could manage.

"It's like this," Razz said. "Here we are, some enterprising men trying to improve the lot of the African-American in America and we hear about this white kid that can do some wild shit, serious juju magic. And I think to myself: Razz, that's someone that we need, someone that can help our cause. So I come here to talk to the sister who's watching over the white chick, figuring she'll do what's right by our people. That she'll give us the white chick, let her work with us and our people."

Kayla glanced nervously at Elizabet, who was being very quiet. *She's not really thinking about it, is she?* Kayla thought, suddenly very scared. *She wouldn't just give me to these guys, would she?*

Elizabet glanced at Kayla and then turned back to the young man. "No," she said.

He blinked, as though he wasn't certain that he'd heard her correctly. "What are you saying, sister?"

"I said no. What I'm saying, *brother*, is that you're not my brother. You're not a hero of the people."

Elizabet matched his glare with one of her own. "My people are making something of themselves. They're doctors, lawyers, preachers, politicians. They're doing something to help the African-American in this country. You, boy, are just a thug."

"Is that what you think, mama?" Razz stood up,

shaking his fist at her. "You don't know jack shit
about it, lady. Fuck this," he said. "Grab the kid.
We're leaving."

"Razz!" It was a shout from outside, "You'd
better get out here, man."

Razz strode to the door; he paused, glancing
back at Kayla and Elizabet. "Don't let 'em pull
any shit," he directed the two lieutenants, who
nodded.

Kayla glanced nervously at the semi-automatic
pistol that was now back in one of the young
men's hands. She edged a little closer to the
edge of the couch so she could see through the
open doorway what was happening outside.

There were more cars in the driveway and in
the street beyond. Kayla instantly recognized the
two standing in the forefront of the small group
of people: Shari and Nataniel.

Razz walked out to the group of elves, quietly
talking with them for a few moments in a voice
too quiet for Kayla to hear. *He can't see them
for what they are*, Kayla thought. *Nobody but
Elizabet and I know what those people are.*

Razz said something else, then turned and
walked back toward the house. Without a word, he
stormed into the house, grabbed Kayla by the arm,
and dragged her outside. Kayla had a glimpse of
Elizabet starting forward, only to have her way
blocked by one of the young gunmen.

"This is what you want, Nate? This little white
girl?" he demanded, shoving Kayla in front of
the Unseelie.

Kayla felt like a mouse surrounded by several
hungry snakes. The Unseelie were gazing at her
with expressions that she didn't want to identify,
and she saw the mix of hate-fear on the faces of
Razz's men.

"That's the girl," Shari said quietly. "You will hand her over to us now, Razz."

"Like hell, mama!" Razz glared at her.

"You little fool," Nataniel said, in a voice like ice. "You don't know what you're dealing with, boy. I would rather see this girl dead, and all of your junior hoodlums with her, than let her remain in your possession." The look in Nataniel's eyes was terrifying, he looked so calm and almost bored with this. He wasn't bluffing, he was absolutely serious. He'd kill all of them with about as much emotion as someone swatting a fly.

Somebody get me out of this, Kayla whispered to herself. *Please, somebody, anybody, get me out of this. . . . There isn't anyone who's going to help me now,* she realized. *Elizabet's back there, being held at gunpoint. There are no cops, no Elizabet, no Ramon, no Billy, nobody.*

Just me.

"What are you going to do, Nate?" Razz asked. "You're surrounded by my bros, who'll shoot you before you can blink, man. You've been a good supplier, a good dude to deal with, but you're not going to walk away from here with jack shit, you understand that?"

"Do you think that matters to me?" Nate said, glancing down at his fingernails. "That your boys are armed with guns? That's fairly insignificant in the scheme of things, I think."

Razz shook his head in disbelief. "You're insane, man. You're fucking insane. We're leaving here now," he called out to his gang. "With the girl."

"I don't think so," Nataniel said calmly. "You have one last chance to reconsider, Razz."

"Like hell!" Razz glared at him. "Fuck with me and you're dead, Nate."

"I couldn't have said that better myself," Nataniel commented.

"Fucking insane," Razz muttered, painfully grasping Kayla's arm again and pulling her along with him in the direction of one of the cars.

Without warning, the world exploded around them.

Blinding light and raging flames filled the air. Kayla felt Razz let go of her arm and fell to her knees, her eyes burning too much for her to see, gasping for breath. The air was too hot to breathe, and someone else's agony washed her like a wave. She quickly crawled away, feeling the asphalt melting beneath her hands and knees. It seared the skin of her hands, but she felt her magic responding instantly, already working to heal her.

She heard a horrible scream behind her, slowly dying away into silence, and knew that she hadn't been the real target of that powerful magic, only close to it. As her eyes cleared, she glanced back and saw Razz's body, engulfed with purple flames, fall lifelessly to the driveway, already crumbling to gray ashes. The T-Men were staring at it in shock, too stunned to move or react.

"Next?" Nataniel said in a bored voice.

One of the T-Men recovered, bringing up his Uzi to fire. Kayla pressed herself flat against the hot asphalt as the air filled with the sound and smell of gunfire. She saw the T-Men diving for cover behind the different cars, and one business-suited elf shoved back against the car by the force of the bullets, as splatters of blood blossomed from his chest.

Another elf leaped toward the gunman with the Uzi. Between one step and the next, the

red-haired elf changed, his business suit melting
away into a suit of glittering silver armor. He
swung the sword that was suddenly in his hands,
cutting through the Uzi and the startled gunman
in one stroke. Then he staggered backwards and
fell, blood trickling from his mouth and the
many gunshot holes in the silver armor.

Kayla felt her stomach turn over and forced
herself to look away. Bullets sang overhead as
she crawled another few feet closer to the
house, hearing shouts and screams from behind
her. The front door of the house hung open, an
inviting rectangle of light, if only she could
reach it. One of Razz's boys was lying
motionless on the steps, his hand outstretched
as though reaching toward her.

*Where's his gun? If I had that, maybe I could
bluff my way out of here, do something, anything! I don't see it, it must be somewhere in the
bushes, it's too dark to see it.*

*I've got to get Elizabet and get the hell out of
here!*

She was at the steps when another sound
pierced the noise-filled air: the sound of screaming tires. She glanced back at the driveway, to
see Carlos, leaning out of the open passenger
window of the Chevy as it shrieked to a stop,
firing the pistol in his hand. Two other cars were
pulling up behind him, homeboys firing through
the windows. Coming up the street behind them,
she could see a black-and-white police car, tires
squealing as it skidded around the street corner.

*Oh my God, I didn't think it was possible for this
situation to get any worse, but it just did. . . .*

Kayla gathered herself and leaped up from the
pavement, diving for the open door into the house.
She dropped hard onto the steps as a hail of

bullets echoed behind her. Kayla crawled through the doorway into the entryway, then stopped short, staring up into the barrel of the gun above her.

The young man behind the gun was looking down at her with terrified brown eyes. Kayla didn't know what to do. She couldn't move, couldn't do anything, just stare at him and wait for him to kill her.

She knew the instant he made the decision, his finger slowly tightening on the trigger . . .

Elizabet slammed into the boy with a football tackle, knocking him against the wall. The gun skittered away across the floor. Elizabet turned quickly and picked up a brand-new glass dolphin sculpture from the table, bringing it down on the young man's head. It shattered, and he blinked at her once and slumped against the wall.

Damn, there goes another dolphin. . . .

"Quickly, child, we're getting out of here," Elizabet said, taking her by the arm.

The world changed to pure white around them.

The force of the blast lifted Kayla off her feet. She landed hard on the floor, rolling. All she could see was brightness, slowly fading. Then she saw Elizabet near the couch, lying very still. She sat up quickly and looked around the room.

Nataniel stood in the doorway, blood dripping from his silver armor, his hands glittering with magic.

Kayla glanced at the pistol, lying on the floor a few feet away.

"Don't bother," Nataniel said. "You've caused me a lot of trouble, girl. I'll take it out of your skin, once we're away from here." He began to walk into the house and stopped suddenly, as though encountering an invisible wall. With an impatient gesture, he brushed his hand at something invisible in front of him, then walked forward. Shari and another elf that Kayla didn't recognize, an older, silver-haired man, followed him through the doorway. All were wearing bright armor from head to foot, bloody swords in their hands.

Kayla shook her head; her throat was too tight for her to speak.

"Oh, defiance from the little kitten. We'll cure you of that soon enough." Nataniel stepped over the unconscious body of the young man, moving toward her.

"My lord?" Shari asked in a strained voice, and Nataniel turned.

She had her sword raised, stained with bright blood. As Kayla watched in total disbelief, she brought it down in a killing stroke, aiming for Nataniel's face.

He ducked back, so that only the tip of the blade creased the side of his face, cutting across his forehead and left eye. He shrieked something Kayla couldn't understand and brought up his own sword, parrying her next attack. Blood coursed down his face from his ruined eye as he countered another attack.

My God, they're trying to kill each other!

Kayla scrambled backwards as the silver-haired elf joined in the fight, swinging a deadly cut at Nataniel, who barely blocked it with his own sword.

"You too, Perenor?" Nataniel hissed.

Kayla crawled closer to Elizabet, realizing that the elves were totally ignoring her for the moment. She rested her hand on Elizabet's shoulder, letting her vision change and show her whether Elizabet was badly hurt.

She was. Kayla could feel the place in Elizabet's skull where the bone had broken, and the fragments were embedded deep in her brain, cutting through blood vessels. *She'll die of this,* Kayla realized. *Or worse, she won't die, but it'll destroy her mind.*

The elves are too busy trying to kill each other; they don't even know I'm still here. I can get out of here, or I can heal Elizabet. . . .

She didn't even have to think about it. Kayla called the magic and let it flow through her. She wrapped the magic around the bone shards, slowly easing them out and back into their proper place, and quickly sealed off the damaged blood vessels.

Distantly, she heard a scream and felt the agony of a sword slicing through flesh and bone, a killing blow. She forced herself to concentrate on Elizabet, as the magic repaired the last of the damage and faded away. She knelt for a moment, resting her face against Elizabet's motionless shoulder. It was too much, everything was too much; the total terror and exhaustion were dragging her down and she couldn't stop shaking. The clashing of swords across the room finally registered with her again, and she looked up, not knowing what she was going to see.

Shari was lying in a pool of her own blood on the floor. Nataniel and the other elf were faced off, standing almost over her body, eyes intent on each other.

"You convinced her to betray me, didn't you, Perenor?" Nataniel asked, gasping for breath. "Shari would never have done this on her own."

Perenor's only answer was another swift block
and cut combination, almost too fast for Kayla to
follow.

Nataniel's mistake was small, and Kayla nearly
didn't see it. His foot slipped slightly in the
blood on the floor, just enough to throw him off-
balance. The other elf moved instantly, closing in
on his blind side and stabbing upward with his
sword. Nataniel made an odd choking sound and
fell back as the silver-haired elf withdrew his
sword from Nataniel's chest. Nataniel staggered
backwards, his back to the wall, then slid to the
floor, leaving a bloody trail on the wall behind
him.

Perenor turned toward Kayla, his sword dripping blood, his eyes bright with insanity. Kayla
was held by that gaze, unable to look away. He
staggered toward her and nearly fell, clutching at
a long gash that cut through his armor along his
side. He straightened slowly, his eyes burning,
breath hissing through his tightened lips. He
brought up the sword with both hands, taking
another step forward. . . .

"Father!" It was a blond woman, walking
quickly across the blood-slicked floor. The sharp
contrast between them, the elegantly dressed
woman and the blood-splattered man in armor,
was so startling that Kayla could only stare at
her.

He looked blankly at her, not seeming to recognize her for a moment.

"Father," she repeated, her hand on his arm.
"You're hurt, and the police will be here soon.
We have to get out of here." She glanced at
Kayla, and Kayla saw something flicker across
those calm blue eyes, too fast for Kayla to see
what it was. Then she turned back to her

father, urging him toward the door. "Quickly, Father, walk more quickly. . . . "

Kayla watched the two leave, suddenly aware of the reek of blood and worse filling the room. She sat there for a moment, just breathing. She heard the sound of a car ignition outside, then the sound of the car pulling away, and realized how quiet it was, so quiet that the loudest sound was her own breathing. Slowly, unsteadily, she got to her feet, walking to the open front door.

Nothing in her life could've prepared her for what she saw. The driveway looked like it had been washed in blood. Elves in armor, T-Men, and Tyrone Street Boys, two uniformed LAPD officers, all lying too still, sprawled on the pavement or against the sides of cars. No one moved, and there was no sound. Except one, the faint voice of someone cursing in Spanish.

Kayla followed that sound. On the other side of a car, she saw Carlos, propped against the tire, his arms wrapped around his middle. He didn't see her at first, lost in his pain as the blood seeped around his fingers and soaked into his jacket. He looked up and saw her. *"Bruja!"* he whispered. *"Bruja,* you're here. You can heal me. Do it, do it quickly."

She could feel the magic in her responding to his words and his pain, and moved closer, her hands reaching out to him.

Carlos smiled, leaning back. "Always you do what I say, *bruja.*"

She stopped in mid-step.

His eyes widened with pain and surprise, staring at her. "Why are you hesitating, girl? Heal me!" He coughed, blood spattering across his lips and chin. "Heal me, *bruja!*"

I can't let him die, I can't . . .

I can't let him own me.

If I heal him, I'll never be free. He'll always want me, he'll always be after me.

But I can't let him die . . .

I can't . . . I can't . . .

Carlos sighed and slumped back against the car. Kayla felt the life fleeing from him, fading away. There was still one last moment, she knew, when she could put her hands against him and hold that life in his body.

She didn't move.

The light left Carlos' body, leaving behind a dark, empty shape, faceless as Kayla's vision suddenly blurred with tears. She sobbed, hot tears running down her face.

Kayla leaned against the doorjamb, holding onto it for support. Everything was too bright and blurry around her, but one thing she saw instantly. Nataniel and Shari's bodies were gone, vanished, just like the other elven bodies had vanished during those long minutes when she'd knelt next to Carlos' body, crying too hard to see anything else. Only the stains of blood on the wall and the floor marked where Nataniel and Shari had been.

She walked unsteadily across the room, hearing the sound of wailing police sirens in the distance. She sat down next to Elizabet and took Elizabet's hand in hers, pressing it against her cheek. *It's crazy the world's all pain and bullets and blood too much blood too much . . .*

She couldn't stop the tears from falling and didn't want to. She could feel the tears washing away the blood from her face, and that was all right; soon she'd be clean again, no blood, no blood ever again. . . .

*   *   *

"Oh my God!"

Detective Cable's face was chalk-white. Walker had never seen her that shocked before, not even when they'd walked into that domestic multiple homicide scene. He'd never seen anything like this, either, not since the Nam.

Cable and the other officers were walking across the driveway, checking the bodies. They already knew that Quinn and Allen were dead, two good LAPD officers dead on the pavement near the gangbangers.

He and Houston walked quickly to the front door of the house. It was quiet inside, but he gestured for Houston to draw her piece and did the same himself. They moved into the house, scanning quickly for any armed opponents.

There was only one live person, and that was a girl sitting, rocking on the floor, blood and tears streaking her face. She stared up at him like a lost soul.

Walker was a father of two grown boys, and his instincts were good. He holstered his gun and knelt beside her, holding her close and letting her tears soak through his uniform, as the other officers walked quietly through the blood-stained room around them.

Epilogue

The sunlight was warm on Kayla's face, warm and very bright. She stood next to Elizabet on the sandy concrete of the Venice Beach walkway and looked out at the crowd of people walking along the beach, playing in the sand and swimming in the water. "Do you see him?" she asked Elizabet, who was also scanning the crowd.

"I don't know what he looks like," Elizabet said ruefully, "so I have no idea who he is."

Kayla saw him then, standing at the edge of the crowd, next to a couple of girls gawking at a weightlifter working out on the sands.

Ramon looks thinner, she thought, *and a little pale.* There were shadows under his eyes that hadn't been there before. He saw her and waved, walking toward them.

"You must be Elizabeth Winters," Ramon said, nodding to her.

"Elizabet," the older woman said. "No 'h' on the end."

He stood for a moment, gazing thoughtfully at Kayla. "You look like you are well, *querida*," he said. "Are you?"

"I'm okay," Kayla said. "How 'bout yourself?"

He shook his head. "It's been very difficult. Mama has not been herself, these weeks since Carlos and Roberta's deaths. It's hard for her."

"I'm sorry," Kayla said, and meant it.

"My life is different, too," he continued. "After what . . . what happened with Carlos, I told the other Tyrone Street Boys that I was through with them, and I went to the *policía*. They offered me a job, working at the prison camp in Malibu where they send young kids from the gangs. And they'll help me finish high school at night, too. Maybe working at the gang camp will make a difference, maybe it won't. I don't know."

He sighed. "I miss my brother. I think I'll always miss him. But I can't go on living his life. It's hard to walk away from my friends in the gang. . . . "

"Most of the time, the right thing to do isn't easy," Elizabet said gently.

"I know, I know. Life is never easy," he said simply. "That's not the reason God put us here on earth. I don't know the reason God put us here, but I know that isn't it. At least, that's what Mama says. . . . I look at Kayla here, at what she's learned to do, the price she pays for helping people, and I think I have to at least try to do the same. I have to try. . . . "

Ramon seemed to run out of words, and stood there looking at Kayla, his eyes lingering on her face.

Elizabet cleared her throat a little awkwardly. "Well, would you kids like some lunch? There's a good sandwich place just up ahead; we can get sandwiches and sodas."

"Thank you, Miss Elizabet," Ramon said. "That would be fine."

They walked in the direction that Elizabet pointed, weaving through the thick mass of people on the walkway. A pair of boys on skates zipped past them, a little too close; Ramon took her hand and pulled her to one side. He didn't let go of her hand, after the boys were past, and they continued walking, hand in hand, following Elizabet through the crowd.

No, it wasn't going to be easy, learning to live with who she was, and what she could do. Kayla knew that. But right now, walking in the sunlight with Ramon, she knew that that didn't matter.

Because it was going to be all right.

Author's Note

This book is a fantasy novel, but the dangers for runaways and homeless youth are very real. Covenant House provides runaways and homeless youth under age 21 with food, shelter, clothing, medical help, counseling, and other services.

If you are a runaway or know someone else who needs help, please call Covenant House at 1-800-999-9999.

MERCEDES LACKEY

The Hottest Fantasy Writer Today!

URBAN FANTASY

Knight of Ghosts and Shadows with Ellen Guon

Elves in L.A.? It would explain a lot, wouldn't it? Eric Banyon is a musician with a lot of talent but very little ambition—and his lady just left him lovelorn in a deserted corner of the Renaissance Fairegrounds, singing the blues and playing his flute. He couldn't have known the desperate sadness of his music would free Korendil, a young elven noble, from the magical prison he has been languishing in for centuries. Eric really needed a good cause to get his life in gear—now he's got one. With Korendil he must raise an army to fight against the evil lord who seeks to conquer all of California. And Eric's music will show the way....

Summoned to Tourney with Ellen Guon

Elves in San Francisco? Where else would an elf go when L.A. got too hot? All is well there with our elf-lord, his human companion and the mage who brought them all together—until it turns out that San Francisco is doomed to fall off the face of the continent. Doomed that is, unless our mage can summon the Nightflyers, the soul-devouring shadow creatures from the dreaming world—creatures no one on Earth could possibly control....

Born to Run with Larry Dixon

There are elves out there. And more are coming. But even elves need money to survive in the "real" world. The good elves in South Carolina, intrigued by the thrills of stock car racing, are manufacturing new, light-weight engines (with, incidentally, very little "cold" iron); the bad elves run a kiddie-porn and snuff-film ring, with occasional forays into drugs. *Children in Peril—Elves to the Rescue.* (Part of the SERRAted Edge series.)

HIGH FANTASY

Bardic Voices: The Lark & The Wren

Rune could be one of the greatest bards of her world, but the daughter of a tavern wench can't get much in the way of formal training. So one night she goes up to play for the Ghost of Skull Hill. She'll either fiddle till dawn to prove her skill as a bard—or die trying. . . .

Also by Mercedes Lackey:

Reap the Whirlwind with C.J. Cherryh
Part of the Sword of Knowledge series.

Castle of Deception with Josepha Sherman
Based on the bestselling computer game, *The Bard's Tale.*™

The Ship Who Searched with Anne McCaffrey
The Ship Who Sang is not alone!

Wheels of Fire with Mark Shepherd
Book II of the SERRAted Edge series.

When the Bough Breaks with Holly Lisle
Book III of the SERRAted Edge series.

Wing Commander: Freedom Flight with Ellen Guon
Based on the bestselling computer game, *Wing Commander.*™

Join the Mercedes Lackey national fan club: Send an SASE (business-size) to Queen's Own, P.O. Box 43143, Upper Montclair, NJ 07043.

Available at your local bookstore. If not, fill out this coupon and send a check or money order for the cover price to Baen Books, Dept. BA, P.O. Box 1403, Riverdale, NY 10471.

KNIGHT OF GHOSTS AND SHADOWS • 69885-0 • $4.99 ☐
SUMMONED TO TOURNEY • 72122-4 • $4.99 ☐
BORN TO RUN • 72110-0 • $4.99 ☐
BARDIC VOICES: THE LARK & THE WREN • 72099-6 • $5.99 ☐
REAP THE WHIRLWIND • 69846-X • $4.99 ☐
CASTLE OF DECEPTION • 72125-9 • $5.99 ☐
THE SHIP WHO SEARCHED • 72129-1 • $5.99 ☐
WHEELS OF FIRE • 72138-0 • $4.99 ☐
WHEN THE BOUGH BREAKS • 72156-9 • $4.99 ☐
WING COMMANDER: FREEDOM FLIGHT • 72145-3 • $4.99 ☐

NAME: _____

ADDRESS: _____

_____

I have enclosed a check or money order in the amount of $_____

ELIZABETH MOON

Anne McCaffrey on Elizabeth Moon:

"She's a damn fine writer. The Deed of Pak-senarrion is fascinating. I'd use her book for research if I ever need a woman warrior. I know how they train now. We need more like this."

By the Compton Crook Award winning author of the Best First Novel of the Year

Sheepfarmer's Daughter
65416-0 • 512 pages • $3.95 _____

Divided Allegiance
69786-2 • 528 pages • $3.95 _____

Oath of Gold
69798-6 • 512 pages • $3.95 _____

Available at your local bookstore, or send this coupon and the cover price(s) to Baen Books, Dept. BA, P.O. Box 1043, Riverdale, NY 10471.